NAILS OF GOD

Nails of God

A Thriller of Faith and Power

Dr. Phillip Stephens

Corporate Publishing

ISBN: 978-0-9747108-3-9

Scripture quotations are generally taken from English Standard Version (ESV) or Christian Standard Bible (CSB) unless otherwise noted.

First Edition –

Printed in United States of America

Disclaimer

This work is a novel and should be read as fiction. While it engages real historical locations, archaeological discussions, ancient texts, and theological traditions, these elements are woven into a fictional narrative and should not be interpreted as definitive historical, archaeological, or doctrinal claims.

The author affirms the authority of Scripture and the historic Christian faith. Any speculative elements are presented for narrative exploration and thematic depth, not as theological instruction or dogmatic assertion.

Notice on the Use of AI Tools

This work was conceived, outlined, and authored by a human author. In keeping with contemporary publishing standards and emerging best practices, artificial intelligence tools may have been used in a limited, assistive capacity for purposes such as research support, fact-checking, editing, proofreading, and stylistic refinement, including improvement of prose clarity and flow.

All creative decisions, narrative content, thematic direction, arguments, and conclusions remain solely the responsibility of the author.

Dedication

For my mother, Jessie,

Steady in faith,

Gentle in counsel,

A quiet steward of the Word.

For my Father-in-Law, Alton,

Firm in labor,

Faithful in service,

Rooted in conviction.

And for the Reader,

This book is for those who pursue truth beyond appearances,

Who recognize that the greatest struggles are not against flesh and blood,

And who are willing to surrender certainty in order to see clearly.

'For we wrestle not against flesh and blood, but against principalities, against powers, against rulers of the darkness of this world."

– Ephesians 6:12

Faith and Fear ask the same: Belief without sight.

-You choose.

Prologue - It Begins…

Innovations Ad Agency, New York

"One guy," the computer operator muttered, running a hand through his unruly hair. His shirt was wrinkled, his eyes bleary. He motioned toward the monitor and shrugged.

"Problem?" Sarah asked, stepping closer.

He tapped the keyboard. "This guy ruined the best shot. We'll have to digitally erase him."

"Show me."

He zoomed in. "This was our money shot. It's on a sidewalk with our model wearing the company jacket, surrounded by people on the sidewalk. A gust of rain hit just as our model raised his collar. Dozens of pedestrians around him did the same. It was instinctive, synchronized. It's a perfect moment. Everyone reacting in unison to the elements. The brand logo on the jacket in the shot is crisp, centered, flawless."

Sarah leaned in, nodding. "Dad's outdoor gear company is going to love it. The weather's real, the reaction's authentic. It sells the product, don't you think?"

He tapped again. "Except for him."

A new section of the image filled the screen just over the model's shoulder.

Sarah squinted. "Oof. Handsome, but yeah...distracting. He's not reacting to the elements at all like the rest of the crowd."

"Exactly. Everyone's bracing against the rain except him. His head is up. Walking straight into the rain like it's a spring breeze. He kills the realism. Throws off the whole dynamic of how to react to a rainstorm."

Sarah frowned. "That's too much contrast. Honestly, if *he* were wearing the gear, we'd have an even stronger message like, '*So effective, you don't even notice the storm.*' But as it is? It doesn't fit."

"I tried every frame. He's always there. Always unaffected."

She stared at the screen again, studying the man. Dark hair. Olive complexion. Strong jaw. His features were striking, like he could be of European descent, maybe Middle Eastern. Or even Latin American. Hard to pin down.

Then she paused. "Wait, why isn't he bothered by the storm?"

Chapter One

New York

By late evening, the rain had stopped. Inside the converted factory, a fire crackled in the stone hearth. One of the few real fireplaces in a city full of fake ones. Its glow warmed the expansive space, casting dancing shadows across concrete walls and steel beams. It was more of a fortress than a home.

The owner ran his fingers through his dark hair, a smile tugging at the corners of his mouth. The flickering fire reflected off his olive-toned skin as he surveyed the space, industrial and raw yet infused with quiet purpose. It reminded him of his roots, of why he was here.

Outside, the building looked like just another forgotten factory buried in a neighborhood that time had abandoned. Boarded windows, a barbed-wire topped fence surrounding it, and dull grey paint made it indistinguishable from other structures in the area. But inside, it was different. Inside was a sanctuary.

The structure hummed with contrast. A stillness against the storm. A pack of dogs patrolled the perimeter, silent as shadows. In the dim glow, it was hard to tell whether they were Dobermans or German Shepherds, but one stood apart: an Akita, aloof and still, like a sentinel over the others. The others simply paced restlessly. The Akita was unmoved.

Inside, polished concrete floors stretched underfoot, and steel beams glistened above. Skylights crowned the ceiling, allowing early light to cascade over an expansive room that defied the bleakness outside. A forge had become a hearth, a warehouse had become a sanctum, and a forgotten space now pulsed with purpose.

On the ground floor, open and windowless save for the second-story skylight above, zones had formed: a study flanked by bookcases near the hearth, a training area, a sleek kitchen tucked in the far corner. Overhead, second-story walkways and offices ringed the perimeter just above the factory floor, now serving as sleeping quarters, sealed behind closed doors that overlook the expansive factory floor space below.

The man moved deliberately. He added wood to the fire, its pop and crackle the only sound echoing in the space. He opened a gleaming steel industrial refrigerator, retrieved a ceremonial teacup, and began to brew tea. His movements were fluid, almost meditative.

He pulled frozen grasshoppers from the freezer, rinsed them, and laid them on a tray. Honey and za'atar-infused olive oil waited for the drizzle. As the oven warmed and the tea steeped, he flowed from task to task with silent precision.

Then a ringtone pierced the silence. He answered on the first ring.

"Alexander Trenfor."

"Alex, why do you always answer the phone like that?" came the voice from the speaker.

Alex smiled. "Would you prefer I answer with *your* name, Richard?"

"Fair. Listen, I need a favor. Can you cover my martial arts class tonight?"

"Of course. Still running about twenty students?"

"Yeah. Good group. I told them you'd be there. They're excited."

"You do important work, Richard. What time?"

Later That Night

New York City wears darkness like a mask. Trenfor moved quietly through it, steady and alert, a gym bag slung over one shoulder. His hoodie, made of stiffer material than most, more gi than garment, shrouded his eyes. His shoes padded silently. His posture was upright and fluid. A shadow with purpose.

Every few steps, he scanned left and right, eyes constantly sweeping. The streets were still. Too still.

After a few blocks, a flash of blue lights suddenly broke the calm as a patrol car pulled alongside him.

Trenfor stopped, pulled down his hood, and nodded at the approaching officers.

"Evening, gentlemen," he said.

One officer, a sergeant by the stripes on his sleeve and a USMC tattoo peeking from under it, approached while the other hovered behind, his hand resting near his weapon.

"ID?" the sergeant asked.

"Certainly." Trenfor calmly set down his bag and handed over two cards. "Driver's license and concealed gun carry permit."

"Are you armed?"

"No."

"You always carry this permit even though there are no firearms allowed in the city?"

"Out of habit. I understand the risk you take every day."

"What's in the bag?"

"Training gear."

"Heading to the gym?"

"No. To teach."

"What kind of class?"

"Martial arts."

"You some kind of black belt?"

Trenfor gave a polite nod. "Am I being detained, officers? I'm simply walking to class and do not wish to be late."

"We're just making sure everything's in order. You don't exactly blend in here."

"I appreciate your concern for my well-being."

"Mind if we search the bag?"

"With all due respect, I do mind. I'm due for my class. Unless you'd like to provide a warrant or articulate probable cause, I'd prefer not. I'm assuming this is a level 1 encounter, and presenting you with my ID itself was voluntary. A search without cause simply delays my travel. I'm sure you understand."

The sergeant narrowed his eyes. Trenfor motioned toward the tattoo.

"You and I fought for those rights. We're both bound to protect them."

A beat passed. The officer glanced at his Marine Corps tattoo that Trenfor had noted, then he looked back at Trenfor. The officer handed back the cards.

"Be safe out here."

Trenfor unzipped the bag completely and laid it open. The officers watched over his shoulder. Inside were a martial arts gi, a black belt, gloves, pads, and a towel as the officers watched. He repacked it calmly and slung the bag back over his shoulder. Trenfor then calmly looked at both officers.

"Appreciate what you do," Trenfor said. "Semper Fi."

"Where'd you serve?" the sergeant asked.

Trenfor smiled then nodded. "If you'll excuse me, I have a class to teach, sir."

Outside the Rec Center

Three men lounged on the steps. One scanned the street repeatedly. Another had an outline of a weapon beneath his shirt. The third pocketed a small plastic bag as Trenfor approached. Trenfor scanned the area for more men before glancing back at them again, noting posture, demeanor, and any hints of more weapons.

Trenfor kept his eyes forward, adjusting his posture, breathing deep. His peripheral vision clocked them.

As he neared, the largest stood and stepped into his path.

"Hold up."

Trenfor stopped, lowered his hood, then smiled. "Evening, gentlemen."

"Gentlemen? Where you from, man? That accent don't match your face. You don't belong here."

"That seems to be a recurring opinion tonight."

"You on the wrong street."

"My destination is just ahead," he said, nodding to the rec center door.

"You got no business here."

The third man shifted. The blocker lifted his shirt just enough to flash a pistol.

Trenfor didn't flinch. "You're right. I don't belong here. But Satan's efforts to delay me are growing predictable."

"You calling me Satan?"

"Not at all. But you may be influenced by the Shedim. Do you know them?"

"Shedim? What kind of gang is that?"

Trenfor glanced at his watch. "Just so you know, in about ten seconds, a patrol car will round that corner."

"You bluffin', bro?"

"No. They are also wary of outsiders."

Right on cue, a vehicle topped with blue lights rounded the corner. The police cruiser slowly rolled into view. The trio hesitated, then quietly scattered, their eyes cast tentatively toward Trenfor.

Trenfor climbed the steps to the rec center without looking back. At the door, he glanced at his watch. Eight seconds.

Christian Intelligence Group (CIG), North Carolina Mountains

"A lady from an ad agency called," Barry said, tossing a slip onto the desk. "She's looking for Trenfor."

Doug McCraken frowned. "Odd. He keeps a low profile."

"She said he walked through a photo shoot in New York. They liked his look."

Doug chuckled. "Alex? A model? That's rich."

"Someone recognized him from his lectures at the university. The agency put up posters trying to identify him. A student made the connection."

"He listed *us* as his university contact?"

"Smart man. We screen his calls."

"I need to speak with him anyway. Thanks, Barry."

New York

Trenfor moved like water in the silent space of his factory home. His motions fluid, silent. His kata echoed elements of tai chi, punctuated with sharp strikes and quick turns. The smoldering hearth cast long shadows, birds gliding across the skylight above, all tracing shapes across the floor.

He finished the form, sweat beading, breath steady.

His phone rang as he dried off.

"Alexander Trenfor."

"Doug here. How's the scholar-warrior?"

"Well. Two lectures this week. A class last night."

"Lectures *are* classes, you know."

"Your semantics are true. In my world, classes are a bit more physical and involve sweat along with some bruises. Only the ego gets bruised in lectures."

"You need a normal job."

"I suspect you've got something in mind."

"Line secure?"

"Of course."

"Good. I need you at CIG next week. We've got new gear. New non-Android, non-iOS phones came in."

"Always with the toys. You realize that any technology is soon hackable by foreign intelligence services. Old ways are often more secure."

Doug chuckled. "True. But we try. We also got a call from a woman named Sarah."

"Ad agency. I know. I saw the flyer."

"She tracked you down through us. Apparently, we're your answering service."

"I'm not interested in being a poster boy."

"Alex, your face isn't exactly a secret anywhere in the world that matters."

"Let them wonder. I prefer shadows. I'll call her though."

Coffee Shop, Lower Manhattan – New York

Trenfor sat in the corner booth, back to the wall, steam rising from his cup as his eyes surveyed the café. He noticed her before she even stepped inside.

Unlike most customers who pushed straight through the door, she paused, checked the address, then cautiously entered. She scanned the room. That subtle hesitation spoke volumes for him. He continued to study her before she noticed him.

Blonde hair. Athletic build. Casual clothes. Likely his age. Right-handed, judging by the way she favored that side for her movements. She soon spotted him. Smiled. He nodded.

"I'm Sarah. Thanks for meeting me," she said, signaling the waiter for coffee before sliding into the booth.

"My pleasure. Is this setting acceptable?" Trenfor asked.

"Oh, sure. I've never been here before." She studied him briefly. "Your university bio says you're a visiting professor."

"Guest lecturer," he corrected.

"Well, more than that. I read that you have a PhD in Early Christian Literature, are fluent in Greek and Hebrew, and are a scholar of the historical Jesus and ancient Judaism. It says you spend most of your time traveling to archaeological digs around the world. Impressive."

"You know a lot about me. I know nothing about you."

"I'm a graduate student. Anthropology."

"And what specialization? Biblical studies? Archaeology?"

"Cultural anthropology, actually. My father owns a large outdoor clothing company. I was drawn to the marketing side at first, fascinated by the cultures that wore his brand. That's what pulled me in."

"An interesting entry point."

"A professor once told me anthropology is simply the study of what makes us human. That stuck."

"So, your plan is to join the family business?"

"That was the idea. I do a lot of photography and marketing work. I'm finishing an internship at a PR firm working on one of my dad's advertising campaigns."

"Coincidentally," Trenfor said, with a subtle smile.

She grinned as the waiter delivered coffee. "I'm also starting a grad project soon. Lately, I've been pulled more toward archaeology."

"Not a direction your father will favor, I imagine."

"My father is... complicated. So, what kind of professor are you?"

"A good one, I hope."

"I mean, are you all theological facts and theory? Or do you lean religious?"

He smiled again. "Not sure I follow."

"I had a religious studies professor once. Total atheist. It just felt... off. Like he didn't believe what he taught. I mean, why did he even teach religion if he was an atheist? The University didn't see the irony."

"Bad experience?"

"Maybe and I guess I shouldn't complain. I'm not religious myself. More agnostic. I just hated the class."

"You're wondering if I'm a Christian professor."

She looked away, embarrassed. "Sorry, that was pretentious. I've just had professors who preach in class."

"My classroom's not about answers. It's about better questions."

She sipped her coffee. "That's rare. Isn't it hard to stay neutral? To let students search for answers?"

"Truth tends to rise when the right questions are asked. I was agnostic myself once. Actually, amoral would be more accurate."

"Amoral? That's honest. And interesting for a theology professor."

"It's been a journey finding God. From the U.S. Marine Corps to a PhD is not the usual path of a professor."

"Where were you stationed?"

"Camp Lejeune, North Carolina. But tell me about the photo you wanted to discuss that brought us here? I don't mean to rush, but I have a flight to catch soon."

Christian Intelligence Group – NC Mountains

Trenfor squinted into the sunlight as it broke through treetops and struck the glass face of the grey building nestled into the mountainside. Chiseled above the stone archway was the inscription:

"The weapons we fight with are not the weapons of the world." – 2 Corinthians 10:4

He smiled and stepped through the doors. A rush of air greeted him. Seamless wall mirrors flanked the narrow hallway he entered. He tapped one, habitually checking for the depth of the reflection. His finger met glass. One-way mirror. Surveillance. He smiled.

He gave a wave at the mirror.

Above him, the ventilation system stirred, scanning for chemical traces emitted by visitors. Trenfor grinned.

"One of these days I'm bringing in explosives, just to test your ion scanners," he said to the receptionist as he entered the lobby.

She laughed. "One of the agents triggered it last week. Residue from a field mission. The alarm was... dramatic. Mr. McCraken is expecting you."

She handed him a visitor badge. Trenfor bounded up the steps.

He nodded to every passing staff member, met with smiles and familiar greetings from each. "Doctor," "Professor," "Alex."

At the top floor, he found the familiar plaque:

Executive Director

Inside, Doug McCraken rose from behind his desk as Trenfor entered.

"Alex!"

Trenfor smiled, admiring the books lining the walls.

"I always love this office," Trenfor said. "Books. Windows to the mind."

"It's more library than office," Doug replied. Trenfor paused by the window, surveying the mountain range before sitting across from Doug. A light fog still clung to the trees amid the rising sun as Trenfor continued to gaze at the rising mist.

"You seem distracted," Doug said.

"That girl who contacted you. Did anything seem... off?"

"We ran her background. Seems legit."

"Spiritually?"

Doug paused. "We didn't sense anything unusual. Daughter of a clothing company CEO. Works in PR. Grad student. Wanted permission to use your image."

"She's troubled."

Doug nodded. "We'll add her to the prayer list. I trust your discernment."

"It's not always a gift," Trenfor said quietly. "What do you have for me?"

Doug pulled out a sealed packet. Inside, photos.

"Take a look."

Two rusted nails, bent. Layers of corrosion. Calcium carbonate.

"Early Roman era?" Trenfor asked.

"Electron microscopy found slivers of cedar wood. Fossilized bone fragments."

"Crucifixion nails?"

Doug nodded. "They were found in the Caiaphas tomb dig."

Trenfor raised a brow. "We find nails all the time in digs. But never in a tomb. Especially not *that* tomb. I'm familiar with the site. I've never heard nails mentioned."

"The discovery of the tomb hit the media in 1990. The ossuary read: *Joseph, son of Caiaphas.* It matched Josephus' records of the High Priest. Ornate. Rare name. Scholars agree that the tomb is authentic."

"I remember. It made headlines."

"What didn't make headlines," Doug said, "was that two nails were found inside. They were documented in the official inventory. The press ignored it."

"Why?"

"All attention was on the ossuaries. The inventory also listed an oil lamp, perfume jar, and a Roman coin in a female skull."

"Pagan influence. The coin was likely Charon's fare for the River Styx, consistent with Greek mythology to ensure the soul could pay the journey to the underworld. But for a Jewish tomb, that's significant. Shows Greco-Roman influence."

Doug nodded. "You understand how important these nails are. Crucifixion nails were considered talismans. A protection in the afterlife."

"Or a memento. First-century Jewish burials occasionally held personal items. But nails? Only if they meant something. Which brings us to the obvious question. Could these be *the* nails?"

"There was a second ossuary in the tomb. Less ornate. It was simply inscribed 'Caiaphas'. Just like the Gospel account."

Trenfor leaned forward. "You realize, there are suppressed traditions that suggest Caiaphas didn't intend for Jesus to be crucified. Some even say Caiaphas became a believer in the aftermath of the resurrection."

"There are quite a few reasons why the nails might be there. Reverence. Regret."

"So, where are they?"

"One was found inside the plain ossuary. The other, just outside the ornate one. They were sent to Tel Aviv University. Misplaced for a while. Now? Gone."

"Gone?" Trenfor's tone sharpened.

"They've vanished, Alex. It was noted in a recent audit."

"That's not carelessness. That's intent. Those types of artifacts just don't disappear."

"Exactly why we were contacted."

"You want me to find them."

"I'm afraid, you're the only one who can. You understand the significance."

JFK International Airport – New York

"Doug, I just landed at JFK," Trenfor said over the secure line. "Heading straight to Tel Aviv. Layover's tight. I did some research before the trip."

"Any leads?"

"Not many. But something strange came up. A group called the *Ashen Veil* staged a protest at the Israel Museum. Vandalized several exhibits. They're demanding inclusion of climate issues and pagan themes in policies. Their presence at the University coincides with the disappearance."

"Ashen Veil?"

"An alliance of radical environmentalists and Marxists. Green and red. They want ancient pagan temple finds given equal status with biblical ones."

Doug's voice then dropped. "Ironically, they're not wrong, in a way. Baal, Asherah, Molech… the Old Testament is full of Pagan worship, and there are certainly archaeological finds that support the Biblical accounts of pagan worship. They just don't get as much press. Pagan worship was pretty widespread at the time of the early church. Until the Gospel challenged the spiritual powers behind those names. But I'm sure their movement is not about fair treatment of archeological finds and more about bringing back pagan worship."

"I've said it before. Christianity was the greatest global exorcism of those spirits." Trenfor then stared at the international boarding gate. "They're coming back, Doug. These pagan principalities. They're not gone."

"I agree. We've been tracking them, Alex. We will check on this latest group who probably believe they have good intentions."

Passengers started filtering past. Trenfor adjusted the cell phone. "As you know, Doug. Most of the evil in the world is done with good intentions."

"I think the phrase is the road to hell is paved with good intentions," Doug said. "They are always passionate and certain of their cause."

Trenfor smiled as he headed for the international terminal. "It is the paradox that explains history's greatest atrocities. Being certain you're right might be the most dangerous idea of all. And being certain that you want pagan gods to return is a dangerous idea."

Chapter Two

JFK International Airport – New York

JFK's Terminal 4 thrummed with the restless rhythm of international travel with announcements echoing throughout the corridors, suitcases clacking, and a thousand lives briefly crossing paths. Trenfor moved through the crowd, immune to its urgency. While others shuffled in line or glanced anxiously at departure boards, he walked with the calm precision of someone for whom time was not a master.

At Gate B22, he found an open seat at the edge of the waiting area, back to the wall, with a clear view of the boarding lane. A routine born not of paranoia but of pattern recognition. He set his leather satchel at his feet and pulled a small, weathered book from within. The cover text was in Hebrew, the spine creased from years of use.

Across the gate, Sarah Whitfield spotted him.

She recognized him instantly. The man from the café, the one who stood in the rain as if it were sunshine. He hadn't even seemed surprised when she approached him back then. He'd simply looked at her like he already knew she was coming.

Now, there he was again. Seated in the terminal, alone but alert. The kind of man who was always aware of his surroundings. She watched as he began to read.

Sarah turned her gaze back to her boarding pass: 14 A. Window seat. Premium economy. She considered letting go of her concerns about her seating arrangement for the long flight. But curiosity had always been stronger than caution. That same trait had pulled her out of corporate PR and into anthropology. Her father hadn't been thrilled when she'd left Elemental Gear full-time, and he certainly hadn't approved of her upcoming dig in Israel. "You should be selling jackets, not shoveling dirt," he'd said.

Still, she was going to Israel. And so, it seemed, was Trenfor.

As passengers began to board, Sarah kept an eye on him. He moved toward the gate with that same deliberate ease. His shoulders were relaxed, eyes scanning, constantly aware. He was in line to board. She kept her distance but peeked over the shoulder of another passenger, hoping Trenfor would not see her. She spied the boarding pass in Trenfor's hand as his line moved forward: 21C.

She moved, too, watching carefully as he handed off his boarding pass and stepped through. She avoided her line and began walking along the lane of passengers waiting to board, glancing at the tickets in their hands. A few minutes later, she spotted a man in a charcoal jacket standing just ahead of her in the jetway, frowning at his ticket as he waited his turn.

Bingo.

"Excuse me," she said, flashing a polite, almost apologetic smile. "Looks like you're not thrilled with your seat assignment."

The man turned toward her, mid-fifties, polished, irritated. "Middle seat in the back," he muttered. "Booked early, too."

"I might have a better option," Sarah offered, her voice casual. "I've got a window seat in premium economy. I'd be happy to trade."

He hesitated. "Premium economy?"

"14A," she confirmed. "A bit more legroom. And no middle seat."

He looked at his pass again. "Why would you want to switch?"

She nodded. "Honestly? You're sitting next to someone I know. We can explain to the ticket agent."

A brief pause. Then he handed her the boarding pass. "Done."

"Appreciate it." She smiled, taking the slip of paper. Her heart quickened. Not because of the switch, but from whatever reaction Trenfor might have when she showed up beside him. There was also this mysterious aura that she sensed around him. But it would allow her to get his advice on her upcoming archaeology experience.

Sarah stepped onto the plane, now holding 21B. If she remembered the layout right, that would put her directly next to Trenfor. She kept her pace even, casual. The cabin lights were dimmed, casting a soft glow on the rows ahead.

And there he was.

Already seated, reading. Still.

As she approached, he never looked up.

"Small world," she said, sliding into the seat beside him.

"I saw you at the gate," he replied. "I take it our seating arrangement isn't by accident."

"I made a deal. Legroom for proximity."

He raised an eyebrow.

"To you," she clarified, smirking. "Figured I could get some insight on ancient relics since we're already acquainted. I'm on the way to an archeological site."

He chuckled softly and closed the book. "The grad studies you mentioned. Fair enough."

Sarah glanced at the book in his lap, noticing the title wasn't in English. "Hebrew?"

"Yes. *Sefer HaRazim.*"

She blinked. "That sounds... intense."

"It's an ancient mystical text. Likely compiled in the Byzantine period. Possibly earlier."

"Light reading for a plane ride?"

"It's work."

She tilted her head. "Is that what's taking you to Israel? Work?"

"In a way." He didn't elaborate.

She didn't push. Not yet.

As the engines revved and the plane lifted off, Sarah felt the familiar rush of the altitude increasing, but this time, tethered to a different kind of anticipation. Something unspoken hung in the air. Not romance, although he was a handsome guy. More like recognition.

They were both going somewhere, and not just geographically. She then shook the feeling.

Sarah settled into her seat, suddenly grateful for the impulse she had followed. For the first time in a while, the unknown no longer felt threatening.

The aircraft soon leveled off, the shift in engine pitch almost imperceptible. Trenfor registered it out of habit. With the seatbelt light extinguished and passengers settling into the low hum of a long-haul flight, he adjusted his satchel and returned to his book.

The cracked leather and subtle wear hinted at decades, perhaps centuries of use. Inside, the yellowed parchment revealed dense columns of text in ancient characters that were structured, mysterious, whispering of forgotten knowledge.

Sarah glanced over. "So, the Sefer HaRazim you were saying?" she asked.

Trenfor nodded. "The Book of Secrets. One of the earliest Jewish mystical texts."

"I've never come across it," she said, tilting her head slightly. "What's it about?"

He turned a few pages carefully. "According to tradition, it was given to Noah by the angel Raziel after the flood. It's not theology, not in the way we use the term. It's more… spiritual anthropology. A catalogue of hierarchies. Angelic realms, cosmic forces, and methods of calling on spiritual entities. Less about God, more about what people feared and how they tried to control the unseen."

Sarah studied the unfamiliar script, eyes scanning the tight curves and slashes of the inked lines. "So…like ritual magic in a Jewish context?"

"That's one way to put it," Trenfor said. "But the interest isn't in the spells. It's in what they reveal about the people who needed them. This text was preserved for centuries even while religious authorities rejected it. It tells us quite a bit."

She hesitated. "Like what, specifically?"

"That which is excluded from canon often says more than what's accepted. The circle of orthodoxy doesn't just preserve truth. It defines what must remain outside. And that boundary can be revealing."

He flipped to a page with concentric rings of Hebrew letters drawn around intersecting lines and sigils. "These describe celestial guardians. Thresholds between spiritual spheres. Entry points. Gatekeepers. You'll find similar patterns in ancient Egyptian texts, early Christian mysticism, even Babylonian incantation bowls. An outline of authority in realms we don't perceive with our eyes."

"Do you believe any of it?" she asked, her voice soft but direct.

"I believe humans have always sensed there's more beyond the veil," he said. "And when they couldn't explain it, they recorded it, coded it into rituals, stories, symbols. That's what this is."

Sarah paused. "So, it's not your theology. It's your data."

He gave a rare, quiet smile. "Exactly. Scholarly reference to put theology into context."

A flight attendant paused beside them. "Your seatmate?"

"We swapped," Sarah replied smoothly. "We're colleagues."

The attendant nodded and moved on. Trenfor raised an eyebrow.

"I'm used to improvising," she said. "Part of working in PR. Or was."

"You're not still with the ad agency?"

"Not anymore. That was just the internship. Technically, I still work for my father's company, Elemental Gear. Outdoor apparel. He didn't mind the ad agency, but he hates the fact I'm flying to Israel to crawl through ancient dust."

"Because it's religious?"

"Because it's impractical," she said. "His world is metrics and margins. Mine… started leaning elsewhere."

She motioned to the book. "There's something about old things. The closer I get to what people once believed, what they did, and why they did it, the more I feel like I'm touching something real. My dad calls it a phase. I call it the only thing that's ever made me pause."

Trenfor listened quietly. "You mentioned a dig?"

"East Galilee. A joint university program. I'll be working on site documentation, maybe some cataloging if I'm lucky. My dad's company also supports conservation and climate groups that wear our gear there. I can count the trip as work if I get some photos of our clothing line in the field. It's the only way I could convince dad on going to the region for school."

He nodded slowly. "That region holds layers that include Jewish, Roman, and Canaanite societies. Pagan rites. Christian miracles. It's where boundaries blurred."

"Places where the veil is thinner? Pagan temples and such. That's what one group my dad supports says anyway."

His gaze turned to her then, just slightly more focused. "What group is that?"

"Someone from our PR department mentioned 'The Ashen Veil'. Said they'd approached us years ago about branding their retreat centers. I think they are in that region."

Trenfor's demeanor shifted a bit. Subtle, but attentive.

"My dad listened to them," she said. "Their pitch had strange language to me, 'energy alignments,' 'convergence points,' even 'tremor lines.' Their words, of course. I remember it because one of our analysts said it sounded more like a cult than a business. It's where I heard the word pagan rites used before."

"Did they name their founder?"

"Eli Weiss as I recall. Obsessed with geography. Ancient temples, ley lines, planetary movement. Said certain sites could 'amplify intent.' He sounded… unhinged."

"He wasn't," Trenfor replied. "At least, not untrained. What they call spiritual alignment, others once called gateway engineering."

"Gateway to what?"

"To power," he said. "But not the kind you measure. Portals to other realms is another way to put it."

The overhead lights dimmed for meal service. For a moment, the world narrowed to the glow above their seats, and the soft current of conversation slowed.

Trenfor closed the book, sliding it gently back into the satchel. "Most people think history is nothing more than the study of the past. But sometimes it's just memory trying to warn us about the future."

Sarah leaned back in her seat, a new stillness settling over her. "You haven't said why you're going to Galilee."

Trenfor paused. He glanced out the window before looking back at her. "I'm following a thread. Something old resurfaced. I want to see where it leads."

"Is it connected to your studies that you mentioned at the café?"

"I'm looking for some missing artifacts."

"How do museums lose artifacts?"

His expression remained calm. "Precisely. Artifacts don't just vanish from museums. In the same way, old references to pagan symbols don't just reappear in the news after centuries. Someone's pulling a thread that I must follow before it unravels. Our quests are not much different."

The meal cart arrived. They accepted their trays in silence, and for a while only the gentle clatter of plastic utensils filled the space between them.

Later, Sarah spoke again. "You said if we want to understand a people, we should look at what they buried. It's why archaeology is so important."

Trenfor nodded.

She turned toward him, eyes steady. "And what they feared."

He looked back at her. "That's why you dig, Sarah?" It was as much a statement as a question.

Her breath caught just slightly, but she nodded. "Yes."

"Maybe it's also," he said, "why you seek."

The rest of the flight passed in a kind of watchful quiet. Outside, the night over the Atlantic stretched infinite and starless. Inside, something had opened between them that was not yet named, but unmistakably real.

Christian Intelligence Group (CIG), North Carolina

Barry Smith's boots clicked crisply on the polished stone as he passed through the hushed corridors of CIG Headquarters. The building, buried deep in the Blue Ridge, projected the quiet authority of an old monastery, but outfitted with modern façade, satellite uplinks and biometric locks.

Barry held a secured tablet blinking red in his hand, a level-five alert. The kind that didn't wait for morning briefings. He gave a curt nod to the guards outside Doug McCraken's door.

"Is he in?" Barry didn't wait for confirmation. He knocked twice, firm, fast, then pushed the heavy oak open at the muted "Enter."

Inside, Doug stood silhouetted against the wide window, the storm outside rendering the landscape a shifting watercolor of gray and pine. Rain beaded and raced down the glass like veins.

"Something's happened in Rome," Barry said, already swiping his tablet to cast the alert up on the main display. "Vatican Square. Three hours ago."

Doug turned slowly. At sixty-two, he carried weight like a man used to bearing it, back straight, silver-haired, not showy. His hands, visibly scarred from an earlier life, hung loosely at his sides as he took in the feed on the larger monitor.

"Casualties?" he asked.

"None. Swiss Guard and Carabinieri responded fast." Barry tapped the screen. Footage played of black-clad figures scrambling up the base of the Vatican obelisk, hauling gear more suited to industrial work than civil protest. "But this wasn't about spectacle. They weren't climbing for visibility. They were going for the cross at the top."

"To damage it?"

"To remove and drop it. One confessed under interrogation. He said the cross had to fall."

Doug's face barely moved, but something in his posture shifted. He lowered himself into the chair behind his desk, glancing once at the security stills of faces twisted in a kind of spiritual delirium.

"They knew what they were doing," Doug murmured.

Barry nodded, tapping to bring up blueprints of the square. "They carried thermal gloves, hydraulic cutters, and carbon-fiber climbing line. But here's what doesn't add up. Vatican security allowed us access to their findings. Toxicology screens came back negative. No amphetamines. No synthetic stimulants. But their core body temps were through the roof. Average of 103 degrees during the climb."

"Fevered. Like mania."

"Exactly what Italian authorities are calling it. Religious mania. But look at their eyes." Barry pulled up a close-up still. "All of their eyes are fully dilated. Have you ever seen pupils like that outside demonic possession cases?"

Doug didn't answer. Instead, he leaned forward, lacing his fingers. "The obelisk... it's not just Roman décor. That's the obelisk from Heliopolis, City of the Sun. Caligula brought it to Rome in 37 AD. They built the circus around it. Peter was crucified in its shadow."

Barry exhaled. "So, the Pope moved it to St. Peter's as a message. Triumph of the cross over the gods of Egypt."

Doug nodded. "And placed a bronze cross on top of the solar globe. A deliberate inversion of power. Legend says the cross at the top holds a fragment of the True Cross, recovered before Constantinople fell. It was moved there as it would have been the last thing St. Peter saw when he was martyred as he was crucified upside down. The obelisk was left to witness the rise of the church St. Peter built."

"Well," Barry muttered, "that'd make it a high-value target."

Rain lashed harder against the windows. Doug activated the main holographic map, a topographic globe rotating slowly above the desk. He drew his hand through the air and lines of light began to overlay: Rome. Jerusalem. East Galilee. Central Africa. All pulsing.

"These incidents are increasing," he said. "Prayer networks in all three regions are flagging spikes of what they call *spiritual turbulence.* And not random. These protest attacks are lining up. All target sites of *spiritual intersection.* Places where boundary lines once separated the sacred from the profane."

Barry stepped closer, his usual humor replaced with tight attention. "So, it's not politics. They're attacking spiritual geography."

Doug nodded. "These are territorial spirits. The ancient kind. Pre-Abrahamic, in some cases. They remember where they were defeated."

Barry pointed toward the map. "Why is Trenfor headed to Kursi instead of Jerusalem?"

"He's not following the nails," Doug said quietly. "Not yet. He's following the tremors. Kursi isn't just a dig site. It's the battleground of the first recorded exorcism. Jesus cast Legion into the swine there. The demons fled, but only for a time."

He expanded the map. Eastern Galilee glowed brighter, the digital overlays revealing seismic spiritual activity beneath the physical terrain. Trenfor's destination pulsed like a flare.

"We're seeing the markers light up again," Doug said. "Rome. Jerusalem. Now Galilee. The Shedim are pressing against the veil."

Barry's voice dropped. "We're not talking metaphor, are we?"

Doug looked up at the rotating map. "They've been returning for a while now hidden behind causes. Behind movements. Politics. Posing as justice, ecology, equity. They've learned to twist good things. That's always been the method. To take truth, distort it just enough, and then demand worship."

He tapped to pull up footage from the obelisk again. "That's not protest. That's spiritual warfare with steel-toed boots and crowbars. These aren't just angry activists. They're vessels."

"The return of the gods," Barry murmured.

Doug didn't disagree. "The modern world opened the door again. We removed the house of the Spirit. So seven others came to fill it. It's prophecy being unveiled."

A moment passed, the rain outside a steady hiss. Then Barry straightened. "Trenfor lands in four hours. Our guy, Shomsky is prepping transport to Tiberias."

Doug nodded. "After that, limited digital contact. Physical drop points only. The electromagnetic noise near Kursi is worsening and satellite comms can't always maintain links. And I don't trust what's interfering with those links."

Barry gave a tight nod. "Cold War playbook."

"No," Doug said. "Older. Think Babylon."

He rose, stepping back to the window, watching the blurred ridgelines vanish into mist.

"Trenfor knows what's coming," he said. "He's not there to document it. He's there to engage."

Barry lingered at the door. "And if he fails?"

Doug didn't turn. "Then this is just the beginning."

International Airspace

Sarah pressed her forehead gently against the cool airplane window, watching the vast Atlantic stretch below like an unbroken slate. Pinpricks of ship lights blinked through the darkness, slow-moving constellations carving lines across the deep. Overhead, stars arced in ancient procession, fixed points once used to navigate the unknown.

Beside her, Trenfor closed the weathered book he'd been reading, sliding it carefully into his satchel. She turned slightly, her voice quiet.

"You ever think about how the ancients memorized the sky?" she asked. "That was their data set. The stars, rhythms, eclipses. It wasn't about wonder. It was about survival. I look at them during archeological digs and think about how we're seeing the same sky the ancients saw."

Trenfor nodded without turning. "Before computer screens captured our attention, the heavens were man's guide. The stars weren't decoration. They were testimony. The sky still speaks to us today. If we look."

She traced a finger through the fogged windowpane, drawing a line. "That's another reason why I like archaeology. We found stone circles in Scotland aligned to solstices and lunar phases. Cultures who never met, building sacred spaces to track the same heavens."

"Because the patterns were written into the sky and the earth. The difference is that some saw them as maps. Others as messages."

Sarah hesitated. "And what about those diagrams in your book. The ones with the circles and letters. Were those maps too?"

Trenfor's eyes remained forward, but his voice lowered. "Yes. Not for terrain, but for realms. The ancients believed there were layers to reality. Not metaphorical. But, actual tiers of existence. And each boundary had a guardian. An angelic being, if you will. A password. A cost to access them."

She looked at him for a moment, unsure how seriously he meant it.

"You think those layers still exist?" she asked.

"I think they never stopped. We just stopped paying attention."

Sarah exhaled through her nose. "Whoa, Ok. You're saying we assume we've evolved past all that. You're saying we've just gone blind to what still moves in realms we can't see?"

Trenfor finally turned, meeting her gaze. "That blindness. That's how the old gods return. Not with announcements. With invitations."

She shivered slightly, whether from his words or the cabin chill, she wasn't sure.

"You said something earlier," she murmured, "about people burying what they fear. I keep thinking about that."

"Fear reveals what a culture truly worships," he said. "What it gives power to. Sometimes we bury our fears in the ground. Sometimes we build monuments on top of them."

They sat in silence for a moment, the white noise of the engines offering an artificial calm. Then Sarah spoke again, quieter.

"I joined the dig at Kursi as an academic exercise. But… it feels like I've already been pulled into something deeper before I even arrive."

He didn't answer at first. Then, gently: "You have."

She looked at him.

"The moment you chose to sit here," he said. "You stepped across a threshold. Not by accident."

Sarah glanced down at the armrest where their elbows almost touched.

"I thought I was just being curious," she said.

"You were," he replied. "But curiosity is the first spark of awakening."

Outside, a break in the clouds revealed the faint outline of the European coastline. Cities glowed in gridded clusters below. Man's order laid over nature's wilderness.

Sarah watched them with new eyes.

"Funny," she said. "They look like constellations, too. Just upside down."

"Because everything above is reflected below," Trenfor said. "That's an ancient belief. Heaven and earth mirror one another."

"And the obelisks, the ziggurats, the towers…" she trailed off.

"Attempts to bridge the two. For good or for power."

The seatbelt sign chimed on. Dawn had begun to push against the eastern horizon, turning the edges of the cloud's gold. The plane dipped gently as descent began.

Sarah straightened, brushing her hair back, blinking herself back to the real world. But something had changed. She wasn't just flying to a dig site anymore. She was being carried toward something deeper. Something she had once longed for without knowing its name. She now had more questions.

Trenfor adjusted his seat slightly and looked out the window ahead. "When we land," he said, "you may find things waiting for you. Answers. Or questions. Just remember that sometimes the ruins we uncover aren't just physical. They're spiritual."

Sarah nodded slowly. She began to think about how her father thought archaeology was a phase to get out of her system. She felt a tug toward it for answers that she intuitively knew could be found by searching the past. But her brief encounter with this mysterious man seemed to make the past relevant to the future. Like connecting some dots, she knew were there all along.

As the plane banked gently eastward and the first full light of day broke across the clouds, she placed her hand against the glass, between her and the ancient land rising to meet her.

And for the first time in years, she didn't feel like a spectator. She boarded the plane for a graduate dig. Now she felt she was stepping into more than the past and Trenfor, who gave her a new perspective. But after the long flight, she still wondered who he really was?

Japan – A mountain Dojo, Kyoto Prefecture

The dojo stood open to the elements, its wooden floors polished smooth by generations of bare feet. Beyond the wide doors, mist clung to the cedars that ringed the mountainside, the air cool and fragrant from a rain that had passed only moments before. The sky remained heavy with clouds, the kind that promised more weather without urgency.

The students knelt in seiza, backs straight, hands resting lightly on their thighs. The cuffs of their gis were still damp, but no one adjusted them. No one seemed aware of the discomfort at all.

The master entered without announcement.

He was older, his hair bound simply at the nape of his neck, his movements precise and economical. Nothing about him suggested haste or hesitation. He crossed the mat and stood at its center, allowing the room to quiet itself before speaking.

"Before technique," he said calmly, "a brief lesson on fear."

His eyes moved across the students, not measuring skill, but attention.

"Fear is not weakness," he continued. "It is information. But a warrior does not allow information to rule him."

He gestured toward the open doors, where mist drifted lazily through the trees. "Rain unsettles the untrained. So does cold. So does pain. A samurai learns early that fearing small things trains the body to fear larger ones. The mind believes what you say to it."

He paused, letting the words settle.

"A samurai fears neither rain nor death," he said. "Not because he is reckless, but because he has already made peace with both."

He stepped closer to the edge of the mat. "Bushidō does not teach us to seek death. It teaches us to live so fully, so honestly, that death loses its authority over us. We learn to fight not because we value violence. We learn to fight so that we do not have to fight. The same discipline that allows peace is the same discipline that survives war."

The students remained motionless, listening.

"A samurai," the master went on, "is one who serves. Service requires clarity. And clarity requires that you confront your own darkness before presuming to confront the world's. A Samurai seeks to understand his world and his service. His fulfillment is in achieving clarity in all things."

One of the younger students raised his hand. "Master," he asked, carefully, "did the samurai all follow the same religion in pursuit of the philosophy of the Samurai?"

The master regarded him for a long moment.

"No," he said. "They were shaped by many traditions, Shinto, Buddhism, Confucian thought. But those were not the source of their oath."

He tapped the wooden floor lightly with his staff. "Their loyalty was not to a system of belief. It was to truth, honor, and the master they served."

He turned slightly, his gaze drifting toward the mountains beyond the dojo. "When foreign missionaries came centuries ago, some samurai recognized something familiar in what they heard, self-sacrifice, obedience, a call to lay down one's life for another. Many converted. Not because they abandoned honor, but because they found its deeper fulfillment. Samurai follow different paths, different masters. But with the same honor. Ultimately, truth follows truth."

The student frowned. "So… which is true?"

The master allowed a faint smile. "Truth does not fear examination," he said. "Where it is genuine, it endures, regardless of where a man first encounters it."

He straightened. "A warrior who understands this is not divided. He is anchored."

The rain began again, softly this time, tapping against the roof in a steady rhythm.

The master bowed. "Now," he said, "we train, not to escape death, but to live without being ruled by it."

The students returned the bow as one, the sound of rain filling the space where fear no longer lived in their pursuit of the honorable way of the Samurai.

Chapter Three

Israeli Airspace

Sarah rubbed the tension from her neck; the ache was a souvenir from hours spent folded into airline geometry. Through the oval window, night was dissolving into violet and pre-dawn blue. The sky peeled slowly from darkness as they edged closer to the cradle of history. She hadn't planned to sleep. She planned to review her notes and ask Trenfor more questions. But the engine's hum and the cadence of his voice had lulled her into sleep she hadn't known she needed.

The cabin remained dim, lit only by a soft amber glow. Most passengers were still suspended in dreams, bodies slumped at angles the human spine was never meant to endure, cocooned in thin blankets against the cabin chill. She straightened, absently smoothing her hair, adjusting to the waking world.

"That passed faster than I expected," she whispered, voice rough from sleep. She turned to Trenfor, who remained as composed as he'd been at takeoff. "Thank you for the conversation. Most people don't make a transatlantic flight feel like a masterclass." She smiled; he acknowledged with a small nod.

A flight attendant moved quietly down the aisle, checking seatbelts as the captain announced descent into Ben Gurion Airport. The aircraft tilted slightly, revealing the contour of the land beginning to form beneath a band of golden sunlight.

"I've been rethinking this whole trip," Sarah said, her eyes on the awakening horizon. She looked back at Trenfor. "When the university approved my research proposal, it felt like resume-padding. Something to toss on an application before drifting back into my dad's company. But now…" Her fingers traced the curve of the armrest between them. "I'm starting to think something here matters beyond academia. Something I need to follow, even if I don't know what it is yet."

Trenfor turned, not surprised, but recognizing. It was the same look he had given her in the café, as though he saw what wasn't yet visible. He let the silence settle, sensing that there was more she needed to say.

"You never said how you know these things," she added, studying him. "About Canaanite rites, biblical accounts, things that most scholars sidestep. You speak like someone who doesn't just study history, but prefers walking in it."

She tilted her head. "What I mean is, when we first met, I asked if you were one of those atheist professors who teach religion without believing it. I've had those types of religion professors. But you don't seem to be in that category at all."

"You've always been suspicious of contradictions," he replied, his voice low but even.

Sarah nodded. "And I didn't sense a contradiction with you, though I still don't know much about you either. Like, how did you become a religion scholar? You said you were agnostic in the Marines?"

He shook his head. "Amoral. I just didn't care."

She nodded slowly. "Still. You seemed to have real-life experiences coming from the military, while other professors have been isolated in academia. I didn't press the question back at the café. But what stuck with me was something more than your theological knowledge. It was what you said about why you didn't react to the rain during our photo shoot. You quoted an old samurai when we me in the cafe. What was it?"

Trenfor's expression barely shifted. "Yamamoto Tsunetomo. He wrote in the Hagakure, *'There is something to be learned from a rainstorm. When you try not to get wet, you still do. But if you resolve yourself to getting soaked from the start, you will not be perplexed. This understanding extends to everything.'*"

"Right. That. You said it wasn't just about accepting what you can't control but even welcoming it. I couldn't get that out of my head. How does anyone live with that much discipline, conviction, or whatever it is? You're kind of a mystery. Ancient philosophy, spiritual discernment, a military background, and a PhD all rolled into one. You're not the typical religion professor. Are you some kind of modern-day samurai?"

She let the question settle like the hush before a storm. It wasn't mockery. It was wonder. A genuine attempt to place him in a frame she could understand.

Trenfor didn't answer right away. A small, enigmatic smile lifted at the edge of his mouth as neither confirmation nor denial. His gaze drifted past her to the landscape appearing below. Galilee was beginning to emerge from night, the ancient stitched to the modern in olive groves, stone ruins, rooftops, and roads. The Sea of Galilee glinted in the distance, catching the sun's earliest light like a blade being unsheathed.

Something shifted in him; subtle, inward. His eyes lost focus, or perhaps found it somewhere she couldn't follow. His stillness changed. Not frozen, but arrested as if something buried in the folds of the terrain below had reached up and touched a scar.

Sarah noticed. The softness that passed over his features made him look younger for a moment, like she'd caught a glimpse of someone just before they became who they are.

The plane continued its descent, pressing gently on their ears. But Trenfor's thoughts had already descended somewhere else in time. A time many years earlier.

Afghanistan – Two Decades earlier

A younger Trenfor adjusted the weight of his tactical gear, sweat carving rivulets down his spine despite the early hour. The Afghan village ahead sat in eerie stillness, a cluster of mud-brick dwellings crouched against the jagged terrain like half-buried bones. The place radiated wrongness, not just foreign, but fundamentally hostile, as though the ground itself rejected their presence.

Three months into his second deployment, the novelty of foreign landscapes had long since worn off. Yet this place felt different. Intelligence flagged it as a nexus for narcotics and human trafficking. Known terrorists had traveled through recently. But Trenfor sensed something deeper, a tension that clung to his skin like a second uniform. It charged the air.

The squad assembled without chatter, running final checks on rifles and radios with silent efficiency. Trenfor scanned the horizon through his scope. No visible movement. Smoke spiraled from a few chimneys. A shaman lived here, known by local intel as a spiritual broker between warlords and tradition. The cartel foot soldiers feared him, whispering of hexes and bone magic even as they sought his favor. Trenfor scoffed at the idea.

A strange chill gnawed at his composure, settling just beneath his sternum. Marines learned to trust gut instinct, but this felt different. Not anticipation. It was more foreboding.

"You feel it too."

The voice belonged to the chaplain. Not the soft-spoken, sermon-giving kind, but a compact man with steel-gray eyes and knuckles scarred from more than prayer. He didn't carry his Bible like a prop. It rode beside his combat knife like another weapon.

"Sometimes the ground is cursed," the chaplain murmured. "You feel it in your gut before your boots hit dirt. The old books talk about veil-thin places. Spiritual rift zones."

Trenfor kept his tone light, but the dryness in his throat betrayed him. "With respect, sir, I chalk it up to adrenaline. No veil. No voodoo men. Just nerves."

The chaplain didn't argue. He simply said, "Always remember Trenfor, you don't have to believe in gravity for it to break you when you fall." Then he turned and joined the unit as the lead gave the hand signal to advance.

The village met them with an unnatural hush. No children. No barking dogs. Even the chickens stood clustered in silence, their heads angled as if listening. A mangy dog sat in an alley, its eyes too still, tracking them without so much as a growl. The villagers emerged slowly, unspeaking, offering no protest, no welcome. They only offered side-eyes that held something closer to pity than fear.

An old man stepped forward, motioning to the village center. He wore a necklace of tightly sewn pouches stitched with crimson thread, maybe protection charms. After a brief exchange, the translator frowned.

"He says we should not remain past sunset. That 'the ones who walk between' come at night."

The squad leader waved the concern away and ordered the sweep.

Behind the largest hut, they discovered a half-buried shrine, scorched earth, and charred bones arranged not haphazardly but with unsettling symmetry. Geometric. Ancient. As though mapped by something not human. The very air around it felt viscous, resistant to movement, like oil in water.

Then the gunfire began.

Short bursts from three directions, none coordinated. It was more harassment than assault, designed to fragment their position. Corporal Rivera dropped near a crumbling wall, his shoulder shredded. Trenfor reached him first, applying pressure to the wound, trying to stabilize the bleeding.

"They were watching," Rivera gasped. "In the smoke. Laughing."

Rivera's eyes were wide and wrong. Trenfor glanced over his shoulder in the direction Rivera was looking. Nothing. Just drifting haze. But Rivera kept staring. Staring into nothingness.

"You don't see them?" Rivera said.

The rest of the day blurred; medevac, recon, radio chatter. By dusk, Trenfor found himself near a collapsed structure, separated from the others during a routine patrol. The firefight was hours behind them. Corporal Rivera's strange visions were written off as shock in the moment he was hit. As Trenfor kicked the ground, his boot dislodged a piece of scorched debris. Beneath it, something gleamed.

He knelt. Half-buried in soot lay an amulet. Dark metal etched with symbols that shimmered subtly, as if unwilling to remain still. Against every instinct, he picked it up.

The metal was cold as he held it. Not desert night-cold but void-cold. His breath caught. Pressure slammed into his chest. The air turned syrup-thick. Not unlike the feeling before the gunfight. He dropped the amulet and stumbled back, watching as the object sank into the ash like it had never existed.

"You shouldn't touch such things," came a voice.

An old woman stood nearby, her cataracted eyes seemingly blind, yet locked with his.

"They are doorways," she said. "For those who fell with the dragon."

Trenfor straightened. "I don't believe in demons if that's what you mean."

"Belief is not required for truth," she said. "The ones who come when summoned are old. Older than your world."

She moved closer, stopping inches from him.

"Do you have a God?" she asked.

Trenfor shook his head. "No. No need for a god." Trenfor then patted his weapon.

She made a sound between a laugh and a sigh. "Then you will need one." Before Trenfor could answer, she was gone.

That night, Trenfor stood guard on the perimeter while the others rested. The air was still, unnaturally so, as if the desert itself were holding its breath. It was the same feeling that had clung to their squad the whole day. Above the village, the stars above were unfamiliar; a lattice of foreign constellations, their light sharp and unforgiving, like watchful eyes. No wind stirred. No insects chirped. An eerie quiet settled around him that night.

He shifted his stance and scanned the horizon, but it wasn't enemy fire or a tactical threat that unnerved him. It was something deeper. The silence didn't feel empty. It felt crowded, full of presence. It was as if the night around him was occupied not by insurgents or snipers but by something older, watching. The old woman's words still echoed in his ears.

He'd fought in cities and deserts. Kicked in doors. Seen blood, chaos and death. But this was different. This wasn't the fear of being killed. This was the fear of being *known*, and not known by a man, but by something that didn't blink, breathe, or move, yet hovered just beyond the edge of vision. It was the sensation of being counted by something eternal. Something was sizing him up. As a warrior, Trenfor knew how to fight almost any enemy. But he sensed an unseen enemy silently studying him. It was an enemy he suddenly realized he was unprepared to face. As a soldier, it was that feeling of the unknown that unnerved him.

The darkness seemed thicker around a scorched tree line to the east. A twisted silhouette that hadn't been there during daylight recon seemed to emerge. Trenfor stared. He could swear it was subtly pulsating, as if breathing. But when he blinked, it was still. The distant hills didn't look like hills anymore, but like shoulders hunched in anticipation.

And then came the whisper; not with sound, but with sensation. A pressure against the back of his neck. Words that weren't spoken but impressed themselves into his mind:

You walk unveiled before the Watchers. The shadows know your name.

He backed away a step, hand hovering near his rifle but knowing instinctively that no weapon in the world would avail him. He'd mocked spiritual things his entire life, dismissed it all as primitive myth or emotional projection.

But nothing in his training had prepared him for this: the certainty that he had just brushed against something real and malevolent. Something that knew his name. Something which did not fear the weapon he held in his hand. It did not fear his fighting ability. And it was stalking him in this forsaken land.

For the first time since childhood; not from belief, but from sheer, marrow-deep fear. He prayed. He prayed because he sensed he had no weapon to fight this enemy pressing toward him in the darkness.

"God… if You're real… show me how to fight what I can't see."

The words felt foolish leaving his lips, but they were all he had. A whisper of rebellion against the darkness. And as the words fell into the stillness, the air shifted; not warm, not cold, just lighter. Not a response. Not safety. But the pressure receded. He realized his heart rate had risen as it began to beat slower as a calm draped over him. The internal fear emerging from the shadowy figure receded.

There was no voice that night. No angelic visitation. But something shifted within him. He didn't know then, but that was the moment his war changed.

The unseen watchers withdrew when he called on the name of God.

Something had heard him, and it wasn't the enemy. It was also his first step from skeptical soldier to spiritual warrior.

Israeli airspace

Trenfor blinked back to the present, the memory of sun-scorched sand and spiritual dread slipped back into its vault as the sounds of the descending plane settled around him. Cabin pressure pressed against his ears, signaling final descent. The engines shifted pitch, a subtle whine beneath the floorboards, and the plane's landing gear thumped into position. He turned his head.

Sarah was watching him.

"So…" she said with a crooked half-smile, "are you like some kind of modern-day scholar samurai?"

The words might have sounded teasing from someone else, but from Sarah they carried a genuine question wrapped in observation. Her tone was curious, not flippant.

Trenfor's gaze returned to the landscape beyond her as the Galilean hills crested under the first touch of gold. "Not quite," he said at last. "The samurai served lords. I serve a King."

He met her eyes. "But like them, I train. Not just for battle, but for discipline. The swords I use are not for killing. They are for cutting away everything false. Slicing through enemies most men do not see. And like the Samurai, I serve. And like a scholar, I study."

Sarah followed his gaze to the window. The terrain rose beneath them like a memory summoned to the surface. Olive groves, winding roads, and ancient ruins half-submerged in modernity. The land wore its history like a second skin.

Their reflections hovered in the glass, fleeting phantoms in a space between. Sarah broke the silence.

"I'm not sure I buy everything we talked about," she said softly. "Some of it sounds beautiful. Some of it is terrifying. There are also some things that sound far-fetched to be honest."

The plane dipped slightly, adjusting its glide path. Trenfor tugged once at his seatbelt.

"Truth usually is both terrifying and beautiful," he replied. "Revelation rarely arrives gently."

Sarah looked down, then up again. "My father never approved of all this. Biblical archaeology, grad work... He's footing the bill, but I always felt like he is waiting for me to come to my senses."

"He supports you, though," Trenfor noted.

"Only because he thinks I'll get this out of my system and come back to retail and marketing: metrics and margins."

"Maybe that was your compromise."

"Maybe." She paused. "But lately I wonder if academia's my compromise. Like I've been playing it safe even there."

Trenfor nodded. "We're all drawn to edges. Some peek over. Some jump."

"Jump?" she repeated.

"No one knows if their parachute works until they jump."

She gave him a look. "So, you trust the chute?"

He smiled. "I trusted the one who packed it."

The words settled between them like a stone in clear water, rippling inward.

Sarah's voice dropped. "You said this wasn't just symbolic. You believe in literal spiritual warfare?"

"I've seen it."

She studied him. "It's a lot to take in."

Trenfor leaned slightly closer, voice low. "Most people think of demons as chaos. But they weren't always cast out. Some ruled domains. We call them territorial spirits that are organized. Hierarchical."

"Not just chaos, but structure?" she murmured. "Like I said, it's hard to believe."

"They don't need belief. Just access."

She raised an eyebrow. "Access?"

"Influence doesn't need belief, only permission."

A long pause. The plane banked through clouds, descending toward the runway. Tel Aviv stretched out below them, modern and alive. She noted buildings appearing as modern glass towers against biblical terrain.

Sarah stared out the window. "My dad said this was a phase. But this feels like more than a dig now."

Trenfor didn't look at her as he checked his seatbelt. "Sometimes what looks like a side quest is the beginning of the real war."

She smiled faintly. "Well, you do know war. Marine, scholar, samurai."

His eyes remained on the horizon. "Only the surrendered survive spiritual battle. And I didn't surrender until I saw what I couldn't fight alone."

The plane touched down with a soft thump. A new day had begun and something ancient had just awakened in her.

Chapter Four

Kursi Excavation Site -
Dawn broke reluctantly over the eastern shore of the Sea of Galilee, dragging fingers of pale light across ancient stones. Trenfor stood motionless at the edge of the Kursi excavation site, his silhouette a solitary interruption against the dim horizon. The air held its breath around him, heavy with history, and something else. Something older, something watching. He had felt it on the ride from the airport. The closer he came, the stronger the weight in his spirit pressed inward.

A thin mist clung to the hillsides, wrapping around crumbling pillars and collapsed walls like a burial shroud. Below, the waters lapped in quiet rhythm, unchanged from the days when fishermen cast nets from wooden boats and crowds gathered to hear a rabbi who spoke like fire. Birds startled from the cliffs, their wings slicing shadows into the morning fog. The ruins stirred beneath the rising sun, as if reluctantly waking to the memory of earth that had guarded their secrets for millennia.

"Dr. Trenfor?"

The voice was soft but broke the spell. Trenfor turned. Dr. Levi Stein, the Israeli archaeologist and site coordinator, approached with measured steps. His sun-worn face was lined with dust and time, his eyes sharp behind the brim of a faded hat.

"Dr. Stein," Trenfor said, extending a hand.

"You arrive early. Most visitors prefer daylight."

"I wanted to see it as it awakens."

Stein nodded, more out of politeness than understanding. He gestured toward the cliff's edge. "This is the site. According to the Gospels, Jesus cast out demons into a herd of swine here. They drowned there, over the rocks."

Trenfor moved toward the precipice, scanning the slope. "And this wasn't Jewish territory. It was Gentile. We know that by the pigs alone."

"Unclean animals," Stein agreed. "A strange detail for the account."

"Not strange at all Dr. Stein. It was strategic," Trenfor said. "Jesus crossed into the land of the unclean to confront the unclean directly. When the demons asked to enter the pigs, they knew what it would cost: they would take what the people valued. It was there last strategic option. The Gentiles didn't see a miracle. They saw a loss of livelihood. It was the only move the demons had left to lash out against Jesus as they were forced to obey, leaving their human prey at his word. In seeing their valuable livestock destroyed, the community asked Jesus to leave. It is a detail many miss on how much the demons hate Jesus even when they must obey him. The Gentiles simply viewed what was happening in the physical, in the moment. But the war was just getting started in the spiritual that still affects us today."

Stein gave a small frown. "Economic fallout. I suppose human nature hasn't changed."

Trenfor's eyes scanned the terrain. "Demons don't need to lie. They only have to twist the truth. That's enough for people to trade freedom for comfort."

The wind shifted. Trenfor knelt near a stone, brushing away the dust. Dust not unlike dust that he brushed from combat boots years earlier. "Do you know about the Roman Tenth Legion? The Legion that was stationed here at the time?"

"Yes," Stein said. "They used the boar as their emblem. I've seen the historical record."

"The demon in the Biblical account said his name was 'Legion' for we are many. Legion was not just the name of the spirits. It was a message. The possessed man called himself 'Legion' for a reason. Jesus didn't just perform an exorcism. He staged a spiritual act of war. It was a prophetic strike against the empire's dominion. When those pigs ran into the sea, it wasn't just symbolic."

Trenfor looked around and continued as he gestured with one hand sweeping the landscape. "The first direct assault on the dominion of fallen ones didn't take place in a synagogue. It happened here. Among tombs. Among Gentiles. The exorcism wasn't a peripheral biblical story. It wasn't isolated. It wasn't even about one demon-afflicted man. It was a signal. The first shot of battle."

Stein's skepticism gave way to silence. He tried to look in the direction of Trenfor's gaze.

Trenfor turned back toward the cliff, his gaze now sweeping across the water. "Every worldly power," he said, "is destined for the bottom of the sea if its foundation isn't based on the one true God."

The wind pressed against him, cool and insistent, and for a moment Trenfor felt the familiar tightening behind his sternum. It was the same pressure he'd felt years ago in a desert half a world away.

He hadn't always spoken like this. He hadn't always known these things. But he remembered when the journey began to learn these things.

The question rose unbidden, not for Stein, but for himself: When had the war stopped being only about what could be seen? His thoughts then drifted to an earlier memory.

Afghanistan – Two decades earlier

A young Trenfor sat on the tailgate of a Humvee beneath a sky scrubbed raw by desert wind, his gear stacked neatly at his feet. His deployment orders were finished. His exit paperwork signed. The war, at least the one with uniforms, coordinates, and rules of engagement was behind him.

Sergeant Martinez stood nearby, methodically cleaning a rifle that didn't need it, the way soldiers did when conversation circled something uncomfortable.

"You're really getting out," Martinez said at last. "Thought you'd ride this longer."

Trenfor didn't answer immediately. His gaze lingered on the horizon, where heat shimmered and the land dissolved into abstraction.

"I've done what I needed to do here," he said.

Martinez snorted quietly. "Everyone says that. Most of them open a gun range. Or teach CQB. You know, you could start a martial arts school tomorrow. You're the best fighter

I've ever seen and half the unit thinks you're the best pure operator we've got. You understand violence better than anyone."

Trenfor smiled faintly, but it didn't reach his eyes.

"Weapons will always be part of who I am," he said. "That won't change."

Martinez finally looked up. "Then what's this about? You don't strike me as the retire-and-reflect type."

Trenfor turned then, measured, controlled, but no longer dismissive.

"You ever notice," he said slowly, "how we train endlessly for enemies we can see, but spend almost no time understanding the ones we can't?"

Martinez frowned. "Meaning?"

"I've spent my life mastering force," Trenfor said. "Control. Discipline. Violence when necessary. But I've come to realize there's another battlefield, one we pretend doesn't exist because it doesn't obey our rules."

Martinez watched him carefully now. "You saying you believe in that stuff?"

Trenfor didn't answer right away.

"I'm saying," he finally replied, "that whether I believe in it or not doesn't change the fact that it exists. And if there's a war being fought that most people can't see, then ignorance isn't neutrality, it's surrender."

Martinez exhaled quietly. "So what are you going to do?"

Trenfor leaned forward, forearms resting on his knees.

"I'm going to learn the rules of the war we've been pretending isn't there."

He hesitated, then added, quieter now, more personal.
"And not just the one out there. Not just bullets and blades. Not just men in uniforms where you know who the enemy is."

Martinez tilted his head. "Then what?"

Trenfor's jaw tightened slightly.

"There's darkness people project onto the world because they refuse to face it in themselves," he said. "Fear. Pride. Rage. The kind that hides behind certainty. That inner refusal doesn't just rot a man, it feeds something larger. Something that wants control."

A pause.

"I've seen what happens when men master weapons but never confront their own shadows. I've stood on ground where none of our training mattered. Where the threat wasn't carrying a rifle or wearing a uniform. Where the atmosphere itself felt… occupied."

Martinez studied him. "That sounds less like tactics. More like psychology."

"Call it what you want," Trenfor said. "Carl Jung wrote that the best way to deal with the darkness in others is to face your own first. I think he was closer to the truth than he knew."

He rose, slinging his pack over his shoulder.
"I think there's a war within us and a war beyond us. And the second feeds on the first. I need to understand those two wars."

The wind kicked up dust between them.

"I'll always be a warrior," Trenfor said, meeting Martinez's eyes. "But I want to understand the ultimate battle."

Martinez watched as he walked away, not toward another deployment, but toward a war most men never admit exists.

Kursi Excavation Site

The sun had climbed higher. Present day Trenfor and Dr. Stein walked deeper into the site, stone columns looming like skeletal remains of a forgotten era. Trenfor's pace slowed as they approached a clearing. "The Byzantine church was built here late," Stein explained, gesturing toward the remnants of a fifth-century structure. "Christians commemorated the miracle here, but the original event occurred closer to the shoreline, where we just…"

He stopped abruptly as Trenfor raised a hand, attention fixed on something other than the nearby ruins Stein described.

Scorched earth. A perfect circle. Around it, stones in a distorted star pattern.

"When did your team last work this section?"

"Three days ago."

Trenfor pointed. "Someone's been here since that time."

Symbols carved into a nearby olive tree. Still moist. Fresh.

Stein knelt beside the scorched circle. "Kids?"

Trenfor said nothing. Instead, he approached the tree. His fingers hovered over the markings.

"This isn't random. Someone inverted early Christian symbols. The fish, the chi-rho. All twisted. Deliberate. This wasn't vandalism. This was invocation."

Stein stepped back. "I should report this."

"They won't understand," Trenfor said. He knelt by the ground, his palm brushing close, but not touching the earth. "This site is no longer dormant. It's groaning."

Trenfor then stood. "Someone's testing boundaries. The veil here is thinning."

Stein looked pale. Trenfor's gaze lingered on the symbols again. "They're not just desecrating. They're calling."

The ruins fell silent once more. But Trenfor heard it. He sensed a low hum beneath the surface, as if the stones themselves remembered something terrible. He had felt this presence before.

He whispered, "They know what this place was before Jesus drove them from it. They're hoping to occupy it again."

Ben Gurion Airpot

The Tel Aviv airport pulsed with constant motion. Travelers rushed toward connections, reunions, or escape. Sarah Whitfield found a quiet bench tucked beneath a frosted window where winter light slanted in muted rectangles across the polished tile. Her hair caught flecks of this cold brightness as she turned her phone over in her hand, rehearsing conversations she wasn't sure she wanted to have. Calling her father shouldn't have been complicated, but lately, every word between them felt freighted with silent expectations.

She had disembarked barely twenty minutes ago, her body still recalibrating to solid ground after hours of pressurized air and recycled light. Now, in this moment between arrival and purpose, Sarah felt the press of what awaited her at the dig site and what she'd left unresolved at home. Her eyes, sharp even through the fog of fatigue, scanned the terminal once more. Trenfor was already gone. Somehow, he'd managed to disappear with the same quiet certainty that marked his presence.

The phone felt heavy as she finally tapped her father's name. Each ring stretched like a thread about to snap, until his voice, warm, confident, and practiced, answered with polished enthusiasm.

"There's my girl! Landed safe and sound in the Holy Land?"

Sarah leaned her shoulder against the cool windowpane. "Just touched down. Flight was smooth."

"How's the weather? You packed that EG thermal jacket, right? The prototype? Won't even hit shelves for another season."

"Elemental Gear's Fall line. Yes, I packed it," she replied, a smile flickering in spite of herself. Her father's pride in his brand's innovations was one of his more endearing traits. "It's actually warmer than I expected."

"Well, desert nights are different. That jacket regulates core temps better than anything out there." A beat passed. "You meet up with anyone from the dig yet? What was the name? Levinson?"

She hesitated. Her gaze drifted to the stream of passengers flooding past. No sign of Trenfor. "Dr. Levinson, yeah. Haven't run into him yet. I think I'm the first to arrive."

The lie nestled uncomfortably on her tongue.

"Good," her father said. "Shows initiative. Listen, before you get buried in your ancient pottery shards, you should know Ashen Veil made the front page of the Times. London march. Full color wearing our shirts."

"I saw it," Sarah said, keeping her voice level.

"Many are even in our outer gear," he continued. "That summit jacket, slate-gray. Better exposure than any paid campaign. When this archaeology phase is over, I'll need you back on the promo side. Your media instincts? Perfect for it."

Across the terminal, a small display caught Sarah's eye. Children's drawings mounted on poster board. A sign beside them read, "To Remember: Stories from Holocaust Survivors." She stood slowly, phone still pressed to her ear, and crossed the floor. On the lead panel, bold, jagged graffiti scrawled over the exhibit: "Free Palestine. Death to the Jews."

Her father's voice droned on in her ear: "…strategic synergy, Sarah. Visibility with moral impact. It's how brand and movement grow together."

She stared at a photo beneath the graffiti as her father spoke. An elderly woman seated beside her grandchild, numbers tattooed on her forearm. A survivor of Auschwitz. Someone had sprayed over her face.

"Sarah? You there?"

She turned away from the display, stomach knotted. "Yeah, sorry. Signal dropped for a second."

"You okay?"

"I'm fine. I need to find transport to the university housing."

"Alright. Keep me posted. And Sarah? Proud of you, kid. Just remember where your future is."

"I know. Love you, Dad."

"Love you too."

She ended the call and slipped the phone into her coat pocket. Her reflection stared back from the terminal glass, poised, professional, the daughter of a CEO. But in her eyes, something new had surfaced, something Trenfor's words had only begun to disturb: "Influence doesn't need belief. It only needs permission."

She fingered the charm bracelet on her wrist, each silver piece a token of some past milestone. Her father's gift on her sixteenth birthday. The weight of memory, of loyalty, of expectation.

And for the first time, she wondered whether those charms had marked achievements or anchors.

She pulled her carry-on upright and moved toward the terminal exit, the graffiti still burning behind her. A maintenance worker knelt before the exhibit, carefully scraping paint from the image of the woman and child. Sarah didn't look back.

But she carried the contradiction with her.

CIG Headquarters – North Carolina

Doug McCraken stood at full posture before the curved digital display that dominated CIG's command briefing room. His silver-tinged hair was cropped with military precision, matching the economy of his speech. The screen's ambient glow lit the lines of his face in flickers of blue, tracing over the contours of a man who had seen too many wars, some visible, others veiled.

The map before him didn't show weather, traffic, or trade. What pulsed across the continents resembled seismic data, fluctuating lines of pressure and disruption. But these weren't tectonic. They were spiritual. Unseen disturbances pulsing beneath the surface of nations.

"These are tremor lines," McCraken said to the room of listeners. Most were interns with seminary degrees, sabbatical pastors, junior analysts still adjusting to the weight of clearance-level truth. "A ninety-day composite of spiritual agitation patterns worldwide. Not metaphor. Not superstition. Spiritual data."

The room carried the air of a war room, quiet, alert, backlit by monitors streaming in satellite telemetry, linguistic overlays, mission logs, and encrypted feeds. Every screen hummed with information no one else dared quantify. CIG didn't monitor rumors. They monitored convergence. They assessed realms. They measured dimensions.

McCraken cycled through overlays, ancient spiritual borders, global missionary footprints, heat maps of prayer concentrations, martyrdom sites. A pattern emerged that transcended geopolitics.

"Here," he said, zooming into a rectangle that spanned North Africa through East Asia. "The 10/40 Window. Latitude 10 to 40 degrees north of the equator. The highest concentration of unreached people groups. Also, the densest spread of non-Christian religions such as Islam, Hinduism, Buddhism, animistic systems, and ancestral worship. But this…" he pointed at glowing red nodes pulsing on the map "…this shows it's not just belief that's entrenched here. It's dominion."

A woman in clerical attire raised a hand. Her collar was crisp, her eyes sharper. "The material said you also monitor 'Shedim' activity. I didn't find anything definitive about that. What exactly are we watching?"

McCraken's response was quiet, firm. "We're watching what governments refuse to name. The Shedim are real. Territorial spirits, root systems of spiritual power tied to geography. Ancient principalities, older than Israel, older than Babel. They operate through ideology, law, bloodshed. And if unchecked, even nature bends around their pressure. The Shedim are the unseen players behind geopolitical events."

He tapped a control, and graphs filled the screen, centuries of revival events layered against uprisings, persecutions, and unexplained disasters. "The intelligence community attributes this to culture, conflict, coincidence. We track causality. We track the disease, not just the fever."

A younger intern leaned forward, loosening a tight tie. "But didn't the Cross break their power?"

"It did," McCraken replied. "Their dominion ended. But not their presence. What was cast out can be invited back in. And humanity is gradually doing just that." He brought up a fresh display: charred churches, broken menorahs, censored religious texts.

"Christians and Jews remain the most persecuted religious demographics worldwide. You wouldn't know that with the propaganda fueled media. The front we face…" he changed the screen again, revealing protest footage, smoke-filled streets, chants carried on digital placards "…is subtle. Deceptive. It wears the language of justice. It doesn't call for revival. It calls for reversal."

Images appeared of protesters wearing slate-gray outerwear bearing a single swirling emblem, smoke twisting like a veil. The Ashen Veil.

"They speak of religious equality," McCraken said. "But equality isn't the goal. Inversion is."

A nervous analyst responded, "But don't they just want all belief systems respected?"

"That's the seduction," McCraken said evenly. "Their demands sound reasonable. But trace the rhetoric: they don't want a seat at the table. They want the table overturned, burned, and the altar rebuilt on its ashes. Many modern ideologies weaponize the language of virtue. Respect as you point out. Justice, fairness, equality. Yet their outcomes mean the opposite. Just because the message is wrapped in virtue doesn't mean it is righteous. The Shedim are masters of using our own virtue as a mask for control. The Shedim know that if you can control the meaning of words, you can control the people who must use the words. Discernment matters."

He stepped back from the display, now showing slogans: Dismantle Hierarchies. End the Old Order. Deify the Earth.

"They call themselves the Ashen Veil," he continued. "They say it's the veil that lifts after the fire of deconstruction, exposing truth. But that's not what ash does. Ash is what's left after something sacred is destroyed. A veil conceals, not to heal, but to hide."

His voice dropped lower. "It's not revelation. It's regression. Smoke and shadow repackaged as progress."

He tapped a control, and voices filled the room, grainy, unfiltered audio streamed from persecution hotspots around the world. Believers whispering prayers from prison cells, children hiding beneath church pews, pastors testifying through crackling static.

"This is our Voice of the Martyrs feed," McCraken explained. "We overlay these incidents in real time, tracking persecution intensity, spiritual atmospherics, and ideological spillover. The pattern isn't fading. It's accelerating."

The global map zoomed in.

A single red pin pulsed along the eastern shore of Galilee.

"Kursi," McCraken said. "A site of ancient exorcism. A spiritual tremor node, long dormant. But something has changed. We fear they are returning. Ancient gods. We see the evidence."

He looked around the room. "We've deployed one of our field operatives. He's not there to dig. He's there to study the source we've identified."

Silence fell. No one needed clarification. They all knew who he meant.

McCraken touched the pulsing marker. The pin glowed brighter.

"Pray for Trenfor," he said quietly. "He's standing on ground where spirits once begged permission to stay. They're back, and they're testing the veil at invitation."

The light dimmed as he bowed his head, and the others followed. "Lord, give eyes to the watcher, steel to the defender, and wisdom beyond what we see. Hold the line at Kursi."

When the prayer ended, the red pulse still blinked. A digital heartbeat.

A single man, reading what others could not.

An Old Monastery, Somewhere in Western Europe

The interview room was small, stone-walled, and colder than expected. Centuries-old monasteries had a way of holding temperature like memory, slow to warm, slower to forget. A single window admitted gray afternoon light, illuminating a wooden table scarred by time and ink. Across from the journalist sat Father Lucien Moreau, his habit plain, his posture unremarkable, his eyes anything but.

The camera's red light blinked on.

"You've said publicly," the journalist began carefully, "that what we're seeing in modern culture isn't ideological drift, but something older. Can you explain what you mean by that?"

Moreau folded his hands, considering the question as if it were poorly framed rather than provocative.

"Modern people," he said at last, "believe gods disappear when belief declines. That has never been true."

The journalist blinked. "You're speaking metaphorically."

"No," Moreau replied gently. "I am speaking historically." He leaned back slightly, the stone chair protesting beneath him. "Before Christianity spread westward, the world was not empty of power. It was saturated with it. Nations were organized around spiritual authorities, principalities, if you prefer the biblical term. Pagan gods were not myths in the modern sense. They were embodiments. Manifestations. Powers that ruled through ritual, law, fertility, war."

"You're saying they were… real."

"I'm saying," Moreau corrected, "that they behaved as if they were." He reached for a book on the table but did not open it. "When Christ entered history, He did not merely teach ethics. He issued evictions. The Gospels record exorcisms not as anomalies, but as signs of regime change. A new authority arrived. And wherever Christianity took hold deeply, Europe, parts of the Mediterranean, the old gods lost their jurisdictions."

The journalist frowned. "Lost… or went underground?"

Moreau smiled faintly.

"An excellent distinction."

He gestured toward the window, beyond which bells tolled somewhere unseen.

"In many regions of the East, parts of Asia, Tibet, sections of the Hindu world, those powers were never displaced. They adapted. Christianity never dismantled their structures there; it simply bordered them."

"And now?" the journalist asked.

"And now," Moreau said quietly, "the West has begun inviting them back."

The room felt colder.

"You mean symbolically."

"No," Moreau said again. "I mean functionally."

He leaned forward.

"Every ancient religion understood the same principle: a god requires embodiment. The Hindus called it avatar, spirit assuming form. The modern world prefers language like ideology, movement, identity, system. These are those forms from which they can manifest themselves to exert their evil influence. The mechanics are unchanged. Powers do not return for nostalgia. They return for dominion."

The journalist shifted uncomfortably. "You're suggesting modern politics, culture, even education…"

"…and leaders, and people, are vessels," Moreau finished. "Yes."

He tapped the table once, softly.

"These entities do not announce themselves with thunder. They arrive through tolerance, through freedom, through the slow erosion of moral clarity. They invert truth. They reward compliance. They punish restraint. Evil, you see, does not create. It corrupts. It exists in defiance of the created order. 'Awakening' culture is a modern example. It claims moral clarity while producing fragmentation, substituting shared human identity with competing victim hoods. It permits cruelty so long as its framed as virtue, and division so long as it is justified as justice."

The journalist hesitated. "And Christianity?"

Moreau looked at the camera now, fully.

"Christianity did not erase the old gods by argument. It displaced them by authority. And authority only operates where it is acknowledged."

Silence settled.

"So what happens," the journalist asked, almost reluctantly, "if a society stops believing any authority exists at all?"

Moreau's eyes were steady.

"Then the strongest claimant to jurisdiction wins. The world has free will. And whatever it chooses to enthrone will answer. We should be very careful. History suggests that's a permission rarely withdrawn without cost."

The camera light blinked off.

Outside, the bells continued to ring, ancient, patient, unconcerned with whether anyone still understood why.

Chapter Five

Tel Adama Excavation Site

The Land Rover jolted over the uneven dirt track, its tires grinding against ancient stone hidden beneath a crust of Galilean dust. Sarah Whitfield gripped the door handle, bracing as the vehicle lurched to a halt near a cluster of canvas tents perched like pale sentries on the exposed hillside. The engine idled for a moment, then cut off, leaving a heavy silence broken only by the wind sighing over the ridges.

Before her, the Tel Adama excavation site unfolded in rugged geometry: trenches, mounds, scaffoldings, all orderly intrusions carved into the bones of a civilization forgotten by history but not by the earth.

Sarah stepped out, boots crunching onto the dry soil. The morning sun hung low enough to slant long shadows across the terrain, casting the dig in bands of alternating gold and deepening blue. A mineral tang filled the air, the smell of disturbed centuries rising around her.

She adjusted the strap on her backpack, its weight familiar and reassuring. Inside were the specialized lenses and imaging tools that had earned her this field appointment, despite her polished background in media production and commercial design.

A cluster of white tents fluttered in the breeze, emblazoned with university insignias and heritage commission seals. Around them, students and researchers moved with the steady, respectful focus of those aware they were walking atop the remains of a buried world.

A check-in table under a striped awning stood near the main excavation trench. A man with silver hair and a deeply tanned face glanced up from a clipboard.

"Sarah Whitfield?" he called, his voice carrying easily across the open space.

She crossed toward him, offering her hand.

"Dr. Levinson?" she confirmed.

"Avraham," he said warmly, his grip firm and dry. "Good to finally meet you. Welcome to Tel Adama."

She smiled. "Thank you. It's a privilege to be here."

"An exciting moment, too," he said, gesturing toward the dig. "Yesterday we uncovered what we believe to be the entrance to a ritual chamber with pre-Roman layers, and some Hellenistic adaptation. Fertility rites. Seasonal observances. All very symbolically charged." His enthusiasm softened the academic gravity of his words.

Sarah scanned the site, noting the gridded trenches, exposed foundations, and careful canopying over more delicate finds. "We are near Kursi?"

"Just northeast. Kursi is less than two kilometers," he said, eyes gleaming. "An intersection of Gentile and Jewish histories. Spiritually complicated land, if one believes in such things."

She gave a polite nod, tamping down the flicker of memory. Trenfor's voice on the plane, speaking of fault lines not just in the earth but in unseen realms. She recalled that Trenfor had mentioned Kursi.

Levinson beckoned her along toward a shaded documentation tent.

"Your photography will be invaluable," he said. "Especially with the pottery. Some of the markings are... peculiar. Not what we expected."

He paused near a table lined with trays of labeled fragments. And there, sorting through a collection of artifacts, stood a figure she recognized immediately.

Trenfor.

He looked up, his eyes locking onto hers. A flicker of acknowledgment passed between them, brief, restrained, but unmistakable.

"Dr. Trenfor," Levinson said, oblivious to the silent exchange, "this is Sarah Whitfield, our documentation specialist. She is a grad student."

Trenfor gave a slight nod, professional but edged with something unspoken. "Ms. Whitfield."

Sarah offered a small smile, masking the jolt of recognition beneath practiced calm. "We've crossed paths."

"Briefly," Trenfor said, his gaze holding hers a second longer than necessary.

Levinson chuckled, arranging papers at the edge of the table. "Well, what are the odds? Trenfor's doing independent research on ancient territorial worship practices. Bit of a philosopher-warrior, this one."

"I've heard," Sarah said lightly.

Levinson frowned, sensing a current he couldn't quite place.

"There are no coincidences," Trenfor murmured, low enough that only Sarah heard.

She lifted an eyebrow. "Given that there are often thirty to sixty licensed digs happening daily in Israel, I'd say coincidence is a strong contender that we were both headed for the same one."

"Perhaps, and I am visiting more than one site," Trenfor said, allowing the faintest trace of a smile. "And, here we are."

The implication hung between them, an invisible thread pulling tighter.

Levinson clapped his hands. "Come, Sarah. Let's get you set up. Then I'll show you something you both might find... intriguing."

As they walked toward the equipment tents, Sarah felt Trenfor's gaze linger a moment longer, as if measuring the invisible shifting of unseen lines.

By midday, the excavation pit had become a crucible of heat, the sun hammering down with biblical intensity.

Sarah crouched at the sifting station, filtering soil and shards through a wide-meshed screen. Dust clung to her forearms and boots. Each fragment that passed through her fingers carried the subtle resonance of forgotten hands, potters, priests, mourners.

She sensed Trenfor approach before she saw him, the slight pressure in the air, a break in the background rhythm of scraping trowels and murmured voices.

He crouched beside her, linen shirt dusted with the honest marks of fieldwork.

"Finding anything interesting?" he asked, voice pitched low enough for privacy.

Sarah lifted a curved shard toward the light, its worn surface catching the sun. "Not yet. But the graduate students have been whispering about... strange symbols near the eastern chamber."

Trenfor's interest sharpened visibly. "What kind of strange?"

"Patterns they don't recognize. Not standard Greco-Roman or Canaanite iconography."

She set the shard aside. Trenfor withdrew his phone, swiping through a file of images.

"This is a site near Kursi," he said, holding the screen toward her.

The photos showed scorched stones, inverted symbols, twisted variations of ancient religious motifs. Forms distorted just enough to unsettle the subconscious.

Sarah leaned closer. "The same. Are these connected across cultures?"

"Across centuries," Trenfor said. "Always where worship turned from gratitude to demand. Where altars shifted from sacrifice to self-exaltation. Many sites find them and they don't match what the students have been taught about the usual imagery to expect."

A shadow fell across the table. Levinson had returned, drawn by the images.

"That symbol," he said, tapping a depiction of an inverted tree whose roots rose instead of its branches. "I've seen that."

Without waiting for an explanation, he beckoned them to the storage tent.

Inside, rows of artifacts rested under careful tags. Levinson retrieved a tray labeled **Sector D—Week 6**, extracting a broken clay vessel.

"There," he said, pointing near the rim.

The symbol was faint but unmistakable, the inverted tree, reaching downward like a corruption of life itself.

Sarah felt a chill ripple along her spine.

Trenfor's voice was quiet. "Not a maker's mark. A claim. An authority."

Sarah thumbed through her tablet and found a file she had saved. She pulled up a news photo of Ashen Veil protesters in Rome, their banners bearing the same contorted symbol.

She turned it toward them.

"Here," she said. "Last month's rally."

Levinson peered closer. "Coincidence?"

"No," Trenfor said simply.

He touched the ancient pot with the kind of reverence reserved for evidence at a crime scene.

"Pagan worship wasn't celebration," he said. "It was invocation. Licensing powers over land, over bloodlines."

Levinson's scientific skepticism warred with the raw certainty in Trenfor's voice.

"And you think the Ashen Veil is...?"

"They're not awakening new causes," Trenfor said, straightening. "They're awakening old allegiances."

Sarah glanced between the pot and the protest banner, a thread of unease weaving through her.

"What do you think they are building toward?" she asked.

Trenfor's expression darkened. "Something old. Something that was once drowned. Something that's clawing back to the surface. This looks like evidence they wish to open a portal."

He checked his watch.

"I have an appointment at the university," he said, gathering his satchel. "There's something I need to verify."

He disappeared into the dusty afternoon, leaving Sarah and Levinson in the tent, surrounded by the brittle remnants of history, and perhaps the first whispers of something older stirring once again.

Tel Aviv University

The archive smelled of climate control and academic pride, a sterile coldness designed to preserve not only ancient artifacts but the fragile reputations of those who cataloged them. Trenfor's footsteps echoed across marble floors, sharp against the hush of the vaulted chamber.

Behind the service desk, a woman with steel-gray hair pinned in a severe knot glanced up from her terminal. Her thin mouth tightened further at the sight of him, the kind of bureaucrat who preferred cataloging relics over dealing with living people.

"I'd like access to the artifact storeroom logs," Trenfor said, setting a leather credential case on the counter between them. He provided documents authorizing his scholarly access to artifacts. His tone was polite, but the weight behind it was unmistakable. "Specifically, regarding materials from the Caiaphas tomb excavation."

The woman, Dr. Miriam Schultz, according to the discreet brass plate, examined the credentials with the slow, methodical suspicion of someone who had denied access to more powerful men than him. She slid the case back toward him with two fingers, as if minimizing contamination.

"These papers are from a private research foundation," she said crisply. "University policy restricts artifact access to our own scholars and designated government representatives. Perhaps you'd care to submit a formal request through the proper channels and state the reason for your request."

"This isn't a matter for bureaucratic channels," Trenfor replied, voice even. "It concerns artifacts that may have been... diverted."

Her chin lifted, academic offense flashing behind her rimless glasses. "Are you implying negligence?"

"I'm implying urgency," Trenfor said, holding her gaze without flinching or apology.

The standoff broke as a man in a tweed jacket emerged from a nearby office, his salt-and-pepper beard neatly trimmed, a faint whiff of pipe smoke trailing behind him.

"Dr. Trenfor!" the man said warmly, extending a hand. "We were told you might be arriving. Professor Abrams, Department Chair."

Trenfor shook it. "Thank you for seeing me."

Abrams turned to Dr. Schultz with a slight nod. "Please assist Dr. Trenfor. His affiliation has been cleared with the Dean's office."

The archivist's mouth compressed into a line so thin it was barely visible. "What, precisely, are you looking for?" she asked tightly.

"The records regarding the Caiaphas tomb artifacts," Trenfor said. "Specifically, the nails."

At the word, something flickered across Dr. Schultz's face, gone in an instant, but noted.

"The nails you seek are no longer housed here," she said stiffly. "There's nothing to review."

"I want to see where they were *supposed* to be," Trenfor replied. "And the access logs for those items over the past decade."

Dr. Schultz cast a glance at Abrams, but the chair merely folded his arms and waited. With visible reluctance, she began tapping at her terminal.

"This isn't necessarily about theft," Trenfor said to Abrams, keeping his voice low. "It's about misuse. Spiritual misuse."

"Misplacement of old nails," Dr. Schultz muttered, not looking up. "Not a haunting."

The tension deepened, thick and still. Abrams cleared his throat. "Perhaps we should continue this discussion privately, Dr. Trenfor?"

"After I've seen the logs, it would be an honor," Trenfor said.

From inside his jacket, Trenfor produced a slim folder bearing international seals. It also included a Christian Intelligence Group clearance. Not something lightly dismissed.

When Dr. Schultz caught sight of the CIG symbol, she paled slightly. Wordlessly, she swiveled her monitor toward him.

Trenfor scanned quickly. Dates. Names. Patterns. His finger tapped a particular entry, sharp and sure.

"This one," he said. "Graduate assistant. Multiple late-night entries right before the nails were reported missing."

Professor Abrams leaned closer. "Aaron Miklos. Brilliant student. Left the program two years ago with no explanation."

"If you'll send a copy of that list to this secure email," Trenfor said, scribbling on a notepad. "I would appreciate it." He handed it to Dr. Schultz.

Abrams nodded, ushering him toward a quieter wing. They entered the chair's office, a booklined refuge smelling of dust, leather, and slow-burning tobacco.

Once the door closed, Trenfor wasted no time.

"The Caiaphas tomb discovery made global news in 1990," he said. "But the discovery of the nails was muted. We both know why."

Abrams settled behind his desk. "Because they were dangerous." He steepled his fingers. "Officially? The nails were dismissed as inconsequential debris. Unofficially... we examined them. Very closely."

"And?"

"Microscopic bone fragments. Slivers of cedar. One nail carried trace elements consistent with human remains." Abrams hesitated, then added, "The political ramifications were... complicated."

"A Jewish archaeological site," Trenfor said, voice quiet, "linked to a Roman execution. Linked to a man called the Christ."

Abrams inclined his head slightly. "It was safer to label them irrelevant." He leaned back, exhaling slowly. "No one wanted to ignite a theological firestorm or invite claims that Israel had stumbled onto relics confirming the crucifixion narrative complicated by where they were discovered."

"Faith, politics, and archaeology," Trenfor murmured. "A combustible mix." Trenfor then leaned forward. "Most modern scholars treat crucifixion nails as relics of shame. They're wrong. In the ancient Near East, nails weren't just instruments of death. They were seals, points where flesh met iron, where the spiritual and physical worlds collided."

He paused. Letting the implications sink.

"In some traditions," Trenfor continued, "nails from executions were buried as warding talismans. Other times... as keys to summon what should remain sealed."

He studied Abrams carefully before adding, "There is also the theory that it could be neither of those traditions. Some scholars suggest Caiaphas may have been haunted by what he had done, regretting the part he played. Burying the nails wasn't just a ritual of control. It could have been an act of desperate repentance."

Abrams said nothing, but the silence in the room thickened, as if acknowledging that some wounds, once opened, were never cleanly closed.

"If the nails from Caiaphas' tomb carry any of that resonance," Trenfor finished, "they're not just artifacts. They're weapons."

"And if the Ashen Veil has them?" Abrams asked, voice almost inaudible.

Trenfor's eyes hardened.

"They won't use them to remember," he said. "They'll use them to re-open."

Galilee shoreline

The road unwound along the Galilee shoreline, the asphalt a thin scar slicing between restless waters and ancient hills. Trenfor pulled off onto the shoulder where the land dropped sharply toward the mist-shrouded sea. The late sun fractured across the water's surface in gold and violet patterns, like writing no living tongue could translate.

He opened the glove compartment and retrieved an encrypted satellite phone. No speed dial needed. He thumbed a code and waited.

Three rings. Then a click.

"Doug here," came the voice, clipped and unshakable across the secure line.

"Update me," Trenfor said, scanning the misted landscape. "Artifact storage access. Caiaphas excavation."

Doug's fingers were audible over the connection, fast, surgical as he clicked a computer keyboard.

"Pulled it," Doug said. "Cross referenced the lists you sent. It's worse than we thought."

Trenfor waited, silent as the hills.

"The nails weren't incidental grave goods," Doug continued. "The University was right. Electron microscopy confirms embedded organic residue. Bone. Cedar. Iron oxidation. Classic crucifixion profile."

Trenfor's hand tightened on the steering wheel. He watched an osprey circling in the distance. "So, they were authentic. True crucifixion nails."

"Confirmed," Doug said grimly. "And they weren't simply buried. One inside an ossuary, one just outside Caiaphas' ornate sarcophagus. Placement wasn't random."

The osprey he'd been watching plunged toward the lake surface, a blur of precision.

"Seals," Trenfor said, voice low.

"Possibly," Doug agreed. "There's precedent. Iron nails used to bind restless spirits. Especially if the deceased was tied to events considered... cosmically disruptive."

Trenfor absorbed Doug's assessment, staring across the fading horizon. "You're suggesting containment."

"Or contrition," Doug added. "As you've always pointed out, older classified notes hint Caiaphas may have regretted his role. That the nails were buried out of guilt or out of desperate precaution."

"Either way," Trenfor said quietly, "they're spiritually volatile."

A long pause.

"And now?" Trenfor asked.

"The nails vanished some time ago," Doug said. "Our trace flags the one link you suggested, Aaron Miklos. Archaeology student. Left under strange circumstances. Now tied to the Ashen Veil's organizational roots."

Trenfor's jaw tightened. "And their intent?"

Doug's voice dropped, almost a growl: "They call it 'reactivating the anchors of dominion.' Ancient artifacts tied to Christ's passion inverted, desecrated, to thin the veil set between the dominions would make sense of their use."

"If they succeed?"

Doug didn't hesitate. "It won't just desecrate. It'll definitely unseal given the worldwide efforts to support it. The artifacts give territorial spirits a foothold as part of the ritual. The consequences won't be just symbolic either. They will claim the populace is demanding their return."

Trenfor closed his eyes for a moment against the wind.

"Then we stop it," he said.

"You're the point man," Doug said. "Find the nails. Break the ritual. And Trenfor..." Doug's voice softened slightly, a rare thing. "This isn't a typical relic retrieval. It's battlefield recovery. And the ground is already moving. We'll handle prayer cover from our end."

The line clicked dead.

Trenfor slipped the phone back into the console. Below him, the Sea of Galilee rolled in the dying light, ancient and restless.

And somewhere ahead, war was waking.

Tel Adama Excavation Site

The late afternoon sun slanted low over the Galilean hills, pouring molten gold across the Tel Adama dig site. Dust rose lazily from the dry earth, swirling in the heavy air like spirits disturbed by the day's labor. Sarah Whitfield knelt beside a grid marker, her journal open across her knee, the ink drying in looping scripts that recorded the day's finds, pottery shards, weathered tools, a broken amulet whose worn carvings had surrendered to time.

Her hand moved, but her mind drifted.

Across the site, near the shadow of the supply tent, Trenfor stood in conversation with Professor Levinson. Sarah caught fragments of the conversation carried on the breeze, something about student logs, artifact access, the university archives. Trenfor's stance was measured as always, yet Sarah sensed an urgency beneath the stillness, a contained force that gave the conversation weight without raising a single voice.

She lowered her pen and watched him from beneath the brim of her hat, telling herself it was habit, observation, the reflex of an analyst. But when Trenfor nodded once in her direction, a simple acknowledgment, something tightened under her ribs. A sudden awareness of herself in the scene, as if she had stepped into a story she hadn't meant to enter.

Sarah looked down quickly, pretending to reread her notes, but the page blurred. Her mind was elsewhere, adrift between memory and uncertainty.

Her father's voice threaded through her thoughts, calm and commanding even from a continent away: *Secure the deal. Build the brand. Control the narrative.* In his world, meaning was currency. Value was measured by market share and influence.

And yet.

Her fingers found the charm bracelet on her wrist, absently turning the silver tokens one by one. Graduation. First major campaign. A commemorative charm from her father's company gala. Each piece a milestone, each one a rung on a ladder she had been expected to climb.

She swallowed. The familiar ache stirred again, gnawing at the edges of ambition. A feeling she had learned to suppress. A sense that beyond every curated success, something vast and unmet waited. Something the metrics could never quantify.

Sarah glanced back toward Trenfor.

There was always a gravity to him she hadn’t encountered before. A kind of rootedness not tethered to success or applause. He moved like someone who understood the fractures beneath the surface of things, who bore witness rather than sought to win.

She drew the bracelet tighter against her wrist.

Can loyalty and longing coexist?

It was a foolish question. But it pressed against her just the same.

Loyalty to her father, to the life he had built, the life she had been prepared to inherit.

Longing, for meaning that wasn't manufactured.

Longing for what Trenfor hinted at without ever naming.

Longing to understand the unseen.

What was it that she really believed?

Trenfor passed by, his boots leaving clean impressions in the dust. His gaze brushed hers, steady, unburdened by expectation. Just a nod, nothing more. But the moment folded itself into her chest like a secret she would not know how to explain.

Sarah dropped her eyes to the journal again. Forced her pen to move.

Somewhere beyond the campsite, the hills bled into darkness. The work lights hummed on one by one, casting artificial halos over ancient stones. Around her, the others pressed on, cataloguing the dead past, dissecting the silence of centuries.

But Sarah felt it in her marrow that they weren't just digging into history anymore.

Something was still digging back.

Chapter Six

Paris, France

The last light bled across the Paris skyline, dragging long shadows over streets lined with stone and history. The ancient façades, their bones older than many revolutions, caught the dying sun in brief flashes of gold before surrendering to gray.

Below, the streets churned with movement. A tide of bodies pressed forward in loose formation, voices rising and falling in practiced cadence. Above their heads, the banners of the Ashen Veil snapped against the evening wind, broad swaths of forest green and muted ash-gray, adorned with sigils of twisted trees and bleeding earth.

At first glance, it looked beautiful, a movement cloaked in the language of renewal.

"Justice for the planet!" The chant rolled like a drumbeat through approaching dusk, synchronized and unyielding. *"Equality for all! Repair what's broken!" "Collectivism over Individualism."*

Most of the faces were young, earnest, illuminated by a zeal that seemed almost too bright for the dimming day. They moved with an almost sacred certainty, their hands lifted in rhythmic gestures. Sustainable fibers clothed their bodies, hemp satchels bounced against their hips, and beaded bracelets clicked softly as they marched, tokens of an earthy spirituality that masked something far older.

Yet beneath the songs of hope, a different rhythm pulsed.

The anger wasn't shouted; it was embedded. It tightened shoulders. It set jaws.

It turned eyes glassy with the kind of fury that could be summoned but not easily dismissed.

When journalists approached, politely asking questions about goals and strategies, the protesters' faces twisted. Many shouted down the inquiries with slogans rather than answers, voices snapping like whips. Others ignored the questions entirely, their gaze fixed ahead as if unable, or unwilling, to break the spell of movement.

Behind the banners, older symbols etched hastily on posters emerged. Tree roots clawing upward instead of downward. Suns inverted into blackened spirals. Circles of ash marked sacred ground that had long been forgotten, until now.

Once a monument to reason and revolution, the city mirrored marches in other cities. It was becoming a stage for something else entirely.

Something older.

Something patient.

Something that had been waiting.

CIG HQ, North Carolina

The secure analysis room hummed with a mechanical heartbeat; the steady churn of cooling systems, the muted whir of encrypted servers feeding streams of data from an unseen war.

Doug leaned back in his chair, rubbing the bridge of his nose as the projection screen bathed the room in a sterile blue glow. Across the conference table, Barry adjusted his chair forward, the image of the pulsing world map reflected ghostlike across his glasses.

Every flare that flickered across the screen was not merely a protest, a demonstration, a harmless social upheaval. It was a wound. A pressure point on the unseen fabric they were sworn to monitor.

"We've logged 583 tremor events in the past seventy-two hours," Doug said, his voice low and sandpaper-rough from too much caffeine and too little rest. "That's a 30% spike from the rolling average."

Barry didn't answer immediately. His gaze drifted toward the dense bloom of flickering lights over Jerusalem, pulsing like a slow heartbeat on the screen. One of many cities being projected before them. "And the pattern recognition?" he asked finally.

Doug tapped a few keys. The main map shifted. Over the blinking data points, faint translucent lines of history appeared; ancient trade routes, spiritual fault lines, crusade paths, the buried arterial systems of a forgotten war.

"It's no longer just political discontent," Doug said. "It's methodical. Surgical."

At the center of it all, the Ashen Veil's symbol burned faintly over Europe and the Middle East.

The Ashen Veil, publicly a banner for climate reform, religious plurality, and human rights. Privately, a machine of ideological warfare, grinding belief and truth into dust beneath the velvet rhetoric of liberation echoed by a willing media.

Doug circled his hand over the holographic projection. "Classic inversion tactics. Marxist playbook with a spiritual edge. Accuse your enemies of what you are guilty of doing. Claim oppression while tightening the noose. Erode language until nothing sacred can stand without sounding intolerant. Control the meaning of words and you control the people."

He keyed in another overlay, ancient maps faded into view, layered over the glowing modern chaos. "Pre-made signs staged to look organic but far from it. Look at their protest sites. Not random."

Barry's mouth tightened. "They're focusing on ancient spiritual strongholds."

Doug nodded grimly. "Every rally. Every demonstration. It's like they're hammering fracture points in the veil itself, centuries-old borders being reawakened."

He traced the arc of glowing events stretching from Jerusalem to Rome to Canterbury to New York, like beads on an unseen rosary.

Barry's voice dropped, more prayer than observation. "They're unsealing the old battlegrounds as we suspected."

Doug pulled up a third layer of intel; incident reports, once background noise, now undeniable patterns. "And it's not just human unrest."

Scrolling down the right margin of the screen were reports:

- **Bell towers** once silent now swarming with bats in cathedrals from Vienna to Madrid.

- **Guard dogs** at sacred sites turning on handlers without warning.

- **Ravens** abandoning the Tower of London, a centuries-old omen of collapse.

- **Animal aggression** selectively targeting Christian symbols and clergy.

Barry rose and stepped closer to the projection, his coffee sitting forgotten behind him. "It's almost like the earth itself is shifting allegiance."

Doug nodded without taking his eyes off the map. "Or the authorities that once bound it are being challenged. They're being challenged as society has slowly weakened that authority over time."

He keyed in another command. Strings of light laced across continents, showing the staggered aftershocks following each protest, vandalism here, a Christian family attacked there, churches defaced halfway across the globe. The influence of the protests lingering.

All linked.

All timed.

"A demonstration in St. Peter's Square precedes violence in Cairo three days later. A rally in Paris coincides with vandalism in Singapore," Doug said, his voice as tight as piano wire.

Barry exhaled slowly. "This isn't activism. It's coordinated insurgency, spiritual insurgency and the media has not idea."

The lights blinked like warning beacons in a storm.

Doug stood slowly, the chair scraping quietly against the polished floor. "Fracture lines are forming across the domains. Every physical outburst we're seeing is the aftershock of something deeper. We're watching a war trying to surface through human hands. The physical is moving the spiritual."

For a long moment, neither man spoke. The room itself seemed to listen, the machines humming like monks chanting a low warning.

Barry finally broke the silence. "Do we alert the field teams?"

Doug's jaw worked once before he answered. "Priority alerts to Jerusalem, Ephesus, and Tel Adama. They're sitting on the most unstable domains."

He turned back to the map, the glimmering network of protests, violence, and spiritual destabilization weaving itself tighter.

"And pray," Doug added, almost to himself. "Pray God stands watch over the gates."

The data continued to pulse behind them, a silent throb of a gathering storm. Data from the most sophisticated intelligence-gathering organization in human history was focused on monitoring the unseen now more than ever.

Yet miles away, under the open Galilean sky, another kind of fire flickered to life, smaller, older, stubbornly human.

Not on a map.

Not in a file.

Not in the media.

But in the quiet hearts of a few gathered souls, leaning close to the ancient rhythms of faith

and story.

Trenfor sat among them, his silhouette cast long by the campfire's glow, ready to speak words the algorithms could never predict and the tremors could never silence.

Tel Adama Excavation Campsite

The flames clawed at the night, casting long, wavering shadows across the Tel Adama camp. Faces emerged and disappeared in the shifting light, half lit, half cloaked, like reflections of the ancient war between seen and unseen things.

Sarah Whitfield lingered near the edges of the gathering, her body angled slightly away, a posture of quiet resistance she barely registered. The night's optional Bible study had drawn a loose circle of students and staff, blankets tossed over sun-hardened ground, knees tucked to chests, murmured conversations fading to silence as Professor Trenfor took his seat on a battered crate by the fire.

Sarah had rehearsed a dozen reasons not to come.

Yet here she was.

Drawn by curiosity or by something she couldn't name.

The ancient stones of Tel Adama still radiated the day's heat, the low walls and broken columns standing sentinel as if listening too.

Trenfor didn't open with scripture.

He didn't open with doctrine.

He opened with memory.

"I don't usually begin these gatherings with personal stories," he said, his voice steady but grave. "Most of you know me as an archaeologist first. A scholar second. Maybe a man of faith third, if at all."

Sarah shifted and sat, crossing her ankles beneath her blanket. She had expected dry exegesis. Footnotes. Intellectual distance. Not this. Not vulnerability.

"I wasn't always any of those things," Trenfor continued. "Before all that... I was a Marine."

A ripple passed through the circle. Students leaned forward. Sarah's skepticism flickered but didn't retreat.

"My final deployment," Trenfor said, his voice dropping lower, "I'd already had brushes with things I couldn't explain. But that final deployment ended in an ambush."

He tapped his sternum unconsciously.

"Shrapnel here. Collapsed lung. Lost on the medevac twice before we even cleared the valley."

The fire cracked sharply, punctuating his words.

"I remember the moment my body quit. Not the pain. Not the fear. Only the sudden clarity as if the world peeled away, and I stood somewhere else entirely."

He paused. Let the silence hold.

No theatrics. No tremor in his voice.

Sarah found herself watching him more closely than she intended.

"There was a gate. Narrow. Almost too narrow. Beside it stood a man robed in simple cloth. His wrists bore wounds. Wounds that bled not blood, but light."

The flames danced in Trenfor's dark eyes as he spoke.

"Beyond the gate," he said, "rose a city, luminous, immense. It wasn't built of stone or steel. It was alive. Peace itself was woven into its walls."

Sarah's fingers tightened around her knees. She told herself it was oxygen deprivation. She tried to rationalize Trenfor had a battlefield hallucination. But Trenfor's even, clinical tone didn't fit delusion.

"I wasn't religious," he said. "Hadn't cracked a Bible since childhood. I thought faith was a crutch for the weak."

A small smile touched his mouth, wry but not mocking.

"But when I woke up weeks later in a military hospital, a chaplain had left a Bible on my tray. Out of boredom, I opened it."

He withdrew several photographs from a worn leather satchel and laid them gently on the cloth between himself and the fire.

"And I found descriptions of what I saw. A City of Peace. A narrow gate. A man with pierced wrists. Written centuries ago about the realities I witnessed. Realities that I saw before I read them. Believe me when I say that I wanted to intellectually disprove what I saw or at least dismiss it. But the more I studied, the more archaeology simply confirmed the writings that I had found in scripture."

He let the photographs circulate among the students, images of crumbling scrolls, inscribed tablets, fragmentary verses.

"This," Trenfor said, pointing to a photograph of an Isaiah scroll from Qumran, "describes a suffering death that mirrors crucifixion centuries before Rome perfected it as public execution."

He let the image pass from hand to hand. "Isaiah wrote these words roughly seven hundred years before Jesus," he continued. "In Isaiah's world, the idea that Israel's Messiah would die a humiliating Gentile execution was unthinkable. Jewish expectation was for a conquering king, not a condemned criminal. Yet the language in the passage, pierced, crushed, numbered with transgressors, buried with the rich, all lines up with one very specific kind of death that didn't become Rome's signature public spectacle until long after this was written. And the scroll you're looking at was already lying in a Qumran cave a century before Jesus was born. No Christian scribe edited this in after the fact. Archaeology doesn't create faith; it many times confirms it. Think deeply about that for a moment."

Sarah felt her pulse hammer harder against her ribs. Her father's voice rose unbidden in her mind: *"They see what they want to see, Sarah. Archaeology is just sophisticated guessing. They wrote things after the fact and pushed it as prophetic."*

But something didn't fit anymore.

Not here.

Not now.

"I didn't become a believer because someone argued me into it," Trenfor said quietly. "I became a believer because evidence found me before I ever sought it. Archaeology didn't create my faith. It simply confirmed it."

Around the circle, no one moved. No one spoke. It was not the pressure of dogma that hung in the air. It was something heavier,

something older.

Truth.

Not demanded.

Simply waiting.

"Truth doesn't need our belief to exist," Trenfor finished, his voice barely more than a whisper. "It only waits to be found."

Sarah stared at the flames, the images of stone and parchment blurring with the rising smoke. Somewhere deep, tectonic plates shifted, fault lines cracking open between the world she had built and the one quietly rising beneath her feet.

When the gathering ended, she slipped away without a word, her steps tracing the ancient perimeter of the dig site. Above her, the stars wheeled slowly in their old, indifferent dance.

But inside her…

Everything was changing.

CIG HQ, North Carolina

The strategy briefing room at CIG headquarters resembled a university lecture hall more than a quasi-military installation; tiered seating rising in gentle arcs around a central presentation floor, muted lighting casting the gathered faces into a landscape of thought and vigilance.

Doug stood near the center, hands clasped behind his back, his gaze sweeping over the newest recruits settling into place. There was a varied assembly of former intelligence officers with sharp, restless eyes; theological scholars who carried centuries of debate behind their pens; field operatives whose bodies bore the calm stillness of men and women who had seen too much and understood it too well.

Doug didn't waste time.

"Spiritual reality," he said without preamble, his voice cutting through the low murmur like a scalpel, "is governed by law, not chaos."

He let that sit.

"Just as gravity binds the physical world, unseen laws govern the spiritual domains. God created order, not disorder. Every system, whether seen or unseen, has its governing rules."

The holographic projector behind him flickered to life, unfolding a shimmering three-dimensional grid, a lattice of light and energy, nodes pulsing softly at their intersections.

"This," Doug said, gesturing toward the projection, "is a simplified model of what we monitor at CIG. Each node represents a documented intersection, points where what we see and what we don't see collide. They are the places where these realities meet."

The recruits leaned forward. Some with instinctual understanding, others with deepening frowns of concentration. Skepticism lingered, but it was edged with curiosity, the mark of minds too sharp to dismiss even the unsettling outright.

Midway up the seating, a young woman lifted her hand. Short-cropped hair, glasses perched on a determined face. "Hi, I'm Dr. Weyland. Theology department. Princeton." Her voice was firm. "Sir, how do you explain realities like the Trinity to rational minds? Spiritual concepts you apparently monitor but that are difficult to understand in our physical understanding. I guess I'm asking how do you explain those intersections. Especially skeptics in the field?"

Doug smiled slightly, the kind of smile earned not by clever answers, but by long battles with the same question.

"Excellent," he said. "You're asking the right question. It's not just about defending the faith. It's about framing reality correctly."

He tapped a control pad. The grid dissolved into a simple two-dimensional plane, a sheet of light stretched flat across the projection space.

"Let's talk about the novella, *Flatland*," Doug said. "Some of you may remember Edwin Abbott's novella from seminary or maybe from math class. Abbott was both priest and mathematician. He struggled to explain higher dimensions to students who could only comprehend the three dimensions in which they lived their entire lives. But he realized they did understand these three dimensions and that would serve to explain higher dimensions."

On the display, a small circle floated across the two-dimensional plane.

"Imagine beings who exist only in two dimensions," Doug said. "They have length and width, but height means nothing to them. The concept of 'up' or 'down' simply doesn't exist. It's beyond their frame of reference. Just like we cannot comprehend anything beyond three-dimensional space. He imagined a flat world that could only comprehend two."

The circle glided along the plane. Then, from above, a three-dimensional hand descended into the flat world. As the fingers touched the plane, three distinct circles appeared; separate, disconnected.

"If I reach three fingers into Flatland from our three-dimensional world into their two-dimensional reality," Doug continued, "the inhabitants see three disjointed shapes. They cannot comprehend that these shapes are part of a single being above them, a being unified in a reality they cannot perceive."

He let that visualization linger, watching as understanding dawned across the room.

"This," Doug said quietly, "is why divine mysteries appear contradictory from our perspective. God is not limited by the constructs of time, space, or material substance. What looks paradoxical from our three-dimensional understanding; Father, Son, and Spirit, makes perfect coherence in higher dimensions where God fully resides and is not bound by our three-dimensional laws. Just like we can understand how three fingers can belong to one person in a three-dimensional world but a two-dimensional creature could not."

Dr. Weyland nodded slowly, the edges of her earlier skepticism softening into contemplation.

Doug tapped again. The hologram shifted, layered planes intersecting, creating a luminous network. Tiny bursts of light pulsed where the planes touched.

"What we monitor," he said, "are these intersections, points where spiritual and material realities graze each other. Not myths. Not hallucinations. Documented fault lines where tremors ripple across dimensions. Where headlines seem to be influenced by something else."

A former Air Force captain in the front row leaned forward. His voice was low but steady. "Are we talking about ghosts? Angels? Demons?"

Doug's face didn't flinch. "We're talking about beings referenced across cultures and epochs, some benevolent, many not. The Bible calls them angels, Shedim, principalities, powers. Other traditions called them gods, spirits, watchers. Names differ. Realities don't."

He tapped another command. Classical paintings, ancient manuscripts, medieval carvings flickered across the screen, depictions of burning bushes, wheels within wheels, luminous beings descending in fire.

"The mistake modern culture makes," Doug said, voice tightening, "is treating ancient encounters as metaphor or worse, myth. Because we no longer possess the dimensional awareness to perceive them properly."

The display faded back to the global grid, points pulsing harder now, hotter, bleeding urgency into the room.

"These aren't random spiritual spasms. They're orchestrated openings. Bleed-throughs."

Silence fell heavy, each recruit absorbing the magnitude of what they were being asked to understand and what they would be asked to confront.

Doug's voice softened, but carried the weight of warning. "At CIG, we do not indulge superstition. We track these spiritualities. We anticipate breaches. We monitor fractures in the veil."

He paused, letting his final words settle like dust on stone.

"And we stand guard where no one else even knows the gates exist."

Tel Adama Excavation Site

Moonlight spilled across the Tel Adama dig site, weaving the ruins into a tapestry of silver and shadow. Trenfor moved quietly between the trenches, his steps deliberate, reverent. Around him, the sleeping camp exhaled faint noises, canvas walls whispering in the night breeze, a distant clink of pottery settling into the sand. But here, among the stones, silence ruled.

His lips moved in steady rhythm, a prayer formed not for others to hear, but for the soil itself to receive. Ancient words, older than the languages carved in the tablets they unearthed, rose invisibly into the cool desert air, sinking deeper into the ground than sound could carry.

At the edge of a newly uncovered wall, Trenfor knelt, pressing his palm against the cold stone. He closed his eyes. Beneath his fingertips, the earth seemed to breathe, a slow, ancient pulse that connected him to the nameless hands who had etched faith into rock when ink and parchment were still dreams unborn.

"Guard this place," he whispered, voice nearly lost in the wind. "Preserve what matters. As you preserved your truth through the storms of history, preserve it still."

The breeze caught his prayer and scattered it across the land, over the barren hills, across forgotten rivers, into distant cities where night still clung to rooftops and alleyways.

And in those distant places, fire answered.

Europe

In Paris, the Square before Notre Dame Cathedral writhed with bodies and torches. Protesters surged like a tide beneath the ancient façade, their faces upturned, lit from below by flames that distorted their features into something more primal than protest or petition.

"Justice for the Earth!" shouted a woman at the front, thrusting a burning torch toward the heavens. Her voice was raw, desperate.

"The church has stolen what was ours!" cried another.

An effigy, robed, crowned with thorns was hoisted onto the base of the medieval obelisk, its silhouette stark against the cathedral's crumbling majesty. The fire took it quickly, hungrily. The crowd pressed closer, their chanting dissolving into guttural sounds no longer shaped by language.

A lone journalist near a barricade watched with a shocked appearance to his face. He lowered his camera, shaking his head as the effigy burned.

Across Europe, echoes answered.

In Rome, gray-cloaked figures circled the periphery of St. Peter's Square, their steps measured to a rhythm only they could hear.

In Canterbury, fires guttered against the cathedral steps as chants in forgotten tongues rose into the night.

In Prague, a silent circle of figures faced the astronomical clock, waiting for midnight not to mark time, but to unlock it.

CIG HQ, North Carolina

Thousands of miles away, in the secure corridors of CIG headquarters, red pulses flared across the world map projected on the main wall.

Analysts moved between stations like bees in a hive suddenly aware the hornets had come. Murmured conversations overlapped, the language of algorithms, of electromagnetic disturbances, of correlation matrices suddenly catching fire.

"The tremor lines are converging," reported a senior analyst, her voice taut as she watched data pour in faster than her screens could parse it. "We've never seen this pattern."

She zoomed in. Jerusalem pulsed at the center, arterial lines stretching outward toward Rome, Canterbury, New York, even into forgotten sites like Kursi and Tel Adama.

"Sir, Tel Adama just spiked," called a young technician. "And Kursi. High resonance with multiple layers of energy disruption."

The senior analyst pivoted. "Kursi?" Her voice dropped. "That's... Legion territory."

Her words hung heavily in the room.

Tel Adama Excavation Site

At Tel Adama, Sarah Whitfield sat cross-legged on her cot, the thin walls of her tent enclosing her in a small, fragile world. A battered photograph of her father trembled in her hands, standing proudly with the author of a book and smiling as the author was signing it for her father, *Faith as Fantasy: How Religion Built Our Superstitions.*

She traced the photo with her thumb, the creases worn by years of keeping it close. It had comforted her once. It confused her now.

"What would you say about Trenfor?" she whispered to the still air. "About the things he's seen? About the things I'm starting to see?"

The photograph offered no answer.

Memories of her father's lectures to her paraded through her mind, religion as a survival mechanism, mythmaking as evolutionary psychology. He had been so certain. But certainty, Sarah realized, felt thin when weighed against Trenfor's testimony, the vision of a city he had never been taught to imagine, prophecies inscribed centuries before the events they foretold, ruins that echoed with the names of gods long denied but never destroyed.

The photograph slipped from her fingers, landing softly on the cot. Sarah pressed her palms against her thighs to steady herself, but the hollow beneath her ribs only widened. The ache of tectonic plates shifting inside her soul.

What if evidence wasn't found only in laboratories and lecture halls?

What if some truths were stitched into the bones of the earth, waiting for those willing to feel them instead of dismiss them?

Kursi Excavation Site

At Kursi, the Sea of Galilee slept beneath a perfect, mirror-black surface. No breeze disturbed the water. No insects stirred the air. Even the ruins, cracked stone walls, fallen lintels, battered mosaics, seemed to hold their breath.

A shadow moved across the rocks. It had no form, no edges, yet its passage thickened the night like oil poured into clear water.

The stones remembered. They had borne witness before. To shrieking voices driven into swine. To spirits commanded to leave. To powers that once fled but had not forgotten.

The shadow slithered over broken altars and ancient inscriptions, drawn by prayers whispered, by fires lit, by doubts awakened in restless hearts, by maps pulsing warnings in a hidden command center continents away.

It moved with purpose.

It moved with memory.

It moved with invitation.

The veil thinned.

The gates creaked.

And the world, oblivious, turned slowly toward dawn.

CIG Headquarters, North Carolina Mountains

The operations floor had dimmed into its evening rhythm, banks of monitors glowing like watchful eyes in the half-light. Analysts moved with hushed efficiency, voices low, fingers precise. The room felt less like a command center and more like a listening post, alert to spiritual movement most of the world couldn't feel.

A young analyst leaned closer to her screen, brow knitting.

"That's not right," she murmured.

Doug McCraken looked up from a tablet. "Define not right."

She rotated her display toward him. A world map pulsed with faint markers, thin threads of activity weaving across continents. Kursi still glowed, residual aftershock patterns spreading outward like ripples from a stone dropped in water.

But another node had begun to brighten.

Rome.

"That region's lighting up faster than projected," she said. "We expected residual disturbance after Kursi, but the Vatican corridor is spiking above baseline. Not protests. Not politics. Something deeper in the spirit realm. Reports are increasing there."

Doug studied the data without comment.

"And there's more," she added, hesitating. Her fingers tapped again, isolating a separate cluster.

East Africa flared softly on the screen.

"Ethiopia," she said. "Lake region. Highlands. Monastic zones. The signal's… different. Older. Slower frequency, but it's intensifying. It's in the middle of nowhere. Reports of odd spiritual phenomenon are rising there as well."

She glanced at Doug, surprised by her own words. "I didn't expect Ethiopia to register this high. Not compared to populated center like Rome with the Vatican at its center."

Doug didn't look surprised at all.

"That's because you're thinking like a modern analyst," he said. "You're weighing influence by visibility. You have to know the historical context to understand it isn't unexpected at all."

He folded his arms, eyes still on the map. "Ethiopia doesn't announce itself. Never has. Ethiopia is a different vault line. This only confirms they wish to open a portal. This is an interesting development as they would otherwise ignore Ethiopia. But they know there is an ancient spiritual stronghold there. Different from Rome. But equally important, if not more important."

Another analyst chimed in from across the room. "Sir, if Rome represents institutional power, empire, authority, spectacle, then Ethiopia's something else entirely?"

Doug nodded once. "Continuity. The theory that they wish to open an ancient portal now makes sense."

The room settled into a thoughtful silence.

"Rome tells you where the fight is loud," Doug continued. "Ethiopia tells you where it's been remembered."

He straightened. "Flag it. Quietly. No alerts outside the division. We need to keep an eye on this development."

"Yes, sir."

As the analyst returned to her console, the map continued its subtle pulse, Rome burning bright and restless, Ethiopia glowing steady and ancient, like an ember that had never gone out.

Doug watched both.

A Lecture Hall, Tidewater Virginia

The lecture hall was small, two dozen students at most, its windows tall and narrow, overlooking a quad where late autumn leaves skittered across brick paths. The room smelled faintly of chalk and old books. This was not a flagship university. No banners. No donors' names etched into marble. Just a place where ideas were allowed to breathe without spectacle.

Ruth Martin, Professor of Comparative Religion, adjusted her glasses and glanced at the clock before continuing.

"Rome," she said, writing the word on the board, "has taught the world to think of itself as the center of Christian history."

She paused, then added another word beneath it.

"Ethiopia."

A few students shifted in their seats.

"Ethiopia surprises most people," Professor Martin continued. "Which is precisely why it matters."

She turned back to the class. "Ethiopia is home to one of the oldest continuous civilizations on Earth. It is the only African nation never colonized. Its spiritual memory was never overwritten by an empire. That alone should make historians cautious."

A student in the front row raised his hand. "But Christianity didn't reach Ethiopia until after Rome, right? Through missionaries?"

Martin smiled slightly. "That's the assumption. It's also wrong."

She clicked the remote, and an image appeared on the screen behind her: an illuminated manuscript, its parchment darkened by age, Ge'ez script flowing in tight columns.

"Christianity was present in Ethiopia before it became institutionalized in Rome," she said. "The Ethiopian Church traces its roots to the first century. Long before councils. Long before creeds. Long before papal authority."

Another hand rose. "Isn't that based mostly on tradition? Like the Queen of Sheba story?"

"Partly," Martin said. "And partly on archaeology. And genetics."

She advanced the slide.

"In 2012, genetic studies confirmed that large segments of the Ethiopian population show admixture consistent with Egyptian, Israeli, and Syrian lineages dating back roughly three thousand years, right around the period associated with the Queen of Sheba's visit to Jerusalem."

A murmur passed through the room.

"Tradition says Sheba bore a son by Solomon, Menelik," Martin continued. "Whether one accepts that literally or not, what matters is this: Ethiopia did not receive Christianity secondhand from Rome. It carried its own lineage, political, cultural, and theological, independent of Western mediation."

A student near the back frowned. "Then why don't we hear about Ethiopian Christianity when we study Church history?"

Martin didn't answer immediately. She let the question settle.

"Because history," she said finally, "is usually written by institutions that survive by controlling the narrative."

She turned back to the board and drew a line beneath the words.

"In 325 AD, the Council of Nicaea met. In 381, Constantinople. These councils determined which texts were considered authoritative, based on authorship, chronology, and doctrinal consistency. That process wasn't evil. It was necessary to preserve what we call the Bible today as the authoritative word of God."

She paused. "But it wasn't universal."

She clicked again.

"The Ethiopian Bible contains eighty-eight books."

That got their attention.

"The King James Version contains sixty-six," Martin continued. "The Ethiopian canon preserved texts, some ancient, some disputed, some rejected elsewhere. Many are what scholars call pseudepigrapha, works attributed to figures who did not write them."

A student interjected, "So… fan fiction?"

Martin allowed a thin smile. "That's a modern term, but yes. Some were rejected for good reason. Others were rejected because they complicated theology. Or authority."

She folded her hands.

"The Ethiopian Church never submitted to Roman papal control. It never passed through the same filters. Its faith evolved in isolation from Catholic Europe, from colonial powers, from doctrinal homogenization."

Another student raised her hand. "Are you saying Rome suppressed Ethiopian Christianity?"

"No," Martin said carefully. "I'm saying Rome became the loudest voice in the room. And history tends to follow volume."

She glanced at the screen again.

"To fully accept the Ethiopian canon would raise uncomfortable questions. About where Christianity truly began. About whether Rome was the center or merely a powerful steward."

The room was quiet now.

"So Ethiopia and Rome are… rivals?" the student asked.

"Not rivals," Martin said. "Axes."

She underlined the word on the board.

"Rome represents institutional memory. Codification. Authority. Ethiopia represents living memory, faith preserved without empire."

She looked at them steadily.

"When you study Christianity, you are not studying a single stream. You are studying converging rivers. And sometimes the river you ignored turns out to be older than the one you built cities on."

A hand rose again. Hesitant. "Why does this matter now?"

Martin closed her notebook.

"Because when societies destabilize," she said, "they don't reach for novelty. They reach backward. To older truths. Older identities. Older powers. They reach for stability over time. The reach for the foundations that stabilized the society."

She met their eyes.

"Rome taught Christianity how to govern the world," she continued. "Ethiopia taught it how to survive without the world. Rome became the steward of Christianity, Ethiopia became its archive."

The room was quiet now.

"To put is simply, one shaped doctrine through councils and empire. The other preserved belief through isolation, persecution, and memory."

She met their eyes.

"When modern structures begin to crack, people don't look to what was recently built. They look to what endures."

"And Ethiopia," she said softly, "has been enduring longer than most are comfortable admitting. Ethiopia is a challenge for those who assume who has always held spiritual authority. Ethiopia has spiritual authority the world has forgotten."

She then paused.

The university had never quite decided what to do with Professor Martin. She opened her lectures with rigor, not reverence, footnotes before feelings, chronology before conviction. And yet she never pretended the texts were inert artifacts. She treated them as living documents, dangerous precisely because they still spoke. She simply taught how to think, not what to think while providing facts. But she held onto the belief that religion students must also learn for themselves why they believed what they believe

When the bell rang, students gathered their things, conversations breaking loose in low murmurs. Martin remained at the lectern a moment longer, chalk dust clinging faintly to her sleeve, eyes fixed on the board as if listening for something beneath the silence.

Some remembered that on the first day of class, before any syllabus, before any disclaimers, she had bowed her head briefly and prayed. Not theatrically. Not insistently. Simply as a matter of conscience. When a student later asked about it, she'd answered without defensiveness.

"You're allowed to study this," she'd said. "And you're allowed to disagree with it. But neutrality doesn't mean standing nowhere."

Now, as the room emptied, she erased the board slowly, the faint rasp of chalk against slate the last sound left behind. She then looked at the two words still written on the board.

Rome.

Ethiopia

Chapter Seven

Ein Gev, Israel – 6 Km southwest of Kursi near Tel Adama

The café near Tel Adama buzzed with idealistic energy, young voices tangled in urgent debate beneath strings of warm amber light. It was a natural harbor town stop for archaeologists, tour guides and academics located on the eastern shore of the Sea of Galilee.

Mismatched chairs scraped tile as activists and academics crowded in, sipping cardamom-laced brews served in clay cups. Posters of endangered species and political uprisings covered the brick walls like devotional icons. A hand-painted banner above the makeshift stage read: **Earth & Faith** - though Sarah suspected only the first word would survive untouched.

She slipped into a chair at the back, notebook in hand, her gaze sweeping the room with quiet precision. The journalist in her hadn't fully died when she changed disciplines. She still recognized a curated atmosphere when she saw one. Everything here from the chipped enamel mugs to the manufactured messiness of the décor. Performative, but effective.

The crowd hushed as a tall man stepped onto the low riser. Eli.

He was younger than she expected, but carried himself with the studied ease of someone who knew when to command attention and when to disguise it. His eyes scanned the crowd not like a preacher seeking converts, but like a conductor tuning an orchestra before the first note. When he spoke, his voice was warm and gravel-laced, like desert wind at dusk.

"We gather on borrowed ground," he began, "not from each other, but from the unborn, whose inheritance we poison with every doctrine that sanctifies dominion at the expense of stewardship."

A murmur rippled moved through the audience.

"The earth groans beneath borrowed scriptures," he said, his cadence rising like a chant. "We must reclaim what the patriarchs buried, buried when they carved gods in their own image and cast the divine feminine into shadow."

Applause broke like soft thunder. Sarah remained still, her pen unmoving, though part of her registered the rhetorical precision. Eli didn't just speak. He invoked. A cadence like liturgy. A fire dressed in silk.

"Equity is not an amendment to faith. It is its forgotten root. Sustainability isn't innovation. It's a right. And our spirituality must be rewilded. Unchained from concrete sanctuaries. Reborn in soil. We must cast off the oppression of organized religion. We must cast off the frigid rigidity of the individual and embrace the warmth of the collective."

Sarah's heart beat faster. Not from agreement, exactly, but from recognition. This was powerful imagery. But like a magnet held too close, it unsettled the compass.

She noticed the way Eli never mentioned names, only forces. No god, no faith, no enemy, no specific religion or political ideology. Just borrowed ground and broken memory. Fairness to all. Vague enough to invoke agreement. And yet, each omission rang louder than a claim.

After the speech, the room dissolved into knots of excited chatter. Sarah stayed seated, half-pretending to take notes. That's when she noticed his shadow fall across her notebook.

"The academic lens," Eli said with a nod, smiling at her closed pages. "I admire the discipline of taking notes."

She looked up. "Old habits," she replied. "I used to work in media before archaeology took over."

He eased into the chair beside her without asking. "That explains the dual gaze. I'd heard a grad student from the States had joined the Tel Adama team. Didn't expect she'd also be a mirror."

She blinked. "A mirror?"

"You reflect things," he said simply. "That's rarer than you'd think."

It should've sounded rehearsed. But it didn't.

They spoke for several minutes, about the dig, the region's environmental fractures, the fragility of ancient sites exposed to modern tensions. His questions were disarmingly precise, threading through historical details and modern politics with disarming ease.

"Dr. Trenfor and I have been comparing some of the site's artifacts to biblical parallels," she said without meaning to. She noticed a pause when she mentioned biblical parallels and Trenfor.

Something shifted. The warmth in Eli's expression dimmed, like a lamp flickering under a draft.

"Alex Trenfor?" His mouth tilted into something between amusement and pity. "A relic among ruins."

Sarah stiffened. "He's a respected scholar. His background in biblical archaeology is…"

"…a means of preserving dead hierarchies beneath the veneer of scholarship," Eli finished. "I know his work. Faith-based science tends to serve only one altar."

His tone wasn't angry. It was worse. It was confident. Assured in the way only conviction unburdened by doubt can be.

"Science gives us models," he continued. "Ecology speaks in data. Why bind ourselves to tales written by men drunk on conquest?"

Sarah hesitated. Trenfor had never sounded drunk on anything unless it was meaning. "Ancient texts still carry relevance. Cultural memory. Even metaphor can guide action."

Eli's gaze softened. "Or confuse it." He reached out, brushing a finger against her notebook. "What we need are not translations of the past, but translations of what the earth is saying now."

He stood. "Let's continue this conversation," he said with a gentle smile. "Minds like yours, they're rare. We need more of them if we're to build something better."

He moved toward another circle of admirers.

Sarah sat unmoving, heart caught in an uneasy rhythm. Eli's fire had a clarity she admired; unapologetic, forward-looking, unflinching in its demand for change. And yet...

His apparent contempt for Trenfor, and what Trenfor represented, still burned behind her eyes. He hadn't attacked ideas. He had dismissed a man. A mentor. Was Eli's dismissiveness jealousy, rivalry, ideology or something more?

And those questions unsettled her more than she expected.

As Eli disappeared into the crowd, Sarah turned toward the door, unaware that a solitary figure remained standing in the shadows beyond the café's entrance, silent, observing, unmoved.

As Eli disappeared into the crowd, Sarah lingered a moment longer, processing the strange weight of their conversation. The scent of roasted coffee still clung faintly to her scarf as she walked along the path back toward camp, dusk settling into the crags and crevices of the Tel Adama hills. Just as she crested a bend in the path, a figure stepped forward from the shadow of an old olive tree.

Trenfor.

He stood with his hands relaxed at his sides, gazing out toward the horizon as if he'd been admiring the last light. But when he turned to her, there was no mistaking the alertness in his eyes, focused, contemplative.

"Evening walk?" he asked, matching her stride.

"Something like that," Sarah replied, adjusting the strap of her bag. "The roundtable at the café ran longer than expected."

He nodded once, then paused. "He speaks well," Trenfor said after a moment. "But some things are meant to dazzle before they divide."

Sarah blinked, thrown off by the comment but not entirely surprised. "You were there?"

"I stopped by," he said evenly. "Long enough to listen."

She glanced over. "He's sincere. I know there's... edge in how he talks, but he's passionate about sustainability. About justice."

"He is," Trenfor acknowledged. "Which makes him all the more persuasive."

They walked on, gravel crunching underfoot. The air was cooler now, and the orange-pink light clung to the hills like fading memory. Sarah could feel her pulse quicken, not out of fear or thrill, but the subtle discomfort of being gently but deliberately scrutinized.

"He said some dismissive things," she offered, as if to beat Trenfor to the punch. "About our work. About religious traditions."

Trenfor stopped walking, and she did too, facing him.

"Not surprising. After he stepped away," Trenfor said, voice low, "I heard him speak to another attendee. Called what we've found here 'primitive mythology masquerading as history.' Not exactly the posture of someone hoping to understand the site. Some call it cognitive bias."

"He's a skeptic. So are a lot of people," Sarah replied, arms crossing. "That doesn't make him wrong."

"No, it doesn't," Trenfor said calmly. "But there's skepticism, and then there's strategy."

Sarah looked away toward the glow of campfires down the slope. "You think he's dangerous?"

"I think he's charismatic. And people follow charisma more easily than they follow truth."

His voice had no condescension, only a wearied knowledge she couldn't quite argue with. It reminded her of old debates with her father, different tones, same gravity.

"He made me think," she admitted. "He frames things in a way that makes... sense. Emotionally. Ethically."

Trenfor studied her for a long moment before speaking again.

"Sometimes we see what we hope for, not what's there," he said quietly. "Just be careful."

The words landed gently but firmly, an echo of something deeper, not a command, but a concern.

"I always am," she replied. But it came out more defensive than she intended.

Trenfor didn't push. "Good night, Sarah."

And with that, he turned and walked back toward the flickering firelight at the edge of the excavation site.

Sarah stood for a moment longer, watching him go. Her instinct pushed her to dismiss the warning. But the problem was, part of her had already started seeing it too. The hints in Eli's rhetoric, the quiet contempt under the eloquence. Something that shimmered like hope, but distorted when you looked too closely. She suddenly felt torn.

Tel Adama Campsite

Later that night, the hush of the dig site gave way to the low, steady hum of Sarah's laptop. Her tent, dimly lit by the screen's glow, felt less like a scholar's sanctuary and more like a confessional. Canvas walls fluttered faintly in the desert breeze, but inside, everything was still, except her thoughts.

She typed the words slowly: **"Ashen Veil organization."**

Just research, she told herself. Due diligence. But the justification felt thin, even to her.

The first results painted a polished veneer: a vibrant website with cascading images of tree-planting ceremonies, eco-poetry, and youth-led workshops in reclaimed urban ruins. Their slogans read like mantras: *Rewild the Sacred. Heal the Earth. Unchain the Past.*

Sarah scrolled further.

The tone changed.

A headline from a Lyon paper chronicled a wave of church desecrations across Europe. Centuries-old icons and frescoes painted over with serpentine runes and inverted sigils. Another article described protests where statues of Christ and Mary were smashed in public squares, replaced by earthen effigies crowned with vines and antlers.

A blog by a former member surfaced next its grainy formatting betraying urgency. The author described rituals invoking Baal and Molech under the guise of *"earth-centered restoration."* Fires lit at the foot of high places. Offerings left in ancient groves long dormant.

Sarah's breath caught when she reached a police report summary from Munich. Ashen Veil affiliates had attacked a climate coalition for including religious groups in their platform. "Compromised by Judeo-Christian restraint," the attackers had scrawled in red paint across the conference hall. Several injuries. No arrests.

She clicked a thumbnail of grainy surveillance footage. Hooded figures spray-painted inverted crosses on the doors of a community center, one that had hosted interfaith dialogue on environmental ethics just the week before. A caption beneath it read: **"Purification action against religious colonization of ecological spaces."**

Sarah sat back, stunned not only by the content but by the silence surrounding it.

Major media outlets, the same ones she followed for environmental news, barely mentioned the incidents. When they did, the tone was reverent, not investigative. Headlines like *"Faithful Revolutionaries or Dangerous Dreamers?"* framed the Ashen Veil as artistic radicals rather than something more calculated. Commentary praised their "courage to deconstruct oppressive myths." The subtext: any concern was conservatism in disguise.

Her pulse ticked upward.

Then she found it. An interview clip of Eli, same gentle cadence, same magnetic delivery, but this time standing before a smoldering wooden structure unmistakably shaped like a church. His hands raised like a conductor's.

"Sometimes the old must burn for the roots beneath to breathe again."

Sarah stared.

The words that had sounded so poetic over cardamom coffee now rang with an edge she hadn't wanted to hear.

Her eyes drifted down to the charm bracelet around her wrist. A small hammer, once gifted by her father. He used to say, *"Build. Don't believe."* A creed that had once felt liberating. Now it seemed... insufficient.

She touched the charm, her fingers curling around the cool metal as if it might anchor her.

Her father's pragmatism. Eli's revolution. Two poles of the same utilitarian compass: *The end justifies the means.* One boardroom, one bonfire.

The blue glow danced in her eyes as she hovered over the tabs, some she closed, others she bookmarked, unable to let go. She had been trained to interrogate ideology, to weigh evidence, to separate symbol from substance. But what she faced now wasn't theory. It was hunger masquerading as healing.

Still, something inside her wanted to believe in Eli's vision. Not the rituals or the rage, but the idea that the earth could be saved. That humanity might still deserve a second Eden.

She sat in that tension, finger hovering over the trackpad, torn between the voice that whispered *hope* and the warning that sounded like Trenfor: *Not all light is light.* Her eyes moved from her hovering finger to the computer screen once again. She then she typed in the search engine: ***Professor Alexander Trenfor.***

The search results populated faster than she expected. Academic journals. Conference lectures. Panel discussions. Interviews clipped into clean, neutral headlines.

She clicked one.

A photograph loaded. Trenfor at a podium, dressed in a dark jacket instead of field gear. Same posture. Same stillness. The caption read:

Alexander Trenfor, PhD — Early Christian Literature, with deep expertise in ancient Greek and Hebrew, applied archaeology, and the historical Jesus.

She scrolled.

Articles written by Trenfor on Second Temple Judaism. On pre-Nicene Christology. On cosmology and creation narratives. One paper examined the philosophical tension between the Big Bang and Genesis without dismissing either. Another explored dimensionality in ancient cosmological texts, not metaphorically, but structurally.

A quote had been pulled for emphasis:

"When we try to understand things like time, creation, or the origin of the universe, we encounter friction between theology, psychology, and cosmology. That friction isn't a flaw. It's what happens when our finite minds attempt to grasp the infinite."

Sarah leaned back slightly.

Another interview.

This one more conversational.

The journalist asked why he devoted so much attention to the overlap between science and theology.

Trenfor's answer was characteristically precise.

"You don't need to understand a combustion engine to drive a car," he said.

"But it's better to know the engine exists. To understand what makes it move. Otherwise, when it fails, you're stranded and you don't even know

why. Einstein said that science without religion is lame, religion without science is blind."

The interviewer had smiled, calling him a *warrior-scholar.*

A Marine turned academic. A man who spoke with the discipline of a soldier and the caution of a historian. One line near the end caught her eye.

"While many theologians pursue the heart of God," the journalist wrote, *"Trenfor seems more interested in the mind of God, not out of arrogance, but responsibility."*

There was a pause after that.

Then a carefully worded addendum.

"Sources close to Trenfor suggest his work extends beyond the university. Though details remain classified, his expertise has reportedly been consulted by unnamed government and international organizations."

Sarah exhaled softly. She then closed the laptop and stared at the ceiling.

A Marine.

A scholar.

A man comfortable standing at the fault line between worlds.

Trenfor wasn't just complicated.

He was layered.

And for the first time, she allowed herself to admit what had been forming since Kursi.

There was far more to Alexander Trenfor than he ever said aloud.

Trenfor sat alone beneath the canvas of his field tent, the night air cool against his neck. A tablet rested open beside him, its screen dimmed but not dark, satellite overlays, spectral readouts, layers of a world most people never knew existed.

He should have been reviewing logistics.

Instead, his thoughts drifted backward.

It was always the quiet moments that did it. When the work paused just long enough for memory to surface.

He closed his eyes.

Not to pray.

To remember.

There had been a time when this war was only a suspicion, an outline without substance. A pressure he could feel but not yet name.

Back when he thought the answer lay in books alone.

Back when the first door had opened.

A University Library – Ten years ago

His thoughts drifted to nearly a decade earlier while finishing his PhD. A younger Trenfor hadn't intended to stay too late studying. He focused on the memory of that night. The night that changed the direction of his life.

The library had emptied around him without ceremony, one light bank clicking off after another until only his desk remained illuminated, a small island of lamplight amid centuries of silence. Greek fragments lay open beside Ethiopic transliterations, marginal notes crawling across the page like living things. Patterns he hadn't been looking for had begun to surface anyway.

He leaned back, rubbing his eyes.

More than answers had emerged.

Infrastructure had formed around his theories. Ideas that seemed unthinkable about time, principalities, and dimensions that intersected with faith.

Footsteps approached, measured, unhurried. Not the aimless gait of a graduate student.

"Still chasing ghosts, Alex?"

Professor Ebert stood at the end of the aisle, tweed jacket, hands folded behind his back. His reputation preceded him: early Christianity, Second Temple Judaism, languages most scholars never mastered. He was simply a brilliant professor. What didn't circulate openly was where Dr. Ebert disappeared to every few months or why certain funding streams attached themselves to his projects without explanation. Not to mention calls from the government forcing him to close his office door at times. Students murmured about such things. Trenfor understood the mystique that surrounded him.

"They aren't ghosts, Professor," Trenfor replied evenly. "They're systems, structured forces shaped by belief, memory, and consent. They behave less like myths and more like terrain. Invisible until you try to move through them. I know my theories of modern science intersecting with ancient faith is a bit controversial to traditional perspectives on theological study. But I believe they are real."

Dr. Ebert studied him, interested. "Go on," he said.

"The mistake," Trenfor continued, "is assuming the spiritual is defined by what the eyes can't see. Science already accepts invisible realities, fields, dimensions, forces that govern outcomes without ever announcing themselves. There are even frequencies in the light spectrum that animals can see but humans cannot. I've started to think the spiritual works the same way across realms and spectrums."

Trenfor paused, choosing his words with care.

"We don't have souls, Professor," he said. "We *are* souls, just temporarily embodied. The unseen isn't less real. It's foundational to my study here. And whatever endures beyond matter…leaves patterns behind. I'm convinced we can track these dimensions, sir."

Dr. Ebert smiled faintly at that and pulled out a chair without asking. He then exhaled through his nose, not impatience, but recognition.

"You don't have to convince me, Alex," he said quietly. "I've read your doctoral work. Every chapter. It is interesting and unsettling to some at the same time. But not in a bad way."

Trenfor's brow creased.

"Unsettling because it refuses to stay where modern theology wants it," Dr. Ebert continued. "The church gets too comfortable. You're not treating belief as abstraction. You're treating it the way a physicist treats fields or gravity, real, directional, exerting pressure whether acknowledged or not. Invisible things controlling visible things. You're asking why certain ideas don't merely survive history, but shape it, leaving measurable effects long after their original carriers are gone."

Dr. Ebert leaned back slightly, lowering his voice even more.

"That puts you at odds with most of your peers, Alex. That's why you are defensive over your findings. Understand that your colleagues will hold to most traditional views. They will play it safe and use their degrees to pontificate. They'll go on to teach. To write. To debate footnotes. Perfectly respectable careers, of course." A pause. A glance around the empty library. "But you're intellect is made for something else."

Trenfor didn't respond.

Dr. Ebert's gaze sharpened. "What you've discovered isn't coincidence or metaphor. It's structure in an unseen world that we pretend is somewhere else. It is structure that isn't speculation or something glamorized from a pulpit as theological history. Theologians tend to treat such things a literary history rather than something real. But there is indeed a system that collides, resists, and reshapes the physical world and whatever moves through it. You've identified a cosmic conflict most just think they understand."

They both let the silence settled on the words for a moment. Dr. Ebert's eyes sharpened, not predatory, but precise.

"What if I told you," he said. "that what your circling isn't new? That scholars like you, rare ones, have already mapped these dynamics. And warriors, like you, have already learned how to move inside them. Inside these realms that you understand are not theoretical. What if there was already an organization already built around your theories? A group where the understandings you have touched on in your PhD work are their daily occupation."

He let that sit.

"You're not late to the conversation, Alex," Dr. Ebert continued. "You just arrived at the classified part of it. The part most people stop when the questions become uncomfortable. Where you realize faith and science don't contradict, they intersect."

That got Trenfor's attention. He nodded still digesting the professor's revelation.

Dr. Ebert reached into his jacket and placed something small on the desk between them.

A lapel pin.

The pin was emblazoned with a red crusader's cross intersected by a vertical sword. Behind it, a faintly gleaming world map etched with coded detail. Scripture markings flanked the blade. The cross guard of the sword was overlaid by an eye.

Trenfor didn't touch it.

"I'm not interested in intelligence work," Trenfor said. "I already did my share of that in uniform."

Dr. Ebert nodded. "It is intelligence work. But this isn't the CIA. This group's jurisdiction is bigger, much bigger."

"Then what is it?"

Dr. Ebert hesitated, not theatrically, but precisely. Choosing boundaries.

"Think of it as an organization that monitors a world most institutions pretend doesn't exist," he said. "One that operates daily, lawfully, relentlessly and without the luxury of disbelief."

Trenfor's jaw tightened slightly.

"And you *see* it," he said. Not a question.

Dr. Ebert met his gaze. "We don't theorize it. This group has moved far beyond the theory phase. Much farther than you can imagine."

Silence stretched between them.

"You're not here to recruit a mere believer to some think tank, I take it." Trenfor said.

"No," Dr. Ebert agreed. "Though you are a believer, belief isn't a prerequisite. Competence is. Competence in science, theology, faith. And being a warrior is a plus."

He gestured toward the open texts. "You've spent years training your mind to move between worlds, languages, epochs, frameworks most people can't hold simultaneously. You don't romanticize darkness, Alex. You dissect it. You have the background we value."

Trenfor exhaled slowly.

"And the Marines? The warrior part?" he asked.

Dr. Ebert's smile thinned. "That's the part you don't try to outrun with this group. Although it is filled with intellectuals, it is far from just a think tank.You'd be at home."

Trenfor glanced at the pin again.

"So this is a war."

Dr. Ebert didn't answer immediately.

"It's governance," he said finally. "Surveillance. Intervention. Containment. Sometimes prevention. Sometimes response."

"And sometimes," Trenfor said, already knowing, "direct engagement."

Dr. Ebert's eyes sharpened, not surprised.

"Yes, engagement. It's why we need warriors."

Trenfor leaned back, studying the ceiling's shadowed arches. For years after the Corps, he'd assumed the answer was mastery of languages, texts, systems of thought. He'd become very good at that. Better than most.

But this…

This was an escalation.

Not a retreat from violence.

A refinement of it.

"I don't want to trade a rifle for a lecture hall and pretend I've retired from the fight," Trenfor said quietly. "If this organization exists… I need to understand the scope. The rules. The limits."

Dr. Ebert pushed the pin closer.

"That's why this isn't an offer," he said. "It's an invitation to observe. Then you decide."

Trenfor finally picked up the pin.

It was heavier than it looked.

"Where does it start?" he asked.

Dr. Ebert stood. "With questions you're already asking and a war you've already stepped into."

He paused at the end of the aisle.

"And Alex?"

"Yes?"

"This isn't the Marines in a tweed jacket."

A beat.

"It's a battlefield most soldiers never realize they're standing on."

The pin rested in Trenfor's palm, warm, not physically, but unmistakably present.

And for the first time since leaving the Corps, the path ahead didn't feel like study.

It felt like deployment.

Midnight, Hidden Church in the Ethiopian Highlands

The sanctuary carved into the cliffs of the Ethiopian Highlands held its secrets with the quiet dignity of the ancient. Moonlight glanced off its stone walls but could not pierce the weight of the midnight air within, thick with frankincense and beeswax. Flickering oil lamps revealed shadowed inscriptions in Ge'ez that seemed to breathe with the walls themselves, their faded strokes still pulsing with spiritual charge.

The faithful entered with silent precision; farmers, midwives, students, and elders. Their numbers were small, but their resolve anchored them to a lineage of believers who had survived kings, crusades, and colonial erasures. They greeted one another in hushed Amharic, knowing that in these highlands, discretion was both tradition and protection.

At the front stood an altar, stone-hewn and wax-slicked from generations of prayer. Beside it stood the elder pastor, his face a weathered map of devotion and discernment. He raised a leather-bound codex, its cracked spine bound more by reverence than thread. His hands, strong despite their age, held the pages open with care.

"We gather," he said in Ge'ez, the ancient cadence slow and clear, "because the spirits have moved again. The watchers stir. And the seals groan."

He turned to a marked passage, and read aloud:

"You were once in heaven. Now your spirits shall wander the earth..."—1 Enoch 15.

The words flowed like an incantation, reverberating off the stone with unsettling precision. The congregation bowed their heads, not just in reverence, but in devotion. For them, this was not just Scripture. It was a warning.

A woman near the back spoke, her netela embroidered with crosses passed down her maternal line. "The hyenas came again. Three times they circled the church. But they didn't sound like beasts. They spoke." Her voice cracked. "They mimicked human mourning."

The pastor closed his eyes. "Then the crack widens." He nodded solemnly. "We must pray fervently."

From the shadows emerged a man of medium build and Western clothing, standing respectfully at the periphery. His name was Kebede, a local by birth, but with American-accented English. His formal posture marked by years of service and intelligence training. He worked for CIG under deep cover but known by the congregation. The pastor had acknowledged him with a subtle glance when he arrived, signaling trust forged not in paperwork but in shared discernment.

Kebede watched, recording discreetly using a modified prayer stone that housed encrypted tech. He was not there as a spy, but was there as a bridge. CIG had long known that

Western threat detection models were insufficient when ancient tremors stirred beneath the earth's skin. This congregation held more spiritual sensitivity than any man-made instrument.

The pastor gestured to the rear of the altar. A younger acolyte brought forth a scroll, bark-pressed and sealed in beeswax. Carefully unrolling it, the pastor began to recite from what he called the *Song of the Gate.* It had never been translated to Greek or Latin. It existed only in Ge'ez and in the oral cadence of this one remote lineage.

"When the iron is torn from tomb and hand,
The watchers in shadow shall speak again.
But iron still speaks, if driven by the righteous.
One shall bind. One shall silence. Both must stand."

The congregation began to hum, a low, pulsing rhythm beneath the recitation. The sound felt like it rose from the ground itself.

"These lines," the pastor explained, turning to Kebede in English for clarity, "were not written. They were sung. Passed father to son, mother to daughter, before Solomon ever saw Sheba. They speak of the nails, not because we possessed them, but because we were charged with the place that their shadow still falls."

Kebede stepped closer to the altar, his voice quiet. "CIG detected tremor convergence. One line ends here. The other points to Rome."

The pastor nodded. "Then we are correct in our discernment . The iron is no longer at rest."

On a flat slab beside the altar, the congregation unrolled their map, one drawn not by surveyors, but by seers. No cities. No rivers. Just tremor lines, spiritual topographies traced over centuries. Red charcoal marked areas of rupture. The highest heat points now pulsed near Debra Ketema.

Kebede scanned the map with his phone. He would send it to Doug within the hour.

As the prayers resumed, the pastor placed a hand on Kebede's shoulder. "We are not enemies of science," he said softly. "But the West has forgotten that some truths cannot be translated. Some spirits do not speak in measurable terms. But they do speak."

Kebede nodded. "And CIG is listening."

Across the mountains, the wind stirred, and a single hyena howled, not a call of hunger, but of something older. Watching. Waiting.

CIG Headquarters, Mountains of North Carolina

The conference room at CIG Headquarters pulsed with a hush that was almost liturgical. Rows of monitors bathed the analysts in soft electric blue, casting their faces like iconography in a cathedral of data. It was 5:00 PM in the Appalachians and midnight in the Ethiopian highlands. The sacred had breached the technological. Across continents and time zones, the ancient stirred within the circuitry of satellites and fiber optics, whispering truths through Ge'ez scripture and encrypted channels alike.

Doug McCraken stood at the head of the room, arms folded, eyes narrowed at a massive digital screen where ancient Ge'ez characters hovered like drifting ciphers. Fragments of the Ethiopian codex, transmitted just minutes earlier by Kebede, danced in high resolution before the team.

"Kebede's file transfer completed four minutes ago," announced a young analyst. Her voice was steady, but her eyes betrayed reverence. "All voice files tagged. Audio integrity high. There's… something in the cadence. Almost a rhythm."

Doug didn't look at her. "Bring in Trenfor."

A secondary screen blinked to life. Alex Trenfor appeared, dimly lit in what looked like a mobile field station, wires and tent canvas blurring behind him. Though his feed was lagging slightly, his expression cut through the pixilation, focused, weathered, and urgent.

"I've reviewed the preliminary transcript," he said, eyes not leaving his own tablet. "There's a passage in the codex we need to address directly."

On cue, the Ge'ez text expanded across the primary display. Trenfor began reading, his voice low and reverent, like a man translating something not meant for light:

"When the iron is torn from tomb and hand,
The watchers in shadow shall speak again.
But iron still speaks, if driven by the righteous.
One shall bind. One shall silence. Both must stand."

The room fell still. No typing. No cross-chatter. Only the hum of machines and the deep silence of comprehension.

Doug finally spoke, nodding toward a gray-haired man seated near the theological archives station. "Dr. Calloway. Initial reaction?"

Calloway stood, slow but certain. "We've assumed both nails were simply artifacts from Caiaphas's tomb. That remains archaeologically true. But spiritually, this codex changes our framework."

He moved toward the main display, calling up the two digital renderings of the nails retrieved in the early '90s. One rotated in a suspended scan, pitted and oxidized, its curve unsettling.

"The codex isn't marking origin," Calloway said. "It's naming function."

"Function?" asked a junior analyst, brow furrowed.

Calloway pointed. "The nail found inside the ossuary, 'by tomb.' It was sealed. Bound. A spiritual lock. Still inert, until it was disturbed."

He gestured toward the second. "The one found outside the ossuary? 'By hand.' Not just touched, but designated for ritual use, its very placement a warning."

Doug's jaw tensed. "So even in the tomb, one was meant for restraint. The other, intended for release."

Dr. Chen called from a side terminal. "Confirming placement records. One nail was recovered from within the stone ossuary. The other… lodged in limestone rubble. Not buried. Just waiting."

Trenfor's voice cut in. "This was not happenstance. The tomb wasn't just a grave. It was a sanctuary. A liturgical configuration designed to hold back something ancient."

The room shifted, the implications darkening the air.

Doug turned slowly. "Matthews. Pattern recognition?"

The archival specialist stepped forward, setting a thin binder on the table. "Every ritual-related relic we've studied with high tremor resonance whether its iron, bone, stone, registers higher activation when passed through intentional human handling. Ritual touch matters. The spiritual designation is not a metaphor. It's a trigger."

Another analyst approached, holding a clear case containing a sealed scroll fragment.

"This fragment hasn't been officially catalogued with the Dead Sea Scrolls. Some believe it originated from a private excavation near Qumran in the 1950s, possibly from Cave 11, but it was never submitted to the Israeli Antiquities Authority." She held up the case carefully. "The inscription is controversial, some call it apocryphal, others believe it was deliberately excluded by the Essenes for being too esoteric." She read aloud: "*Those who pierce the veil with iron shall reap voices from the pit.*" The words hung in the room, heavy and vivid.

There was a collective intake of breath. Calloway looked at Trenfor. "You said something about a source that might help interpret all of this Dr. Trenfor?"

Trenfor nodded grimly. "The *Sefer HaRazim*. The Book of Mysteries."

A few analysts exchanged uneasy glances. One muttered, "That's necromancy material, communication with the spirit world, isn't it?"

"It skirts the line," Trenfor admitted. "It's a legitimate mystical text originating in the third or fourth century. Jewish sages used it to summon angels for healing, protection, even altering fate. But some later rituals begin to mirror techniques associated with spirit contact, especially in the syncretic versions found in Alexandria and parts of Mesopotamia."

He tapped his tablet, projecting a translated segment onto the nearest screen. "This fragment isn't in the main HaRazim corpus. It's from a composite scroll unearthed in the Cairo Geniza, a mixing of HaRazim and other apotropaic writings. It's been referenced in only two peer-reviewed footnotes I could find. The translation reads:"

"'*He who parts the veil with forged flame shall divide the heavens not as the prophets, but as the violators. Then shall the voices of the under deep stir—those long sealed. Let no man summon save by the purity of command, for the unbidden return not gently.*'"

A hush followed. Trenfor continued, "The original Hebrew uses rare verbs, *ḥotem* for 'seal' and *tzolel* for 'to churn the deep.' The tone shifts from angelic invocation to eschatological warning. It's not typical *HaRazim*, but it may reflect a darker layer of mystical tradition that formed as Judaism interacted with Hellenistic and Babylonian ideas."

Doug leaned forward. "So, whoever's using these nails… isn't just drawing power. They're tearing something open as we've already suspected. This only confirms the gravity of what they are doing. The question is whether they know what they are unleashing?"

"Exactly," Trenfor said. "And doing it with tools and texts once meant to bring order. This is inversion, like building a temple with weapons."

Doug's eyes narrowed. "So, the Ashen Veil isn't just dabbling. They're activating something they believe works."

"They're not wrong," Trenfor replied. "But they don't understand consequence. They're mimicking Enochian and Razimic texts without discernment. There is a reason mainstream scholars avoided these texts."

Another screen lit up. Two points pulsed: The identified convergent points of activity. One in Ethiopia. One in Rome.

The theology division lead stepped forward. These two regions are getting the most spiritual activity. "The 'nail by tomb', the binding nail, must be returned to containment. Our assessment is Ethiopia, likely near the Ark's spiritual epicenter. A domain of preservation. The original seat of God hidden in Ethiopia. The one they wish to use quietly."

He swiped the screen to zoom on Rome. "The 'nail by hand', that's the active one. The one they intend to use openly. We suspect it's headed to the Vatican Obelisk. A symbol of empire, of conquest. Where Peter fell. Represents the seat of mankind."

Doug stared at the two points, the tremor lines stretching like veins between them.

"They're using the nails," he said quietly, "to tear open what was sealed. Two keys. One lock. One gate. Not unlike a nuclear submarine, which requires two keys to launch a nuclear weapon."

"And not just to awaken the Shedim," Trenfor added. "To give them voice again. Rome and Ethiopia aren't arbitrary marks on the map." Trenfor continued, his voice tightening. "Rome was indeed the seat of mankind when the Shedim were exorcised from Kursi by Jesus. It is the ground where apostolic blood was spilled and human authority tried to crush the church as Saint Peter, who was martyred there was the foundation of the church. Ethiopia, on the other hand, is the seat of God. A place of preservation, where the Ark's shadow still lingers and ancient faith has never broken. They need both. If both sites are opened at once, the old boundaries won't just weaken. They'll collapse."

The silence that followed felt less like uncertainty and more like the pause between breaths in a battlefield prayer. Everything now seemed clear.

Doug turned slowly to the room. "Send everything to field ops. Trenfor, get ready to move. And make sure Kebede knows about these potential target sites. His site may be the last tether still holding. We have our locations."

On screen, Rome and Ethiopia pulsed like eyes opening in a long-slumbering face.

Tel Adama Campsite

Sarah sat cross-legged on her cot, the pale nylon walls of her tent drawn tight against the desert wind, forming a flimsy cocoon that offered the illusion of solitude. Outside, the night murmured, low gusts threading through stones, a distant animal cry echoing from the hills. But inside, beneath the lamp's amber glow and the soft hum of her laptop, she had assembled her own sanctuary of inquiry.

Books, printouts, and digital devices formed concentric circles around her. Modern ritual tools arranged with unconscious reverence. The Dead Sea Scrolls clustered closest, followed by translated fragments of 1 Enoch and scribbled notes from recent lectures. Academic journals, historical dig site records, and linguistics references formed the outer ring, like guards at the gate of understanding.

Her charm bracelet caught the lamplight as she shifted, its metal hammer charm flashing like a warning. She tapped her pencil on each document, recalling the data she gleaned from each.

Eli's voice still lingered, like incense after ceremony: *"The earth groans beneath borrowed scriptures. We must reclaim what the patriarchs buried."* His words were more than rhetoric. They were liturgy masquerading as activism. Seductive. Noble. And dangerous.

In counterpoint, Trenfor's restraint hummed in memory, quiet and solemn: *"Not all light is light. The most dangerous lies wear the face of justice."* He had spoken not just as a scholar, but as a watchman, burdened with the kind of discernment that resisted both outrage and applause.

She was suspended between those two voices. Between poetics and prophecy. Between the call to action and the caution to wait.

She typed slowly into her search bar terms from her notes of Trenfor's lectures at the dig site: **"Watcher spirits Ge'ez."**
A pause.
Then enter.

Articles unfurled across her screen, academic papers, fringe theology posts, old Orthodox homilies. The Watchers: divine beings assigned to guard humanity. Some remained faithful. Others fell, took mortal women, birthed abominations, and were bound. But their spirits, the *Shedim*, wandered still. Ancient texts warned of doors, gates, and tremors in the veil. Warnings not unlike what Trenfor had been tracking.

Sarah opened a forum thread titled *"Veil-Weakening Phenomena in the Ethiopian Highlands: A Comparative Theology."* She scanned notes on spiritual tremor lines, subtle shifts in ritual patterns across cultures, and the terrifying possibility that some boundaries, never intended to be touched, were being deliberately eroded.

Her skeptical training offered an anchor: *this is mythology*, she told herself. But mythology often concealed something else, encoded truths, collective memory, or trauma retold through story. And when myths echoed across Mesopotamian, Hebrew, Ethiopian, and Greco-Roman traditions, it became harder to dismiss them as mere fiction.

The canvas rustled behind her, a breeze sneaking through the zipped seams. Desert air crept into the tent, dry, mineral-rich, touched with the scent of ancient earth. It whispered like an echo of something older than the scriptures she studied.

A soft buzz broke the silence.

Her phone screen flared to life on the cot beside her. She had signed up for email lists.

Message from Eli:

"Come with us tomorrow. We're planting something beautiful."

She stared. The words were innocuous, almost pastoral. They could mean anything, an ecological initiative, a symbolic ritual, a spiritual demonstration. But paired with her research into the Ashen Veil's more radical branches, the phrase pulsed with ambiguity. What exactly were they planting?

She reached for the device, her fingers hovering above the screen. Curiosity and caution grappled in silence.

The scholar in her knew this was a rare opportunity. She could witness their rituals from within, observe the gestures, the words, the myth-making machinery. She could record, analyze, question.

The environmentalist in her still felt drawn to their zeal, even if it frightened her. They cared about the earth in a way few movements did, with intensity, with belief. And belief was in short supply.

But beneath all of that was something unsettling. A warning hum in her chest that bypassed reason and curled around instinct. Trenfor's concern no longer seemed quaint. It felt, prophetic.

Her thumb brushed the screen as the hammer charm shifted on her wrist, catching the lamplight once more. *Build. Don't believe.* Or maybe… *build wisely, and believe with care.*

The cursor blinked in the reply field. Waiting.

CIG Headquarters, Mountains of North Carolina

The Monitoring Room at CIG Headquarters pulsed with a kind of reverent focus, its ambient light kept low to heighten the luminous spill from a dozen active screens. It felt like a digital sanctum, less war room, more cathedral of data. To Doug McCraken, it always recalled medieval scriptoria: scholars hunched over texts, though now the parchment was silicon, and the ink was code. But there were the obvious similarities to a modern-day NASA control room as well.

The central wall-sized monitor flickered with overlays of codices, map data, seismic readings, and transcriptions from ancient languages. Ge'ez scrolled alongside Hebrew, Aramaic beside Latin. AI-enhanced translations pulsed softly as algorithms adjusted for nuance, context, and theological ambiguity.

Doug stood before the display, a dark silhouette against its glow. With practiced gestures, he summoned layers of scripture and spiritual mapping. "Cross-reference the Ge'ez codex with the Ethiopian tremor overlays and the Qumran site reports again," he instructed.

Lines arced across the digital globe, connecting ancient prophecy to modern coordinates. To the untrained eye, it might have looked like chaos. To the CIG team, it was a clarifying pattern.

A theological analyst with wire-rimmed glasses and a calm, clipped voice chimed in. "Seismic data, spiritual disturbances, and artifact movements all still triangulate toward the two locations we projected. Reports of natural phenomena changes are coming in as well from both regions." The globe spun, zoomed, and stabilized on two glowing markers: the Ethiopian highlands and the Vatican Obelisk at St. Peter's Square.

Doug nodded. "Spiritual fulcrums indeed. Ethiopia, home to the Ark's last rumored resting place and one of the oldest uninterrupted Christian communities. Rome, the site of Peter's martyrdom, crowned by a former pagan monument now repurposed to symbolize Christian triumph. Let's stay on these two."

A theological analyst whispered, "To be clear, they're not trying to undo the cross, but to bypass its seal. To reopen what Christ closed, or at least to invite the return of the pagan gods."

Doug exhaled slowly. "To reverse the exorcism of the world. They can do it if they provide the authority. They are blinding the world to ask for the old gods to return."

On screen, the two red points continued to glow, Ethiopia and Rome, flared in synchronization. Between them, new threads emerged, like circuits igniting. A spiritual circuit.

"They're attempting to complete a ritual at these points for sure," Trenfor said over an adjacent screen. "A convergence of ideology, artifact, and geography. Not through fire from heaven but through cultural subversion, ideological spread through re-enchantment of the world under a different authority giving permission back to the fallen angels."

Doug stared at the pulsing map. "So we agree that possession of the nails isn't just symbolic. It's catalytic. Whoever controls them controls the means of access."

The two markers flared again. One stood atop martyr's blood. The other guarded the shadow of the Ark. Ancient tremor lines trembled, unseen to most, but clear to the CIG's instruments and their faith-trained instincts supported by ancient literature. They had analyzed the data then rechecked it over and over again.

Doug's voice, quiet but resolute, cut through the room: "Then we stop them. Before the keys turn."

Chapter Eight

Kursi Excavation Site

The usual dawn mist clung to the Kursi hillside like a secret reluctant to part from the land. It wove between the tents of the dig site, softening the outlines of equipment and turning the distant Sea of Galilee into a silver mirage. In this gauzy light, the excited voices of the students carried a peculiar clarity, cutting through the morning stillness with the sharp edge of discovery.

Alex Trenfor lifted his gaze from the site map spread across a folding table, his attention caught by the commotion. Three undergraduate students, two young men and a woman with her hair tied back in a practical knot, were gesturing animatedly to Professor Stein, the lead archaeologist. Trenfor set down his coffee, the steam rising to mingle with the morning fog, and approached with measured steps.

"It's behind a thick growth of brambles, Professor Stein," the female student explained, her words tumbling over one another in her eagerness. "We wouldn't have found it except that Rami's drone caught an anomaly in the thermal imaging."

The taller of the two male students nodded, eyes bright with excitement. "The entrance is small, but it definitely opens into something larger. A chamber, maybe."

Professor Stein adjusted his glasses, the lenses catching the pale light. "Where exactly?" Stein turned to the site map as Trenfor joined them. The students crowded around, pointing to a section marked in quadrant D-7.

"That's outside our permitted excavation zone," Stein mused, his brow furrowing. "We'll need to notify authorities before we proceed."

"Unless it presents an immediate safety concern," Trenfor interjected, his voice low and measured. "In which case, a preliminary assessment would be prudent."

The professor considered him with a long gaze. The introduction of Trenfor as a "consultant" on the site was an honor considering his credentials. Those alone had been sufficient to quiet academic skepticism, though the exact nature of his expertise remained deliberately vague. Stein knew of Trenfor's military background and connection to CIG. He also knew Trenfor's true interest lay in missing nails from the University archives.

"Show me," Stein decided, nodding to the students.

They made their way up a narrow path that wound through stands of scrubby trees and sun-bleached rocks. The brambles came into view, a dense tangle of thorns that had grown to conceal what appeared to be a narrow fissure in the hillside. Two other students were already there, carefully cutting back the thorn bushes to reveal more of the opening.

Trenfor knelt beside the entrance, studying it with the careful scrutiny of someone reading fine print. His fingers traced the edge of the stone, feeling for marks or patterns that others might miss.

"Natural formation?" Stein asked.

"No," Trenfor replied without hesitation. "The cut is too precise. This was sealed deliberately." He stood, brushing dust from his hands. "I'll check it."

Stein hesitated. "We should wait for proper equipment. Protocol—"

"Protocol permits emergent investigation," Trenfor assured him, already retrieving a flashlight from his pack. "I'll just confirm its stable enough for a proper team to enter later."

Trenfor ducked through the entrance before anyone could raise further objections. Dr. Stein instructed the students to stay put while he headed back down the path to retrieve his phone to call in the find. Sarah watched as Dr. Stein headed down the path back to camp quickly then turned her attention back at the narrow cave entrance.

As Trenfor entered, the narrow passage opened quickly into a broader chamber that smelled of earth and something acrid, like burnt herbs. The beam of his flashlight cut through the darkness, revealing walls that bore the unmistakable marks of human handiwork, smoothed in places, with crude niches carved at irregular intervals.

"You shouldn't go in alone." Sarah Whitfield's voice came from behind him, startling in the confined space.

Trenfor turned, his expression unreadable in the shadows cast by the flashlight. "Dr. Stein asked you to wait outside."

"And I chose not to listen." She stepped fully into the chamber, her own small flashlight adding its beam to his. "I'm the team's documentation specialist. If there's anything worth noting, I should see it."

Trenfor's jaw tightened, but he didn't argue further. Instead, he moved deeper into the cave with deliberate steps, careful to avoid disturbing anything underfoot. Sarah followed, noting how he seemed to instinctively know where to place each foot despite the uneven ground.

The chamber widened further, revealing a space roughly circular in shape. Trenfor's light swept across the floor, highlighting a series of stone alignments that seemed deliberately placed. But many were inverted from what one might expect in a sacred space. Between these stones, faint patterns of ash were stamped into the earth, remnants of something burnt in precise locations.

"Is this a ritual chamber?" Sarah observed.

Trenfor made no reply. He moved to the center of the room and stood perfectly still, his eyes closing as if listening to something beyond human hearing. His hands hung loosely at his sides, fingers slightly spread, as if sensing vibrations in the room.

His breathing slowed, becoming nearly imperceptible. In the beam of Sarah's flashlight, his face appeared carved from stone itself, all sharp angles and deep shadows.

While he remained motionless, Sarah took the opportunity to examine the chamber more thoroughly. Her light traced the walls, catching on irregularities in the stone. She noted the still air, the dusty smell and silt filtering through the beam of her light. She moved toward one edge of the room. On the dirt floor something caught her eye that didn't fit the surroundings. She reached down and picked up a button. It was small, metallic, and stamped with a familiar logo: Elemental Gear.

Her breath caught. She looked at briefly toward Trenfor. Without conscious thought, she slipped the button into her pocket, a reflexive action that surprised even her. When she turned, she found Trenfor's eyes open as he glanced in her direction, though he remained in the center of the room. His gaze held a question, but he said nothing.

Sarah stepped back to his side, meeting his look with one of feigned innocence. Something unspoken passed between them like a knowledge that they were both keeping secrets, both seeing more than they acknowledged.

Trenfor's attention returned to the chamber, his gaze sweeping the space one final time. The silence stretched between them, heavy with implications neither was ready to voice.

"They've already called something this place," he finally said, his words echoing slightly in the enclosed space. "And they've moved on."

The declaration hung in the air like the mist outside, both revealing and concealing at once. Sarah shivered, though the cave wasn't cold. Her fingers brushed the pocket where the button rested, its presence burning against her consciousness like a small, accusing flame.

The darkness of the cave wrapped around them like a confessional booth, intimate and isolating. Sarah broke the silence.

"What did you mean?" Sarah asked, her voice hushed yet insistent. "About something being 'called' here?"

Trenfor studied her face in the crossed beams of their flashlights, his expression a careful neutral. "Following me in an unknown cave can be dangerous. You're not easily frightened, are you?"

"It takes more than a cave to scare me," she replied, meeting his gaze with a steady one of her own.

"What I meant was that this place bears the marks of a specific ritual. One I've seen before. But it was performed recently, and those who did it have already achieved their purpose here."

"Which was what, exactly? And while we're on the topic of your expertise, I've been hearing the other graduate students talk. You're not just here as a consultant or visiting professor, are you?"

He hesitated, then continued. "I'm here to find something that was taken. Something powerful. Two nails were found in the tomb of Caiaphas, the high priest during the trial of Jesus. Both were taken from a university archive where they were quietly being studied. The Christian Intelligence Group, my organization, believes they're being used in a sequence of spiritual rituals. And the calling that happened here may have been one of the first."

Sarah frowned. "Caiaphas... as in the Gospel accounts?"

"Yes. The nails were discovered during a tomb expansion years ago. The nails were first century, with biological evidence embedded. They were religious relics. We believe they're being used not as symbols, but as spiritual instruments."

Sarah swallowed hard. The implications landed like stone.

Trenfor nodded toward the inverted stones and ash. "Whatever began here, it was part of something larger. And it's already in motion."

Sarah took a step closer, suddenly aware of just how much larger this story was than her original academic interest. "So, you're here to stop it."

"I'm here to prevent the unsealing of things that should remain sealed."

They stood together in the silence of the chamber, ancient dust rising around their ankles.

Sarah was quiet for a long moment. Then: "Look, I don't mean to offend. But sometimes I wonder what the real difference is between all this talk of demonic rituals and the sacrifices in your own scriptures. My dad used to say God demanded the same things the pagans did. Isaac on the altar. Blood on the stone. What's the difference?"

Trenfor didn't flinch. "And what do you think the story meant?"

"That God asked Abraham to kill his own son. Just like Molech or Baal demanded."

"You've been near the scorched altars we've excavated," he said gently. "You've seen the tiny bones."

She nodded slowly.

"Then remember this," he said. "Those demonic gods demanded sons and took them. The God of Scripture stopped Abraham from sacrificing his son. God was never seeking Isaac's death. He was exposing the difference. Abraham believed God would keep his promise, even if Isaac died. Hebrews says he expected God to raise Isaac from the dead. And in the end. God stopped Abraham's hand and later gave his own Son instead. That's a huge difference."

Sarah absorbed that in silence. The mist of her breath hung briefly in the cave air. Her hand moved almost unconsciously to the button in her pocket. She was beginning to realize how little she understood of what she had dismissed for so long.

The afternoon sun had burned away the mist that once cloaked the Kursi hillside, exposing the cave entrance in unforgiving clarity. What had felt mysterious that morning now looked startlingly ordinary under the glare, except to those who could still sense what lingered beneath the surface.

Professor Stein moved around the mouth of the cave with the slow deliberation of a man reading a text no one else could see, his steps light on the earth, his thoughts weighted with questions. Trenfor stood a few paces off, scanning the ground like a sentry rather than a scholar. His focus not just on the physical markings, but on something less visible, as if listening for spiritual echoes that had not yet faded.

"These scorch marks are deliberate," Stein said finally, crouching to trace a perfect arc blackened into the stones. "Controlled burn. Not vandalism. Not weather."

Trenfor nodded, noting the trampled brush around the entrance. The marks are too erratic for fieldwork, too patterned to be animal. "Someone meant to leave no trace, and left one anyway."

Stein rose slowly, his joints protesting. "That quadrant was scheduled for next month. No team was assigned here. Whoever accessed it did so under cover of the calendar."

A hush hovered among the nearby students, gathered in quiet clusters around the path. They watched the professors with sideways glances, half-sensing the seriousness of what had been uncovered. Stein called over his assistant, a woman with a sun-scorched face and the sharp focus of someone who'd worked too many field seasons in forgotten corners of the world.

"The Antiquities Authority has been informed," he said. "Until they arrive, I want full documentation; photos, soil cores, and a motion-triggered camera at the threshold. No one goes inside again. Understood?"

The assistant nodded, already issuing instructions. Trenfor stepped away, allowing the team to work. His gaze drifted down the slope toward the Sea of Galilee, glittering in the distance like an ancient memory. He didn't move until Sarah appeared beside him.

"You're leaving, aren't you?" she asked. Not confrontational, but curious, watchful.

"I will be," he said. "The nails aren't here anymore. This site was a beginning, not a destination."

"You sound sure of that."

"I am."

They walked together along the path, dust rising soft beneath their steps. The students had resumed their work in low-voiced collaboration, their excitement tempered into methodical reverence. Sarah glanced sideways. "So… students. You think they're involved?"

"They make good cover," Trenfor said. "They move through institutions freely, they get access to restricted archives. Ideal intermediaries for groups like the Ashen Veil."

Sarah stiffened. "You say that like they're part of some global conspiracy."

"Global activism needs global funding," he replied. "The Ashen Veil didn't print banners for a local protest. Their language is coordinated. Their events choreographed. They span multiple nations. That kind of reach takes more than idealism. It takes money."

Sarah didn't respond immediately. Her thoughts flashed to the boardroom at Elemental Gear. Her father had signed off on several large donations to "forward-looking ecological organizations." At the time, it had felt like justice and ethical capitalism. Now the thought made her stomach tighten.

She changed direction. "What makes you so sure all of this is spiritual and not just… theft? Or some bizarre performance?"

Trenfor stopped. The sun cast shadows across his face, deepening the lines that conviction had carved. "Have you heard of the 10/40 Window?"

"I've read about it. Missionary stuff. The tenth and fortieth meridians on earth."

"It's more than that," Trenfor said. "It's the most spiritually contested territory on earth. Where persecution is normal, and ancient spiritual structures have had millennia to root themselves into culture, ideology, even land."

Sarah raised an eyebrow. "And you think Kursi fits that?"

"Historically and spiritually," Trenfor said. "The archaeology confirms the rest such as altars to Canaanite deities, sacrificial remains. And then, Christ came here. Not to preach, but to cast out."

She frowned. "You said the bones found here. Some of them were children."

Trenfor nodded. "Pagan worship demanded blood. Always. That's the contrast."

Sarah folded her arms. "And yet I still can't get out of my mind our discussion that God told Abraham to sacrifice Isaac. I know you say it was different."

Trenfor didn't flinch. "Because it was," he said simply. "We've already talked about that. It wasn't divine cruelty. It was divine contrast."

"A contrast to what?"

"To everything else the ancient world believed about the gods," he said. "Abraham lived in a culture where sacrificing your child was seen as the highest form of devotion. God was testing his obedience, yes. But not because God desired Isaac's death. When Abraham had faith that even if he killed his son that God would raise him from death, that was trust, not resignation."

Sarah blinked. "So, God never intended for Isaac to die?"

"He interrupted the act and provided a substitute. That's the point," Trenfor said. "Pagan gods demanded sons. The God of Scripture gave His."

They resumed walking, slower now. Sarah didn't speak. Her hand drifted to her pocket, where the Elemental Gear button still rested like a stone; smooth, small, heavier than it should be. The camp was ahead, tents forming an uneven skyline across the hillside.

Under the canopy, simple food waited in shared trays, but Sarah barely noticed. She looked at Trenfor again. "You really believe that all this isn't just metaphor or myth."

"I do," he said. "I've seen the patterns. The rituals. The consequences."

"And if you're wrong?"

"Then nothing happens," he replied. "But if I'm right and they're trying to reopen something Christ once closed, then we won't have the luxury of ignorance much longer."

Professor Stein's voice carried across the camp, calling Trenfor back to examine a newly unearthed inscription. Trenfor turned, giving Sarah a final look, measured, steady, and somehow sad.

As he walked away, Sarah slipped her hand deeper into her pocket. The metal edge of the button pressed into her palm like a seal she hadn't meant to carry. Not yet.

University Campus, Israel

The quad near the university's eastern edge had been transformed into a tapestry of earth-tone banners and grassroots zeal. "Planting Peace," "Justice for Gaia," and "Sacred Soil Revival" waved in the breeze, their slogans painted in fonts that managed to be both militant and poetic. What should have felt familiar to Sarah as just another environmental gathering, another cause cloaked in canvas and conviction, felt somehow off-kilter.

She moved through the gathering with careful neutrality, her press badge clipped to her side from her marketing days, a camera resting on her shoulder more as camouflage than intention. She'd covered dozens of rallies like this. But as she stepped into the orbit of the event, something intangible prickled at the edge of perception. The air hummed with a quiet, anticipatory rhythm like a ceremony waiting to begin.

At the far end of the quad, a stage draped in dyed fabrics rose in understated prominence. Participants weren't arranged in rows but concentric circles on the grass, their formation too symmetrical to be accidental. The geometry read more like liturgy than logistics.

Sarah paused at the edge of the outer circle, scanning the crowd. Professors in weathered blazers stood shoulder to shoulder with barefoot students. A beekeeper in full gear shared a thermos with a woman who wore her dreadlocks like a crown. Despite the diversity, there was a coherence beneath the aesthetics, something like shared intention. It set off an instinct honed during years of academic observation and quiet reporting.

"First time?" asked a woman beside her, offering a ceramic cup. The tea inside steamed gently, its scent earthy with a trace of something unfamiliar.

"I've seen my share of protests," Sarah replied, accepting it. "This feels more… choreographed."

"We don't call it protest," the woman said, her silver-streaked braid falling over one shoulder. "We call it remembrance. The Ashen Veil believes the land remembers what the world has tried to forget."

"Forget what?"

"Pathways, justice," the woman said simply. "Between realms."

Before Sarah could reply, the woman turned and melted into the gathering.

The circles began to move, slowly at first, bodies swaying in quiet rhythm, then more deliberately as participants aligned themselves in mirrored patterns. It was movement with intention, like a dance without music, though the silence itself pulsed with a sound Sarah couldn't hear. She felt it in her chest.

Then the chanting began. It emerged like vapor, indistinct at first, then rising in harmonics that wove through the air like thread through cloth. The language wasn't Hebrew or Arabic, Greek or Latin. It sounded ancient. Designed, she realized, to sound like something older than language itself. The chants were clearly practiced, a ritual more than a song.

Participants pulled pouches from cloaks and satchels, extracting small handfuls of rich, dark soil. With reverence, they began forming symbols on the grass, glyphs of a kind Sarah couldn't place, yet disturbingly familiar. They resembled the ash patterns from the chamber at Kursi. Geometric. Alive in their arrangement. Meaningful in a way her training could not explain.

A few began to anoint the soil with oils, fragrant, resinous, sweet. The air grew dense with scent and silence. Sarah lifted her camera and captured a few discreet frames, but her instinct told her she wasn't just photographing a demonstration. She was witnessing something masquerading as ecology that reeked of invocation.

Then the chanting ceased.

A man ascended the platform. His presence quieted the murmurs like a hand pressed gently on water. He wore earth tones and charisma with equal comfort. His face was sharp with conviction, his posture loose but intentional. The crowd oriented toward him as if by magnetic force.

"Brothers and sisters of the earth," he began, voice warm, resonant. "We gather in continuation of the oldest tradition, communion with the soil that remembers us."

Sarah recognized him instantly: Eli. The center of the Ashen Veil. His voice balanced seduction and command.

"For too long," he continued, "the soil has been stolen. Colonization wasn't just the theft of land. It was the theft of tradition. The sacred pathways our ancestors walked were paved over. Replaced by the cold geometry of empire."

The crowd murmured assent.

"Today, we reclaim. We unseal what was buried. We call down the roots that remember."

Sarah flinched. The language; "reclaim," "unseal," "call down" It echoed Trenfor's warnings that she could now see hidden in the words. Eli guided them through a series of refrains, call-and-response. Hands pressed seed, symbol, or soil into the earth. They were not just planting. They were burying something.

As the circles dissolved into fellowship, Sarah scanned the crowd again with new eyes. What she'd dismissed as choreographed now looked ritualistic. Familiar. Too familiar.

A voice spoke just behind her.

"Enjoying the revival?"

She turned to find Eli beside her, smiling. His expression was open, affable. But his eyes were assessing.

"I guess. It just seems more ritual than rally," Sarah said.

"The distinction is recent," he replied. "We're just remembering what was forgotten. Earth and spirit were always meant to be in covenant. Our ceremonies are about coherence. Justice."

"With seeds. And soil. And symbols."

"And objects," he added, with a tilt of his head. "The land responds to our calling. So do we."

Sarah kept her voice even. She then took a deep breath. "I've been covering the Kursi excavation. There are rumors of missing relics. Ritual signs in a chamber. A consultant you know named Trenfor is... concerned."

Eli's expression didn't change, but something in his stillness did. A flicker beneath the mask. "Archaeological thefts happen all the time in this region," he said smoothly. "Though I'm not aware of anything recent."

Then his tone shifted almost casually. "Your father's company does beautiful work. Elemental Gear has done a lot more than just outfit hikers. His support is appreciated."

The statement dropped like a stone into her thoughts.

Sarah blinked. "So you know who I am."

Eli smiled, wide and warm. "Everyone here knows who contributes. Your father's generosity has advanced our educational initiatives more than he realizes. Or maybe he does."

Her gaze slid to his jacket. Elemental Gear's Alpine Series, limited edition. Her eyes locked on a gap where one button was missing. Where a specific type of button should have been. She helped design it and knew every detail.

"I should take a photo," she said. "For my father."

"Of course." Eli turned slightly, obliging her lens.

Click.

"I hope you'll return," he said. "Curiosity is a kind of loyalty."

And then he was gone, folding into the crowd like vapor through a veil.

Sarah stood still. The button in her pocket burned with new weight. Eli's words echoed louder than the chants; reconnection, memory, unsealing. This wasn't just activism. It was reenactment. And she was no longer sure who was using who.

Hidden Church in the Ethiopian Highlands

The chapel clung to the mountainside like a secret whispered between earth and sky. During the day its features were clearer. Hewn from living rock, its walls bore the quiet scars of centuries with chisel marks, candle soot, and unspoken prayers. The air carried the familiar scents of midnight vigils; beeswax, old stone, and frankincense.

Seven elders sat in a half-circle, their faces carved by age and weather and waiting. No vestments adorned them. The wore only simple wool garments with the kind of authority that came not from title but from decades of unbroken observation. In the center, a fire crackled within a carved basin, its smoke drawn upward through a narrow chimney cut into the rock like a throat opened to heaven.

The wooden door creaked open, and a gust of mountain wind curled through the space, bending the flames with its breath. Kebede entered, shoulders dusted with the long journey, his frame bowed more by the burden of knowledge than fatigue.

"You've returned sooner than we feared," said the pastor, his beard streaked with white, voice softened by wisdom but sharpened by discernment.

Kebede bowed his head briefly in greeting and took the final seat in the circle. "Because the signs came sooner than we hoped," he said, voice low but resolute. "The seal at Kursi has been disturbed. The spirits seem to move toward us with intention."

A ripple moved through the elders, not surprise but confirmation. The woman nearest the fire closed her worn prayer book and folded her hands atop its leather cover.

"What did you witness?" the pastor asked.

Kebede's eyes held the stillness of a man who had seen too much and not enough. "The birds were first; raptors, doves, even scavengers, circling in unnatural spirals. Not riding thermals or avoiding predators. They traced geometries, concentric, intersecting, intelligent."

The pastor nodded solemnly. "Sentinels of the air. They see what we miss."

"Then the animals," Kebede continued. "Sheep refusing pasture. Dogs pacing perimeters and growling at emptiness. Even the elders of the flock stood with eyes turned toward hills they once grazed blindly."

The old man with the gnarled hands leaned forward. "And the people?"

Kebede hesitated. "The dreams began two nights ago. Villagers awoke with identical visions: nails driving through flesh, blood that defied gravity, and wounds that whispered in tongues no living person remembers."

He reached into his satchel and unfolded a sheet of paper. At its center was a child's drawing. It was circular, crude, disturbingly precise. Inverted crosses radiated outward from a central eye, each ending in what could only be a nail, inked in heavy, deliberate lines.

"Children have begun drawing these in dust and ash," Kebede said. "Unprompted. From memory that is not their own."

The pastor's fingers hovered above the paper but did not touch it. The air above it felt warmer, as though the ink retained more than just pigment.

"These markings here match the ash patterns discovered at Kursi," Kebede added. "The local team believes them to be vandalism, perhaps the work of amateur mystics. They do not see the pattern. But Trenfor does. We've compared notes."

"Trenfor?" the elderly woman asked.

Kebede nodded. "Yes. He recognizes the signs. He has seen this convergence before. But he's not alone. Others are moving as well. Those who serve other masters."

The pastor's gaze deepened, drawn inward to some private reservoir of memory and prophecy. "The veil thins. The tremors widen. The gates strain."

"CIG requests your discernment," Kebede said, his voice almost reverent. "They wish to confirm whether the tremors here align with those felt in Rome as well."

The woman closed her eyes briefly, lips moving in silent intercession.

The pastor answered without hesitation. "They do. We have already seen the signs: birds in odd migration, strange weather moving against wind patterns, and one of our own hearing voices in the night, psalms never memorized, in languages never spoken."

His tone changed slightly, more formal now, weightier. "Rome may be the seat of mankind. But our land… this has always been the seat of God. We agree with their assessment."

Silence fell like a curtain. The fire in the center shifted, popping once as a knot of resin ignited.

"The second gate stirs," the pastor said, not as a warning but as a liturgy. "There will be two. Their symmetry is not by accident. Heaven is mathematical. So are the powers beneath."

"And their symmetry," Kebede said, "is what allows them to anchor influence. To reverse what was once expelled. We can expect escalation here and Rome as initiation rites seem complete at Kursi."

The elders exchanged glances, acknowledgment without panic. They had waited too long, studied too deeply, to be surprised. They had stood as spiritual sentinels while empires rose and fell. This was not the first tremor they'd felt. But it might be the most significant.

A candle near the pastor flickered, then curved as if pulled toward the center of the room. Others followed suit, their flames bending subtly in the same direction. None of the elders moved. The pastor only whispered, "So it begins."

And in the hush that followed, the mountain chapel seemed to breathe, not with wind, but with something older than weather, older than stone. Something watching. Something remembering. Something awakening.

Somewhere in Italy – Just outside Rome

The Italian estate unfurled across the hillside with the serene dominance of a dynasty untouched by time. Renaissance gardens unfurled in symmetrical harmony, their precision betraying the deeper order beneath. From above, the sprawling villa appeared like a sacred sigil, hedges tracing patterns of invocation older than any blueprint. The sun, now low over the western hills, turned the villa's limestone façade to gold, cloaking the ancient stones in a glow that belied the quiet calculations happening within.

In the west wing, a mahogany-paneled study served as a temporary operations center. The room exuded aristocratic elegance with coffered ceilings, inlaid floors, oil portraits that watched with generational indifference, but beneath the old-world aesthetic pulsed another language. A geometry of intent. Every arch, panel, and carving seemed to bend subtly toward unseen alignments, drawing the eye into spirals too precise to be decorative. Symbols hidden in design. Purpose disguised as beauty.

On a sleek laptop resting atop a 16th-century writing desk, Eli's face glowed in grid formation beside six others on the computer screen. The soft light of the screen caught the angles of his face, emphasizing the deliberate stillness with which he held his posture. Around him, the shadows of the study retreated as if making room for what the conversation invoked.

"The Kursi site is complete," Eli reported, his voice smooth, professional, eerily calm over the digital display. "The ritual matrix is anchored. The site's resonance lines are stable. We've begun phase two earlier than projected."

A woman with silver hair pinned in an elegant chignon nodded from her screen. Behind her sat marble busts and classical columns, likely a museum office or private gallery. "The Foundation was concerned about the disruption at archeological sites near the university," she said. "We were told security was heightened."

"Our teams anticipated that," Eli replied. "Institutional security guards just watch for metal tools and missing vases. Our students blend in."

A man in a tweed jacket with an East Coast accent asked, "And the artifacts?"

Eli's hand idly traced a sigil on the desk surface, an unconscious echo of the one drawn by children near Kursi. "The nails are attuned. They resonate. They remember what they pierced. That memory is… active. They are now ready."

Another donor, his face blurred and voice digitally altered, leaned forward. "What of interference? The CIG operative, Trenfor, has been seen in the region."

Eli allowed himself a smile. "Trenfor is gifted. But he's still operating on the defensive. He follows traces. We're setting the tempo."

They spoke next of logistics: crates moved as eco-donations, financial channels masked by sustainability initiatives, and a ceremony in Rome masked as a summit on ecological justice. Every detail rehearsed. Every front polished. Then came the final question.

"The Whitfield girl," the blurred man said. "We understand she's asking questions about the nails."

"The heir to Elemental Gear," added the silver-haired woman. "Your proximity to her needs reviewing."

Eli's smile grew wider. "Sarah Whitfield is simply observing. That means she's awakening. Curiosity is loyalty in embryonic form is a favorite quote of mine."

"She must not interfere," the woman warned. "Her father is too valuable. Witting or not, he's been a pillar of support."

"She won't interfere," Eli replied. "Not before she's seen what lies behind the veil. And by then, she won't matter."

There was silence on the call, agreement disguised as caution. Finally, the silver-haired woman said, "Proceed. But carefully. We've come too far."

Eli inclined his head. "Understood. I depart for Rome tonight. Ensure the site is cleared. The original items should already be in place."

The screens of the conference call blinked out one by one, leaving Eli alone in the fire-warmed silence.

The lights in the study gradually adjusted. As the shadows receded, the room's hidden activity revealed itself. Two assistants, dressed in simple black, approached a large shipping crate stamped with the Elemental Gear logo. They moved reverently, as though opening a reliquary.

Inside were not hiking supplies, but something far more ceremonial.

Robes of deep ochre and earth-tone silk, embroidered with gold that shimmered unnaturally in the low light, were lifted from their compartments. The symbols stitched into the hems shifted subtly as the garments moved, ancient geometry threaded with something more alive than ink or pigment.

The male assistant examined a dagger, its blade forged from a dark metal that didn't reflect the light but seemed to consume it. "The thread was mixed with gold?"

"Yes," the woman replied. "Just as the manuscript specified. Each robe follows the alignment pattern precisely."

Beneath the garments lay a second layer: tools of ritual. Silver bowls lined with micro-inscriptions, tuning forks forged from an unknown alloy, a rod etched with increments that did not match any modern system.

At the bottom, in a case of leaded glass and velvet lining, lay a single iron nail.

Aged. Blackened. Seemingly inert. And yet the air above them pulsed with a strange weight as though space itself bent slightly around their presence.

"One of the originals," the assistant whispered. "It just arrived from Israel. The other one is already enroute to Ethiopia."

"This one will be installed into the primary array at the service," she continued. "The readings show total resonance."

Outside, the sun finally dropped behind the Italian hills, casting shadows that grew too long, too quickly. In the courtyard, the olive trees shifted though the air was still. Somewhere in the distance, a bell began to toll the hour. But the sound came warped, as if filtered through water or time. Within the villa, silence thickened like incense.

The ritual had not yet begun.

But the ground was already listening.

Chapter Nine

Tel Aviv University - Israel

The alert on Trenfor's phone pulsed without sound, its presence urgent and unmistakable. It was an update from CIG. He scanned the data: spiritual tremors – precise and layered. This wasn't tectonic movement. Spiritual activity seemed to be focusing with some scattered activity near Trenfor.

Coordinates pointed to a neglected ruin outside Tiberias, classified publicly as a pagan synagogue but long flagged by CIG as a dormant nexus. He pocketed the device and walked the sterile halls of Tel Aviv University's archaeology wing. Its walls were lined with display cases and scholarly artifacts, faith stripped into fragments.

Professor Stein was hunched over a ceramic shard when Trenfor approached.

"Professor," Trenfor said, voice firm but even, just enough to cut through the hum of the overhead lights. "Would you accompany me to a site near Tiberias tomorrow? There's a structure worth reviewing. Possibly a transitional form between Jewish and early Hellenistic design."

Stein looked up, blinking. "We were just finishing a survey out that way. What sort of anomaly justifies pulling away this late in your visit?"

Trenfor spread a series of satellite prints on the table. Then, he added a few old scout photographs from the CIG files. Partial, ambiguous, but compelling. "Certain overlapping features suggest hybrid worship patterns. The sort that could predate established chronology. Satellite imagery shows a pattern of these sites, but we only have a couple of old photographs to see what might be there."

The professor adjusted his glasses and leaned in. "Unusual alignment here... these motifs are clearly Judaic. But this configuration? Not Second Temple. Not exactly."

"That's why I'd like your opinion on site. Before erosion takes what little of evidence remains. The site has almost no documentation and has not been properly excavated."

From behind a display cabinet, a flicker of motion caught Trenfor's eye. Blond hair. Intent green eyes. Sarah Whitfield, quiet as always, but not idle.

"I'll arrange a team," Stein began, but Sarah stepped forward.

"Forgive the interruption," she said, tone casual, timing precise. "But for undocumented sites, a photogrammetric model from the outset would preserve context that can't be recovered later. I've been refining my method."

Trenfor hesitated, but just barely. She noticed.

"She's been invaluable this season," Stein added. "And she won't interfere."

Trenfor nodded. "We leave at three. Late light will serve both fieldwork and photography."

The drive unfolded in quiet calculation and unasked questions. Sarah sat in the back of the field vehicle, her camera gear packed with precision. The hills beyond Galilee stretched long and gold under the sinking sun.

"It was logged in the nineties," Stein said from the passenger seat. "Catalogued but deemed low-priority. No funding, no urgency."

"Some sites choose their own hour," Trenfor murmured.

They arrived just as the last rays grazed the slope. The ruin emerged halfway up the hillside, half-buried, partly revealed, like the vertebrae of something ancient trying to rise.

Sarah stepped out and froze. No birds. No hum of insects. Just silence. Not natural.

"It's too still," she said.

"Stillness can preserve what movement forgets," Trenfor replied. Then added, "Hadrian built a temple to Venus atop Christ's tomb. What he meant to desecrate, he protected. Some of these sites hold surprises, with all the levels of civilization built on top and around them."

The main chamber devoured light as they stepped inside. Stein's portable LEDs created white islands amid the dark, throwing shadows across the carvings.

Sarah set up her tripod, methodical but unsettled. She watched them move: Stein cataloging layers of age; Trenfor moving like a man reacquainting himself with the familiar.

"These symbols," Stein murmured, tracing a wall. "Second Temple syntax, but imagery that parallels Isaiah, even Daniel. Look: 'wheels within wheels.'"

"And 'ancient of days,'" Trenfor added. "Some of these inscriptions reflect scripture."

Sarah looked up sharply. "You speak as if the prophets recorded events, not visions. As if scripture were history."

Silence. Stein looked surprised. Trenfor simply paused. They both let her statement hang between them. Sarah could feel their skepticism without either man saying a word.

"I mean, that's not rigorous archaeology is it?" She pressed. "You are referring to scripture as if the Bible is actual history."

Stein responded gently. "The Moabite Stone, Sarah. Found in 1868. Mentions Mesha, King of Moab. Confirms 2 Kings in scripture. And it was carved by Israel's enemies. So, we know its authentic and simply support the validity of the Bible."

He showed her his portable tablet. "Then there's the Tel Dan Stele, ninth century BCE, references the 'House of David.' Once dismissed as myth. Numerous rigorous archeological finds like these confirm scripture over and over as a historical document."

Sarah frowned. "My father taught me these were legends. Crafted to explain nationhood."

Trenfor turned toward her. "The stones remember what empires buried."

Stein added, "Carbon dating, linguistic markers, they place texts where tradition always claimed. Not centuries later, as critics suggest."

Sarah stared at the wall.

"Archaeology, keeps confirming more than critics expected," Stein added quietly. "Not just history, but the way the theology is rooted in real events."

She swallowed, camera trembling slightly. She had come to document stones, not to have her worldview excavated.

Trenfor traced a sigil resembling wings. "Documentation is vital. But understanding requires more than light. It requires sight. Cognitive bias is a powerful thing to overcome."

Sarah looked again through her viewfinder. But this time, she saw more than just lines on stone. She saw a fracture forming in the story she'd always believed. A silent crack, widening even more.

The afternoon light soon began to thin, casting long golden shafts through the crumbled gaps in the stone ceiling. Dust floated in the beams like slow-moving embers, visible only at just the right angle. As the sun receded, the chamber darkened, and the LED lamps scattered about the room took on a deeper hue, shifting the atmosphere from documentation to something more intimate. The past didn't whisper here. It held its breath and waited.

Trenfor had moved off quietly, away from the altar inscriptions they'd been studying. He now crouched near a section of wall mostly hidden behind a fallen lintel stone, its position awkward, its relevance uncertain, at least to anyone else. But Sarah, watching through her lens, recognized purpose in the way he moved. His fingers brushed away layers of dust with reverence, not haste. It was a gesture not unlike comfort.

Symbols emerged as he brushed. Sharper than the others. Older. Not just stylistically different, but almost... defiant. These weren't the stylized Hebrew lines they'd been working with. They were angular, their corners cutting against the stone as though the carver had been in a hurry, or in grief.

"Here," Trenfor said, low enough that Sarah barely heard him.

Stein joined him, the edge of his flashlight catching the freshly uncovered inscription. Sarah followed, abandoning her camera for the moment. The air around that corner felt cooler somehow, not in temperature, but in depth, like the wall had been holding something in.

Trenfor's lips moved silently for a few moments before he translated. His voice was measured, and Sarah could feel the weight behind every word.

"Before the garden was planted, a covenant was broken. The luminary cast down claimed dominion over the dust."

Professor Stein furrowed his brow, stepping closer, the words scratching at something in the back of his mind. "That phrasing… it doesn't conform to any post-exilic theology. It doesn't even sound like late prophetic metaphor."

Sarah tilted her head. "Is it... biblical?"

"Not in the way most people mean," Trenfor replied, eyes still on the stone. "It's older. The idea shows up in pre-canonical writings, texts that didn't make it into what we now call the Bible but weren't dismissed by early believers either as part of the circulating literature of the early church."

Stein adjusted his glasses, clearly intrigued. "You're referring to the gap theory."

"Among others," Trenfor said. He sat back on his heels and looked at Sarah directly. "There's a view that between Genesis 1:1 - 'In the beginning, God created the heavens and the earth', and Genesis 1:2 -'And the earth was formless and void', that something happened. Something catastrophic. The fall of Lucifer and the wreckage that followed."

Sarah's expression gave nothing away, but she didn't look away either.

"The theory suggests," Trenfor went on, "that what we see in Genesis isn't the first act, but the second. That the world Adam entered had already been corrupted. That the rebellion of celestial beings had ravaged creation and that God was restoring, not simply creating as evidenced by the fact that Lucifer was already present in the garden. 'Dominion over dust' refers to that false claim, to Lucifer's theft of what he was never meant to rule. And what he wants to control now."

Stein whistled softly, eyes back on the wall. "And this... this would be one of the earliest references to it. Certainly, in Hebrew context."

"It's not a settled doctrine," Trenfor said carefully. "But the fragments persist. The Book of Enoch, preserved by the Ethiopian Church, details watchers, fallen angels, who descended, corrupted the bloodlines, and taught forbidden knowledge. It was controversial, but never entirely cast off. These ideas were once taken seriously."

Sarah stepped forward slowly, her eyes locked on the inscription. "Why didn't we learn any of this in Sunday School? I mean... I even took religion courses. Comparative mythology. We talked about creation myths, sure, but never this."

"Because orthodoxy wins wars," Trenfor said. "Theologies, like empires, are shaped by what they survive. But these older accounts weren't stories to the people who recorded them. They were warnings."

Stein, surprisingly, nodded. "You see similar myths in Mesopotamian texts, a divine being attempting to mirror creation, but twisting it. Then a flood. A reset. It's all there. But this," he tapped the inscription gently, "this is different. Less mythic, more... judicial."

Sarah's brow creased. "Judicial?"

Trenfor stood, dusting his hands. "It implies legal stewardship. That the earth was under lawful guardianship before Adam. And that rebellion wasn't just cosmic rebellion. It was cosmic theft."

Silence settled for a moment.

"And this is why people want this site?" Sarah asked.

Trenfor met her gaze. "Some want to remember what happened before Eden," he said. "Others want to undo what happened after."

He didn't name them. He didn't have to. Something unspoken passed between them, and Sarah understood. The Ashen Veil weren't just protesting. They were calling back to the gods referred to in the inscriptions who ruled before Eden.

Professor Stein broke the moment, glancing at his watch. "We should go. I don't like those switchbacks in the dark."

Trenfor ran a final hand along the stone, almost like sealing it again. "Yes. Let's not test what might still linger here. But I get the sense that if someone has visited this site, they are now gone. Like they are done with Kursi."

As they packed their equipment and began moving toward the entrance, Sarah noticed Trenfor lag behind. He stepped into a shaft of fading light and pulled out his phone. The screen lit his face in stark contrast to the gloom. His expression shifted. Subtle, but sharp. Alerted.

Sarah instinctively lifted her camera again, zooming in, not to photograph, but to see. Trenfor's body language had changed. The weight in his shoulders now seemed calculated, his eyes scanning not just for light but for exit points.

She caught up as they emerged from the ruins into the dusk.

"Everything all right?" she asked.

"A colleague," he said. "Another site. But I'll handle it when we're back in Tel Aviv."

But Sarah saw the tension in his neck. Heard the distance in his tone. And she knew instinctively that whatever that message said, it wasn't about another dig. It was about this one. And something had just shifted.

The trail back down the hillside crunched underfoot. But in Sarah's mind, it wasn't her footsteps she was hearing. It was those ancient words echoing again: *Before the garden was planted, a covenant was broken...*

Something had remembered. And now, something else was responding.

Tel Adama Campsite

Dusk gathered between the white canvas tents like spilled ink, turning the dig site into a scatter of lantern-lit islands in an otherwise encroaching sea of night. Researchers clustered at folding tables, heads bowed over artifacts and notes, their voices hushed by the desert wind, like the past itself had asked for silence.

Sarah sat slightly apart, transferring images from her camera to her laptop. Each photo caught a nuance her eye had missed; edge flares in ancient inscriptions, mineral discolorations tracing old trauma into stone. The image of the pre-Adamic inscription glowed on her screen, the angular script rendered with stark precision. It looked older than the rest of the ruin. It felt older than memory.

Professor Stein approached, his shadow stretching long across the gravel in the lantern light. He moved with the worn grace of someone used to fragile things, pottery shards, ancient truths, his own joints. He sank into a camp stool beside her with a sigh that doubled as punctuation.

"Exceptional work today, Ms. Whitfield," he said, peering at her screen. "You've managed to capture not just the artifact, but the atmosphere. That's not easily taught."

"Thank you," Sarah replied. But her tone lacked enthusiasm. The image on her screen had too much weight behind it. The words Trenfor had spoken still pulsed at the edges of her mind, luminaries cast down, dominion over dust. All echoing in her thoughts.

The professor removed his glasses and cleaned them with his shirttail, a tic Sarah had already come to associate with approaching formality. "Actually, there's something else I'd like to discuss. A bit of a professional detour, but one I believe you'll find worthwhile."

She paused her work.

"We've just reestablished communication with a partner team in Ethiopia," he continued. "Near Lake Tana. They're working on ancient Judaic inscriptions, possibly linked to the earliest diasporic traditions. Some of the texts that Mr. Trenfor referenced today have corollaries in their findings."

Sarah looked up. "The Ethiopian Orthodox manuscripts?"

"Exactly. They're under-documented and underfunded. And they've asked specifically for assistance in visual preservation. I told them about your photogrammetry work. They were... impressed."

"Ethiopia?" she repeated.

"The timing is short," he admitted. "They're racing the rainy season. They need someone by the end of the week. It would be a quick assignment, two weeks, perhaps. And a remarkable one."

Sarah absorbed the offer, though her mind was already reaching beyond it.

"No need to decide tonight," he added, rising. "But I hope you'll consider it."

She nodded slowly as he stepped away. Lanterns flickered in the wind, and across the camp, the night settled like a verdict.

Back in her tent, her laptop bathed the interior in a soft blue light as she sifted through more images, trying to ignore the weight building behind her ribs. That's when her satellite phone buzzed. Her father's name blinked on the screen.

"Dad?" she answered. Apparently, she had sounded more surprised to hear from him than she intended.

"Can't a father check in on his daughter?" His voice was a smooth, professional warmth, more boardroom than bedtime story. "I hear from the school you may be traveling this week."

Sarah narrowed her eyes. "You know about the Ethiopia offer?"

"Of course. The foundation's funding an eco-initiative in that region with solar generators, water filtration kits. We're shipping them out next week and it would be great if you could be there when they arrive. Small world, isn't it?"

Too small.

"I haven't decided."

"You should. It's a rare opportunity. Field work. Ancient monasteries. Gorgeous topography." He was already selling it. "Prime material for your portfolio. Plus, Elemental Gear's planning a new campaign. We're testing weather-resistant gear in extreme climates. Cameras, packs. The trip checks all the boxes."

She bristled. "So, you dropped my name to the University. You realize I'm not doing product shoots for the company. It's archaeology."

"You can do both. You're always good at improvising. Practical. Creative." He paused. "And it gets you away from all that theological nonsense. Those people you're with now, they're trying to resurrect fairy tales with broken pottery I hear."

She bit back a response.

"Pack light, shoot heavy," he said cheerfully, and hung up before she could answer.

Moments later, her phone lit up again. A voicemail from an unfamiliar number.

Eli's voice spilled into her tent, recorded but somehow still urgent.

"Sarah. The land of beginnings holds answers. You should go."

No explanation. No sign-off. Just that cryptic fragment.

She stared at the phone. Her father wanted her in Ethiopia. So did Eli. Different motives. Same destination. The precision of it chilled her. Neither of them should have known this fast. Some unseen hand was moving them.

She found Trenfor just outside his tent, packing with methodical calm. Each item folded, coiled, tucked into place like a ritual of preparation.

"Stein offered me Ethiopia," she said. "Lake Tana. Monastic inscriptions."

Trenfor paused mid-zip. "I've been many times. It's a place that doesn't forget."

"I thought you'd try to talk me out of it."

He shook his head. "If you feel drawn to go, that's reason enough."

"My father already knew about the offer. And Eli. Both of them nudging me toward it for different reasons." She studied him. "And you, what do you think?"

He didn't answer immediately. Instead, he stepped away, made a short call on his own satellite phone, coded phrases, clipped tones then returned with something in his hand. A small wooden cross on a leather cord, the carving was rough and worn at the edges from years of being touched.

"For the road," he said simply.

She hesitated, then took it. Their fingers touched, just for a second. But long enough for something unsaid to pass between them.

"I have friends there," he added. "People who understand the deeper layers of this conflict. If the nail is involved, they'll know."

Sarah slipped the cord over her head. The wood was warm against her collarbone, or perhaps she only imagined it was.

"I think I'll go," she said. "I won't take it off."

Trenfor nodded once. "Then go. But go open-eyed. There's more than archaeology waiting for you in Ethiopia. And some forces, maybe both good and bad, want you there."

She turned to leave, the cross catching briefly in the edge of her collar. She didn't adjust it.

Let it stay visible.

Let the watchers see it.

Let them wonder which side she'd chosen. Because she wasn't yet sure herself.

Ben Gurion Airport

Ben Gurion Airport gleamed in the early morning light, all clean lines and glass facades, modernity set against the ancient stones Trenfor had left behind. He moved through the terminal with practiced anonymity, a man engineered to vanish the moment he stepped beyond view. His carry-on, a worn leather satchel more professor than operative, concealed nothing outwardly remarkable: a change of clothes, toiletries, a weathered copy of Herodotus. But false linings and hollowed bindings held tools for an entirely different journey.

Inside were compact instruments disguised as ordinary items: a pen that fluoresced ancient inks under UV light, a tablet loaded with restricted theological archives, microfilament tools tucked into a travel grooming kit. The satchel's most guarded contents were text fragments, translations never digitized, protected under layers of innocuous-looking travel brochures.

Near the diplomatic lounge, a woman in a charcoal suit approached, her airport security badge flashing under the terminal light. She fell into step beside him without breaking stride.

"Intel says Eli's timeline has accelerated," she murmured. "He acquired transport credentials yesterday under a new alias. One we hadn't seen. He's moving fast."

"Artifact confirmed?"

"Partially. Thermal scans of his baggage showed trace minerals that match, but no actual artifact. We think the nails were smuggled out of the country or mailed discreetly." She handed over a leather passport wallet. "You've been granted clearance via Vatican diplomatic cover. Full archive access is waiting."

"Extraction protocol?"

"Standard. Unless you signal escalation. Protect the asset if Ashen Veil forces appear." Her eyes flicked toward his satchel. "Tools embedded in your secure digital download from CIG. Authentication calibrated for pre-Nicene material and references for artifact verification."

At the next checkpoint, uniformed officials scanned his credentials with deference. The woman turned away as he passed through, her voice low and final: "The girl's in motion too. We're tracking."

Twenty minutes later, Trenfor boarded the CIG-arranged flight to Rome. He settled into a first-class seat offering both discretion and a clear view of the cabin doors. As the aircraft taxied, he flipped open Herodotus to a dog-eared page, an old habit masking the forward gears already turning in his mind.

In a neighboring terminal, Sarah Whitfield sat by her gate, watching her plane edge toward the runway. The final glimpse of Israel framed in her window with sandstone hills dissolving into a sliver of sea. It felt less like departure and more like crossing a line she hadn't known existed.

A week ago, she'd arrived as a graduate documentarian, trained to analyze relics and capture their surfaces. Now she carried something far heavier: questions her training had never prepared her to ask.

The wooden cross at her throat caught the morning light. It pressed against her collarbone with a weight that seemed to shift with every breath. Her fingers found it unconsciously, already attuned to its unfamiliar gravity.

Her father's involvement troubled her more than she cared to admit. That Elemental Gear's foundation happened to be aiding the exact region she was being sent. Where ancient manuscripts and sealed monasteries lined Lake Tana's shores. It was too timely to dismiss as coincidence. Especially after his flippant dismissal of the Israeli dig as "religious nonsense." Either he was willfully blind to the parallels... or pretending to be.

And then there was Eli.

His voice still rang in her voicemail - "The land of beginnings holds answers" - a phrase that now echoed unsettlingly in her memory, folded too neatly over Trenfor's earlier translations.

She pulled out her tablet. On the screen, the inscription Trenfor had uncovered sharpened under digital zoom: *Before the garden was planted, a covenant was broken.* The ancient script seemed to pulse with its own current, as if aware it was being read.

The plane lifted smoothly. Israel shrank beneath her, boundaries blurring until the landscape resumed its ancient form of hills and rivers, not states and roads. Modernity dissolved into myth. A few thousand feet up, everything looked old again.

Sarah realized she wasn't really flying to Ethiopia as a documentarian anymore. She wasn't just going to record artifacts or assist a team. She was heading toward something layered, something woven into time itself. Her father wanted her there, or at least wanted her out of Israel. Eli wanted her there. Even Stein, with his careful academic framing, had nudged her more forcefully than usual. Trenfor had simply handed her a cross. No persuasion. Just a gift.

Her fingers brushed the wooden pendant again. It held no signature, no brand. Just a shape carved for meaning, not marketing. She had followed the path of logic and found it intersecting with something older than logic. Faith. Memory. Conflict. Whatever lay at Lake Tana wasn't a matter of coincidence. And it wouldn't be neutral.

Outside her window, the Mediterranean unfolded below a sheet of steel and scattered clouds. Somewhere beyond that horizon waited ancient texts, silenced histories, and people who had preserved truths the modern world had forgotten.

She closed the tablet.

Trenfor's parting words surfaced once more.

"For finding your way back."

Back to what? she wondered. Truth? Belief?

As the plane cut eastward toward the Horn of Africa, Sarah leaned into her seat, the weight of the cross grounding her as the sky opened ahead.

CIG Jerusalem Outpost

Beneath an unassuming office building in Jerusalem's German Colony, far below the sidewalk cafés and cobbled charm, the CIG outpost monitoring station pulsed with silent urgency. Shielded behind biometric vaults and interference dampeners, its subterranean chambers bore no resemblance to anything aboveground. The air vibrated not with noise, but with information as streams of raw data, spiritual telemetry, and seismic signatures filtered through systems designed to track what no satellite or microscope could detect.

In the center of the operations floor, Miriam sat encircled by curved displays. Her workstation a cockpit of convergence.

The light from her primary monitor bathed her in spectral blue, casting faint shadows across the room's matte-black surfaces. A single pulsing alert blinked red at the corner of her interface.

She tapped her headset. "Priority ping. Pattern recognition. Unprecedented correlation across dual coordinates."

Her eyes swept across the topographical map projected in front of her: Lake Tana, Ethiopia. Vatican City, Rome. Two crimson dots pulsed in perfect, metronomic unison. They were not seismic events. Not weather anomalies. The rhythm they kept did not match the heartbeat of the earth, but something older. More deliberate. Physical points pulsing from nonphysical origins.

Miriam adjusted the interface, peeling away surface data until only the spiritual substrate remained, tuning to frequencies below electromagnetic detection, yet measurable through refined resonance analytics. What she saw made her blood chill.

Runic overlays, ancient symbols cataloged from shattered altar stones, unearthed scrolls, and forbidden codices, aligned with the tremor maps precisely. These weren't artifacts of ancient memory. They were signatures. Matching glyphs from pre-Babylonian strata appeared in real-time pulses echoing through the ether, like a code rehearsed over millennia now returning to full signal strength. The archeological data provided context to the spiritual reports.

"Convergence time confirmed," Miriam said softly. Her voice was automatically transcribed, appended to a real-time dispatch already compiling. "Tremor alignment at 89 percent. Temporal cadence increasing. AI model suggests this isn't a warning system but an invocation countdown."

With practiced precision, she flagged the alert. Routing: Executive Director McCraken. Copies to Mediterranean and North African regional nodes.

SUBJECT: CONVERGENCE PATTERN MATCH – COUNTDOWN INITIATED.

Attachments: [Data Packet – Tremor Sync][Runic Overlay Confirmations] [Atmospheric Anomalies][Temporal Acceleration Indicators][Spiritual Activity Reports]

Across her peripheral screens, supplemental data cascaded into view.

In Cologne, visitors inside the cathedral had reported waves of identical emotion followed by identical dreams. In the highlands near Mount Ararat, shepherds claimed their flocks wouldn't graze beneath open skies. In the Old City of Jerusalem, water in ancient mikvehs had begun displaying unnatural stillness, interrupted only at certain hours when surface tension spiked and held like crystal before resuming flow.

Miriam's fingers moved faster now, correlating field reports. The global pattern wasn't weakening. It was tightening thread by thread. The algorithm showed acceleration curves. The convergence pulse was no longer static. It was quickening. Reports were increasingly being added to the database. They may have a time table.

Her eyes narrowed. A new variable had entered.

The Rome–Tana tremor cycle had begun to shift, subtly but unmistakably. What had first appeared as summoning coordinates were now fluctuating. Adapting. Reacting.

As if... now responding.

She updated the dispatch with fresh analysis. "Revised hypothesis: Convergence sites no longer fixed points. Movement suggests adaptive behavior. Response to agent interference likely. Trenfor en route to Rome. Subject Whitfield now airborne to Lake Tana. Probability of unintentional alignment: <0.000001%."

For a moment, the hum of the chamber dimmed to silence. It was too sudden to be mechanical failure. Monitors blinked once. Then again.

Then everything in the room synchronized.

Screens, lights, processors and equipment isolated by redundant protocols and electromagnetic shielding, flickered and aligned to the same unbroken frequency. Not a system error. A spiritual mirroring. For three full seconds, every display showed a single image:

The pre-Adamic inscription from Tiberias. **"Before the garden was planted, a covenant was broken. The luminary cast down claimed dominion over dust."**

No one had entered that inscription into CIG's database. Not yet.

Then the image vanished. Logs reset. Diagnostics showed no anomaly. No record of intrusion.

Only Miriam had seen it.

Her heart pounded. It wasn't just a glitch. It was a message. Not from within.

From them.

The returning powers. The old dominions. The watchers of the watchers. They knew who was watching. And they wanted CIG to know.

Miriam rose slowly, her breath tight. She authorized Protocol Eliakim, the highest alert classification outside global catastrophe. It opened a silent, encrypted channel to McCraken's secure tablet, flashing a single phrase across his encrypted screen:

"They know."

As her hands returned to the console, she stared again at the convergence dots. Rome. Lake Tana. The pulse now visible to the naked eye, rising. Hungry.

Seventy-two hours.

"May God help them," she whispered, her voice almost lost in the quiet hum of re-stabilizing systems. "And God help us all."

Chapter Ten

CIG Jerusalem Outpost

The red pulses rippled across the monitors in deliberate rhythm, throwing the analysts' faces into alternating bands of light and crimson shadow. Thirty feet beneath the German Colony in Jerusalem, the subterranean station hummed with unseen voltage and quiet dread. Once a British military bunker, then a Cold War shelter, the compound had been repurposed by CIG into something altogether different: a nerve center for watching tremors of a kind no seismologist would recognize.

They didn't call them earthquakes. They called them *disturbances*. But only behind soundproof doors. On the outside, the analysts had been particle physicists, linguists, or data architects. Now, they mapped what the visible world denied. The glowing grids on the screens didn't track fault lines, but fault *realms*, invisible frictions where ancient things shifted in the dark, tracking activity in a dimension operating beyond our own.

"Amplitude spike over the Ethiopian highlands," a woman said without looking up, her glasses reflecting a spiraling data stream. "Thirty-two percent jump in the last hour."

"Rome's trending too," murmured a second analyst. His silvering hair caught the red glow as his fingers summoned harmonic overlays. "Pattern alignment confirmed. They're syncing."

At the center of the command floor, surrounded by curved displays and rolling equations, stood Miriam. Her hair was wound in a tight bun, her eyes shadowed by long hours, but there was a stillness to her posture that silenced the room. She nodded to the technician at the main console. He tapped in a sequence of commands. One screen blinked, shifted then became a live channel.

Doug McCraken's face then appeared on the main screen, drawn and alert. The lighting in his office was dim, the wooden shelves behind him lined with books and a single iron cross. He spoke without preamble.

"What are we looking at?"

Miriam stepped into frame, her voice even. "The epicenter in Israel has gone quiet. Not dormant, but *quieted.* We believe its deliberate. Meanwhile, Rome and Lake Tana are in phase-lock." She gestured to her technician, who split the screen to show the oscillation graphs: two distant waveforms pulsing in mirrored sequence.

"The rhythm's shifted," she continued. "This isn't residual. It's *strategic.* They've changed the axis. We've cross referenced the data with on the ground reports."

Doug leaned forward slightly. His eyes moved between graphs, the tension in his jaw sharpening. "They're moving the stage," he said finally. "Not because they failed in Israel, but because Trenfor saw too much."

The name moved through the room like an electric pulse. Trenfor wasn't often mentioned aloud. But everyone had read his reports. Watched his debriefs. Studied the anomalies that always seemed to cluster around his assignments.

Miriam didn't flinch. "They're splitting attention, but this doesn't look like division. It looks like expansion. They're dividing the battlefield and spreading out as planned. Maybe even earlier to try to get ahead of Trenfor. The other theory is maybe they completed their rituals in Israel and left early. Either way, they've moved on."

Doug nodded once. "Diversification of assets. Trenfor can't be in two places at once."

He tapped his desk console. "Activate prayer protocols. Full global coverage. Flag Rome and Lake Tana as primaries. I want intercessors in rotation every hour."

The room moved immediately. No one hesitated. Typing accelerated. Red lines began triangulating across global maps. Churches around the world would be notified to join in focused prayer and intercession.

Doug's voice dropped a note. "And Miriam, cross-reference the current harmonic schema with the Jerusalem signatures from last month. I want to confirm this isn't a decoy set."

"We already run side-by-side comparisons," she said, eyes flicking to a nearby terminal. "The waveform structure is identical. Only the amplitude has grown. And the cohesion… is stronger. We think the clock is now ticking."

Doug's expression darkened. "Then they're using both nails."

That sentence hung in the air like smoke from a blown fuse.

A historian at the edge of the room cleared his throat. "If that's true, then we're not looking at an invocation anymore."

"No," Doug said grimly. "We're looking at an installation now. This may be the primary summoning of demons."

Miriam tensed. "What's the endgame?"

"Dual fronts," he said. "A mirrored gate in both Rome and Ethiopia. And possibly a fallback channel in case one fails."

"We don't have field teams in Ethiopia," Miriam said. "None of our mobile teams are in position yet. It's an isolated region."

Doug exhaled. "Then the Remnant will have to hold the line there. God provides."

The feed blinked off.

In the quiet that followed, the display maps continued pulsing. Rome. Lake Tana. Two beating hearts, miles apart, synced like twin drums of an old war chant.

"Ma'am?" the silver-haired analyst said quietly, breaking the silence. "We just clocked a twenty-five percent acceleration in the pattern. We've hit the three-minute cycle."

Miriam watched the converging waves. She felt the pressure in her ears shift, like altitude change in a sealed room.

"We need to move faster," she said, lifting the secure line again. "Enlist every prayer team you can contact."

The red light held steady now, a fixed beat. Not a tremor.

But a countdown.

Lake Tana, Ethiopia

The wooden boat swayed gently beneath Sarah Whitfield's feet, her balance intuitive despite the rhythmic pull of the water. Morning mist rose from Lake Tana in curling tendrils, as if reluctant spirits still lingered above its ancient depths. Pale sunlight filtered through the fog, gilding the lake in soft hues of gold and tarnished silver. The monastery emerged slowly, first as shadow, then stone, rising from the rock like memory surfacing from forgotten depths.

The structure appeared more grown than built. Hewn from the same basalt it rested upon, the Ura Kidane Mehret Monastery clung to the cliffside like a secret kept for centuries. Moss and vine softened its silhouette, but nothing obscured the sense that it had been planted here deliberately, positioned with spiritual precision on a land that had never bowed to time.

The boat bumped softly against the stony shore. Kebede stepped forward, sure-footed and calm, his frame upright despite the decades his weathered face suggested. His eyes, the color of dark tea, glinted with welcome as he reached for Sarah's hand.

"Ms. Whitfield," he said, his English precise and faintly lyrical. "Welcome to Ura Kidane Mehret Monastery."

Sarah accepted his hand and stepped onto dry land, her boots crunching softly on the gravel path. The earth beneath her felt still in a way she hadn't experienced in weeks.

"The lake is massive," she said, gazing toward the horizon. "How many monasteries are here?"

"There are thirty-seven islands," Kebede replied. "Nineteen hold monasteries." Then, with a hint of a smile, he added, "That we know of."

Sarah raised an eyebrow. "That we *know* of?"

"The lake keeps secrets," Kebede said. "It has hidden emperors, entombed relics, and so we believe, it once sheltered the Ark of the Covenant."

"And this monastery. Would you call it the most important?"

"They all guard something," Kebede said. "This one holds manuscripts that predate many Western canons. It preserves stories, laws, prayers. Some written in Ge'ez when Rome was still young. But the Ark… its journey passed through here."

He continued, his voice lowering with reverence. "After Solomon's Temple was defiled by King Manasseh around the seventh century BC, the Ark was believed to have been taken first to Elephantine, a small island near Aswan, where a Jewish community built a temple. Two centuries later, it traveled down the Nile, arriving at Tana Qirqos. There it remained for over 800 years before being moved to Aksum, where a single Guardian still tends it, never leaving the compound until death."

Sarah absorbed his words in silence, the air around her laced with incense and history.

Kebede added softly, "Ethiopia has never been colonized, Ms. Whitfield. Not by the Ottomans, nor the Europeans. Perhaps that is because something has always protected us. Our church has always known peace with our Muslim neighbors. You will find no war here, only endurance."

As they moved inland, the mist began to lift. Two elders waited at the top of a narrow path, robed men with skin like weathered teak and eyes framed by beards white as limestone.

Their presence radiated stillness. They bowed their heads in greeting, their robes brushing the earth like wind through parchment.

"These are Remnant elders," Kebede said. "Guardians of an oral line that traces back to Solomon's time."

They spoke to her in Ge'ez, the ancient liturgical tongue of the Ethiopian Orthodox Church, its syllables sharp yet sonorous, like wind through carved stone.

A third figure stepped forward. He was in his thirties with steady eyes and scholar's poise. "I am Dawit," he said. "I will interpret for you."

Sarah nodded, following as they began the slow ascent toward the monastery. The path curved through archways and sunlit courtyards, where stone altars rose like standing stones, scarred but unbroken. Sunlight caught the corners of these stones, creating moving shadows that seemed almost conscious.

"These altars," Dawit said, "have stood since long before the time of Christ. Our tradition holds that the Queen of Sheba, on her return from Jerusalem, stopped at stones like these to offer prayer after receiving Solomon's wisdom."

The elders walked with slow precision, their fingers brushing near, but never on, the ancient stone, as if afraid to break some invisible membrane between worlds as they entered the monastery.

Frankincense hung in the air. The corridors narrowed, growing darker. The walls were lined with faded murals, winged angels, crowned kings, fire in bowls. A chamber opened ahead, lit only by oil lamps hanging on iron chains. The flickering light cast slow-moving shadows that drifted across the stone walls like ghosts untroubled by time.

At the center stood a glass case, modern, yet humble, containing manuscripts that pulsed with quiet authority. Parchments the color of sand, etched in inks that had weathered centuries, rested under meticulous preservation. Some were written in Ge'ez, others in scripts Sarah did not immediately recognize.

The elder gestured to one particular scroll and spoke softly.

Dawit translated, his tone hushed. "This text is among our oldest. It speaks of a covenant that predates Adam. A pact between realms, sealed long before Eden."

Sarah leaned closer. Symbols she had seen only in fragments back in Jerusalem now took full shape. A flame encircled by waves. Stars inverted over mountains. Threads woven between heaven and dust.

She pointed to one symbol. "This here. What does it say?"

The elder's response came slowly, as if he weighed each word. Dawit took equal care in translating.

"It speaks of the sealed flame beneath the waters. A force contained in the earliest age. It says the flame calls to men in dreams, offering power in exchange for release. That it has no shape, only memory."

A chill passed through Sarah. The phrasing echoed inscriptions from the Tiberias site, references to containment, to something once bound.

"And Ethiopia?" she asked. "Is this connected to the Ark?"

The second elder stepped forward. His hand pressed reverently against the glass, tracing the script as if reacquainting himself with an old friend.

"He says the Ark came here not just for safekeeping, but because the land was chosen," Dawit translated. "Chosen for its faith. Tradition. The ground here remembers prayers older than iron."

Sarah felt her throat tighten. The monastery was not merely old. It was *alive* with memory. And something was stirring beneath that memory now.

Dawit continued. "They say when Solomon's son brought the Ark, he followed ancient pathways and not just physical, but spiritual. This monastery stands on one of those crossings."

Sarah's hand hovered over the case but did not touch. "Do the texts say anything about now? About what's happening today?"

The elders exchanged a glance. Then the first elder spoke again, his voice darker.

"He says," Dawit relayed, "when the world forgets the sacred, the sealed things stir. That disbelief is not safety. It is invitation."

Sarah's fingers trembled slightly. The chamber felt heavier now, as if the air had taken on the weight of an unseen watcher.

She whispered, "Thank you, for letting me see this."

The elder's eyes reflected lamplight and something older than it. He nodded, but his gaze lingered, measuring not her presence, but her purpose. Not her arrival, but what she would carry with her when she left.

Twilight pressed against the window of Sarah's quarters, reluctant to relinquish the monastery to darkness. The stone walls had absorbed centuries of incense and whispered prayers. They radiated a quiet that wasn't the absence of sound, but the presence of something ancient and listening.

Sarah sat cross-legged on the narrow cot, her laptop dark. She powers it on and opened a video call. The screen flickers momentarily, resolving into the crisp, polished image of her father as he answers the call.

Behind him, the skyline of the city gleamed through glass walls, boardrooms and ambition etched in steel and LED. He sat in a modern chair behind a sleek desk, dressed in a charcoal suit, his silver hair immaculate. His smile appeared by habit more than emotion, professional warmth that didn't quite reach his eyes.

"Sarah," he said, tilting his head. "You made it to Ethiopia."

"I did," she replied. Her tone was even, unreadable. "It's quiet here. A different quiet."

He chuckled faintly. "Looks like you're roughing it, he said, gesturing to the meager surroundings behind her. "Still chasing the Ark of the Covenant, are we?"

Sarah shifted the angle of her screen slightly, letting him glimpse the stone walls behind her. "I know you're teasing me," she said. "But actually, the monks say the Ark did pass through here. Some believe it never left."

"Well, if you get a photo of it next to one of our jackets, I'll triple your bonus," he said, smiling wider.

She returned his smile, thin, deliberate. "Is that because you don't believe it exists," she asked. "After all, you're funding the Ashen Veil."

His smile faltered. "Excuse me?"

"I traced the ESG pipeline," she said, her voice calm but unyielding. "Three nonprofits - shells, really. The money flows straight into Ashen Veil operations. I recognized one of the directors from a sustainability retreat. He's also on the board of an Elemental Gear subsidiary."

He leaned back slowly. "Ashen Veil is an advocacy organization. Progressive, yes. But hardly subversive. I thought you, of all people, would appreciate how they challenge outdated traditions. They are getting a lot of media exposure right now."

"Advocacy groups don't perform rituals in restricted archaeological zones," Sarah said. She reached into her pocket and held something up to the camera.

A silver button. Polished, embossed. Subtle, but distinct. She held it up to the screen.

"From a limited-edition Elemental Gear jacket," she continued. "Issued during the Geneva conference. Only fifty made. You wore yours. So did Eli. I found this where a subversive, outdated in your terms, ritual was performed. So much for challenging the old. More like summoning pagan gods back, while wearing our clothing line."

He didn't blink. "Thousands of executives wear similar jackets. It proves nothing."

"I have photos," she said, pulling up an image and zooming in. "From the planting ceremony in Jerusalem. Eli's jacket is missing a button. This button. I found it while our team was investigating desecration of an archeological site."

There was a pause. Just a breath too long.

Her father's voice sharpened. "You're drawing dangerous lines from thin connections. Eli coordinates community projects. You know how optics work. The jacket, the ritual site, it's circumstantial evidence."

"So is laundering money through ESG grants," she said. "But circumstantial evidence piles up. And you want to talk about optics, the company could get the wrong kind of publicity."

He exhaled through his nose. "You're getting too close to things you don't understand. I was relieved when you left Israel. I thought you'd reset, regain your balance. Ethiopia doesn't have the religious overtones if you want to do your archaeology thing."

"If you only knew," she said. "There are things here that have even deeper religious implications. The media just ignores Ethiopia. You're the one who is playing with forces you don't understand, Dad."

His expression hardened, the paternal mask slipping into something colder. "You sound like those zealots you've been documenting."

"No," she said quietly. "I'm still figuring out what I believe. But at least they don't lie about who they are."

He leaned forward, voice low. "Come home, Sarah. You have a position waiting. Your name still matters."

She matched his intensity. "I won't use my name to shield your compromises anymore."

Silence stretched between them like a wire pulled tight.

Then, with a flick of his hand, he cut the call. The screen went black, his face frozen mid-expression. Not concern. Not anger. Just calculation.

Sarah sat motionless. In her hand, the silver button caught the last of the light through the window. Outside, the air deepened to black. The monastery exhaled the day's final heat, as if sighing at things spoken aloud for the first time in years.

She closed her fist around the button. Its edges bit into her palm, sharp, small, undeniable. The morning couldn't come soon enough.

The elders beckoned without a word, their calloused hands motioning Sarah toward a narrow archway carved from volcanic stone. It absorbed the morning light rather than admitted it, a mouth into the earth. She followed, heart steady, the heaviness of ancient prayers coiling around her like unseen incense.

Beyond the threshold, the monastery descended into silence. Each stone step was worn smooth by centuries of barefoot pilgrimage. The air shifted, cooler, denser, laced with faint traces of frankincense and the subterranean breath of long untouched soil. Sarah felt it press against her skin, not unpleasantly, but with gravity, like entering a place that did not care for the modern world or its assumptions.

Oil lamps flickered from iron sconces, their flames trembling in unseen drafts, casting shadows that moved with intent. The procession was quiet, deliberate. The monks' robes whispered against the stone, the cadence of their movement like a ritual unto itself. Dawit followed close behind, a calm interpreter between two worlds, hers and the one that had never stopped believing.

"Where are we going?" Sarah asked softly, her voice muffled by the stone.

Dawit translated, receiving a faint smile from the elder ahead. "He says we are not traveling by distance, but by depth. We are headed toward the heart of the truth."

The passage narrowed, forcing them to walk single file. Sarah reached out, fingers grazing the ancient walls, textured here, smooth there, like tactile memory etched in basalt. The flickering lamps made their shadows stretch and retract, giving the impression of unseen companions walking alongside. The further they descended, the less she trusted her senses. The world she knew was thinning.

After a final descent of seven precisely cut steps, the corridor opened without warning into a circular chamber carved from the living rock. The air was still, reverent. The domed ceiling was geometrically flawless, unadorned by icon or image. There were no crosses, no saints, only patterns: interlocking lattices of shapes carved in deliberate precision, their symmetry forming a subtle rhythm that hummed against the skin like distant thunder.

"The Chamber of Echoes," Dawit whispered. Even his voice was swallowed oddly, rippling through the space like a voice underwater. "Built long before the monastery itself. Some say Solomon's men left the designs in secret."

The eldest monk stepped forward and entered the circle at the room's center, a copper ring inlaid in the floor, now dulled to sea-green by centuries of exposure. He whispered a single phrase in Ge'ez.

The walls answered.

The sound didn't simply echo, it multiplied. It leapt along the carvings, fragmented and rejoined, surrounding Sarah in layers of identical voices. Dozens, even hundreds of harmonics that defied logic. It was as if the room remembered every prayer ever whispered and had been waiting to reply. Then, slowly, the sound returned to its origin, drawing inward until it faded completely. The silence that followed was not absence, but fullness. A silence that had weight.

Sarah stood still, gooseflesh rising along her arms. "How is that possible?"

Dawit's eyes shone. "The geometry resonates with perfect harmony. Sound flows along encoded paths. This chamber was designed not to simply hear prayers, but to store them and to echo them. The prayers are given resonance, vibration, frequency."

She walked slowly around the circumference, her fingertips grazing the carved stone. The grooves vibrated faintly, not from present sound, but memory. Vibrations of past centuries, perhaps millennia, remained embedded in the walls like ghost-notes in an ancient instrument.

"It's remarkable," she murmured. "But why show this to me?"

In answer, the elder motioned toward a recessed alcove she hadn't noticed, shielded by a transparent barrier and controlled by modern preservation systems. Scroll fragments, mounted between protective layers of glass, rested within. The ink had faded to rusty brown, the parchment browned like autumn leaves, yet the text remained legible. Symbols she'd seen only in obscure footnotes in Jerusalem seemed to repeat here, like forgotten verses frozen in time.

"These scrolls," Dawit said reverently, "predate the Book of Enoch. They speak of things remembered only in whispers, fragments too dangerous to transcribe, too sacred to destroy."

One of the elders leaned forward, indicating a section of the text. Dawit's voice shifted, heavy with reverence.

"This line reads: " 'When man acknowledges the fallen one, his legion returns. When the old ways are remembered, the gate begins to stir.' "

Sarah froze. "These resemble the ash-circle glyphs I found outside Jerusalem. This is ritual language."

The elder nodded, speaking softly again. Dawit listened, eyes narrowing slightly as he absorbed the message. "He says the lake stirs beneath us. That we stand on what was once sealed. There are those calling for it to be unsealed. They have guarded it for generations, not just from people, but from forces that do not dwell in the seen world."

Sarah swallowed. "The Ashen Veil are trying to unseal it. But why would my father support people who might, awaken it?"

The elder responded without hesitation. Dawit translated.

"Because your father only believes in what earns a return. He does not believe in demons. But demons don't need belief," Dawit translated. "They need ignorance."

The word landed like iron in the room. Sarah stared at the scrolls. She stared at words written before any modern system of thought had tried to explain them away.

"Demons," she repeated. "You're saying they're real."

The oldest monk placed his palm against the wall where the carvings shimmered in the flickering lamplight. Through Dawit, his voice emerged calm, resolute:

"Satan's greatest lie was not that he was powerful," Dawit translated. "It was that he didn't exist. The modern world forgets not because it has no memory. The modern world forgets because it chooses not to remember."

The chamber's acoustics carried his words deeper than mere ears. They vibrated in her bones, in her blood. Sarah felt her skepticism begin to fracture, not entirely, but undeniably. A fissure had opened.

"And if the gate opens?" she asked.

This time, the elder didn't speak aloud. His whisper was lost in the room's strange acoustics. Yet Sarah heard it, somehow, not with her ears, but in the chambers of her own perception.

Then what was sealed away returns, and the world you know ends.

Rome, Italy – The Vatican

Trenfor entered St. Peter's Square with the studied casualness of a man used to blending in. Dressed in a conservative charcoal suit with a priestly collar pin and a modest tie, he passed unnoticed by tourists and clergy alike, just another quiet functionary in the Vatican's daily theater. His credentials, clipped from a lanyard, identified him as a visiting consultant on early Christian relics. They were legitimate. So was the quiet authority in his step.

Sunlight gleamed off his AI glasses, catching the curve of each lens with the occasional flare, just enough to obscure his eyes. The device streamed encrypted feeds directly to CIG, offering facial recognition analysis and thermal imaging overlays of the square in real-time. But it also concealed Trenfor's gaze, letting him observe without revealing what he saw.

The square was alive with the choreography of the faithful and the curious: pilgrims trailing rosaries, children chasing pigeons, priests whispering into phones. Trenfor moved through it like a shadow with purpose, pausing occasionally to study his phone or admire a statue. Each stop allowed CIG's systems to catalogue thermal signatures, electromagnetic fluctuations, and spectral data invisible to the human eye.

He drifted toward the center, where the ancient Egyptian obelisk rose in stark defiance of time. Imported from Heliopolis under Caligula, re-erected by Sixtus V in a Christian age, it stood now as a contradiction of symbols, once crowned with pagan worship, now topped with a cross. Trenfor circled its base slowly. The granite was ancient, but he noticed faint discoloration at the lower tier, barely perceptible even to trained eyes. He marked it. Noted the angles. The alignments. The geometry.

Then he turned and made for the side entrance beneath Bernini's colonnade, nodding at the Swiss Guard posted there. The soldier checked his credentials and waved him through. Trenfor descended into the basilica's lower chambers with practiced ease, moving past chapels and vestries, down into older corridors where polished marble gave way to worn stone steps slick with centuries of moisture and reverence.

Beneath the Vatican, time blurred.

Here, among the catacombs, lay the bones of martyrs. Unnamed. Forgotten by most. But not by Trenfor. He walked with quiet familiarity, his footsteps echoing through the subterranean hush until he reached a secured chamber lit by low, indirect LEDs. It was a strange hybrid of ancient faith and modern vigilance, stone alcoves cradling relics in gold, beside laptops, infrared scanners, and motion-detection grids. This was the Vatican's hidden pulse, a place where past and present conspired to watch what came next.

Father Anselmo stood waiting. His frame was stooped, translucent in the sterile glow. A scholar-priest, his face was carved by fasting and thought, and his fingers, though gnarled by time, moved with surgical clarity.

"You've come just in time," he said without greeting. His Italian accent softened his English, but not the urgency behind it. "The signs accelerate."

He gestured to a bank of screens. On the central monitor, satellite imagery displayed St. Peter's Square from above, live, detailed, annotated. He tapped a timeline on the overlay, tracing a curved trajectory.

"The ritual is scheduled for the eclipse," he said. "Seven days. Eleven forty-two. The obelisk will stand directly beneath the shadow path."

"And the Vatican approved it?" Trenfor asked, already knowing the answer.

Father Anselmo's jaw tightened. "They filed for a permit under the name of an interfaith climate initiative called, 'Planetary Healing Ceremony.' Denying it would have sparked accusations of religious intolerance."

Another screen blinked to life, a heat map. In the dead hours between two and four a.m., invisible glyphs were being traced around the obelisk with ash and oil by hooded figures. Not graffiti. Not vandalism. Ritual inscriptions rendered in sympathetic patterns invisible to ordinary light, but perfectly legible to thermal scans. Then the recording blinks off.

"They move like clockwork," Anselmo said. "Each night. Security's been told to ignore them. From above our level. The excuse is that what they are writing cannot be seen with the naked eye. So our orders are to simply monitor it."

Trenfor nodded, studying the complex geometry radiating from the obelisk's base like veins from a heart. "They're laying a resonance lattice. A sympathetic grid designed to amplify whatever they intend to channel."

He looked up, as if he could see the sky through the many meters of stone above them. "They're turning Peter's martyrdom on this plaza into a gate. A reversal of sorts. From sacrifice to summoning."

At a nearby workstation, a younger priest in a white clerical shirt, Father Marco, spoke up hesitantly.

"But surely this is just symbolic. We're not in the Dark Ages. The Church isn't hunted anymore."

Trenfor's reply was calm but absolute. "Christians are still dying in Asia, parts of Africa. The intensity has increased, not diminished. Quiet martyrdom doesn't make headlines. It never stopped."

Father Marco looked down, chastened. Trenfor stepped forward and set a tablet on the ancient table, bringing up a high-resolution image of a bent iron nail. The scan showed irregular surface pitting and some corrosion.

"This was stolen from a secured archive in Jerusalem. From Caiaphas's tomb. It matches known relic patterns from early Christian execution methods, pre-Constantinian metallurgy."

Father Anselmo crossed himself. "One of the crucifixion nails?"

Trenfor nodded. "We believe so. They're using relics as keys, objects already charged with belief, trauma, blood. Physical links to the spiritual. Their goal isn't metaphor. It's access to invoke ancient spirits who were cast out by Jesus."

Another priest spoke from the back, voice cautious but curious. "We value relics. But how can an object affect the spiritual realm?"

Trenfor turned. "Because it was once used in an act that tore the veil. And now, its residue carries a memory. It carries a vibration. The spiritual world isn't bound by time. It echoes. Their rituals resonate more powerfully when tethered to real sacrifice."

He looked around the chamber, at the fusion of relics and fiber optics, of incense and algorithms. "They're counting on modern skepticism. On our need to rationalize."

"The veil between worlds," Father Anselmo said quietly, "is thinnest when no one believes it exists."

Trenfor met his gaze. "Exactly. And they're counting on that silence."

Outside, the Egyptian obelisk cast its long shadow toward the basilica. It had once served the sun gods of Heliopolis. Then it watched a fisherman crucified upside down for refusing to renounce a risen carpenter.

Now, it waited.

Seven days.

And a gate prepared to open again.

CIG Headquarters, North Carolina

The CIG command center beneath the Blue Ridge Mountains hummed with quiet intensity, its operations as seamless as the forest canopy that concealed it. Within the fortified compound, analysts of the Christian Intelligence Group continued their round-the-clock surveillance of what the rest of the world still refused to acknowledge: a spiritual war unfolding in tandem with geopolitical events.

Inside the main chamber, the atmosphere had grown denser. Floor-to-ceiling displays lit the room with spectral overlays displaying supernatural activity translated into live geospatial data. Across the digital globe, pulses of red bloomed with synchronized rhythm over two critical sites: Rome and the Ethiopian highlands. Not seismic. Not electromagnetic. These were signatures of something ancient, pre-linguistic energies woven into the earth's foundations.

CIG's proprietary systems converted the invisible into measurable metrics. Algorithms, refined by centuries of missionary field data, apocryphal texts, and machine-learned pattern recognition, tracked frequencies too subtle for conventional science. What the world had relegated to folklore, the analysts here rendered into heatmaps and harmonic signatures, evidence of an unseen convergence accelerating toward manifestation.

The room vibrated with a quiet urgency. Analysts moved deliberately between terminals, voices low, fingers scanning control surfaces and touchscreens calibrated to filter metaphysical interference from earthly noise. The hum of high-performance processors was undercut by a deeper tension, less mechanical than spiritual.

At the heart of the chamber stood Doug McCraken.

His military posture was undiminished by the pressed civilian shirt and dark slacks. He suddenly was commanding a war most of the world denied was happening. The flicker of harmonic anomalies illuminated his face as he watched the main display.

"Social context overlay," he said.

Dr. Eleanor Reeves stepped forward. The lead cultural analyst. A former professor, now a field theorist of ideological erosion. Her silver-streaked bun was precise; her tone, clinical.

She transferred data from her tablet to the wall screen. Graphs surged into view, generational faith loss, doctrinal fragmentation, theological drift.

"Church attendance continues to decline," she said. "But the real shift is epistemological. We're not just losing congregants," she said. "We're losing shared metaphysical language. The old structures, ritual, tradition, oral transmission of warnings, have collapsed in most regions."

She brought up correlation layers. Heat maps. Spiritual vulnerability indexes.

"The more the world flattens its beliefs, the more receptive it becomes. Paganism no longer needs temples," she continued. "It wears hashtags. It codes itself in sustainability jargon and wellness retreats. The Ashen Veil isn't simply introducing the gods. They're reminding us we already worship them but by other names," she paused for a moment before continuing. "Our assessment of the scripture and historical record is that if a civilization that has been set free of the gods and cleansed of paganism ever empties itself of the true God, then that which was cast out will return in greater measure than before if allowed to return. A re-paganization will then occur. A repossession if you will. And it has already occurred in many ways. The Ashen Veil is simply conducting the final rituals for their return. It's not the beginning. It's the end."

A hush followed. Not shock. Recognition.

Julian, a tech specialist, broke the silence. "We're seeing pattern drift."

He magnified a waveform. Peaks and valleys deviated from projected summoning profiles.

"This isn't just a ritual grid. These are response curves. They're not pulling energy in. They're synchronizing with something already awake."

Barry, senior systems engineer, stepped forward, grizzled, blunt, Australian.

"Looks like defense staging to me, mate," he said. "Not invocation. Positioning. Reactionary posture."

McCraken's eyes narrowed.

"Which means we're late."

No one disagreed.

"Bring up the Vatican feed," he ordered.

The central screen flickered, cutting to live infrared footage from a high-altitude drone orbiting over Rome. St. Peter's Square appeared in spectral relief, cold stone and residual heat. The timestamp read 03:17 hours.

In the thermal spectrum, seven humanoid figures moved around the obelisk, hooded and deliberate. Each occupied a quadrant of the ritual array being laid in ash and oil. Their placements mirrored ancient schema, predictive patterns CIG had modeled from apocryphal liturgies and unclassified Vatican archives.

"Zoom," McCraken said.

The drone complied, edging closer. They watched as the figures placed bowls, marked sigils, and poured lines of viscous fluid invisible to the naked eye but perfectly legible to thermal scans. The choreography was too precise to be rehearsal. This was execution.

Then one of them paused.

The figure's hood lifted slightly. Not enough to reveal a face, but enough to suggest awareness. Slowly, it turned.

Not in panic. Not in confusion.

The figure looked directly at the drone.

Thousands of feet separated them. No noise betrayed the drone's presence. But the figure raised its hand.

A gesture. Deliberate. Not hostile. Not theatrical. A symbol.

Recognition.

"They see us," someone whispered.

The figure's fingers formed a configuration, two intersecting shapes. Cameras captured it, AI already parsing the signal.

And then—

The feed stuttered.

Once. Twice.

Static rippled across the image. When the signal returned, the square was empty. The obelisk cast the same shadow. But the figures were gone. No heat traces. No displacement.

Vanished.

"Replay," McCraken said, voice taut.

The loop showed the same. Ritual in progress. Eye contact. Static. Nothing.

Julian ran diagnostics. "No drone malfunctions. No environmental interference. They disrupted the signal without touching it."

Barry stepped back. "That's not summoning," Barry said quietly. "That's announcement."

Dr. Reeves nodded. "They wanted us to see them. And to know they could vanish at will."

McCraken faced the command floor. "Send full spectral analysis of the gesture to linguistics. Activate secondary prayer protocols globally. Increase watch on Rome and Lake Tana."

He turned to the comms operator. "Contact Trenfor. Tell him they know. And they want him to know it. They want us to know they have power and that we're dealing with more than some young activists who don't know what they're summoning," McCraken rubbed his chin before continuing. "They believe they are far enough along with the rituals that they no longer fear who we serve."

The command center returned to motion, every station pulsing with the hum of coordination.

Above them, two red pulses—Rome and Ethiopia—throbbed in perfect symmetry on the wall-sized display. Twin signals. Twin gates. Twin warnings.

Or perhaps... an invitation.

Chapter Eleven

Rome, Italy – The Vatican

The ancient stone exhaled centuries as Trenfor descended a series of stairs beneath the Lateran Basilica. Each step echoed with ritual symmetry, the sound of leather soles and cassock hems trailing through a corridor that had once hidden saints and secrets. Unlike the polished sanctuaries above, this tunnel held the uncurated truth of Rome: bloodstained, contested, and holy in spite of itself.

Father Benetti led the way, his silhouette wavering in the torchlight. They passed beneath groined arches where soot had darkened the saints painted into the plaster, watchers now almost erased by time.

At a junction where the corridor narrowed into darkness, a black iron gate emerged like a scar from the stone.

"The first checkpoint," Benetti murmured. His voice was crisp, European, trained.

He drew a brass key, smoothed by centuries of anxious hands and unlocked the gate with a hollow click. The sound lingered like a warning.

"How many have access to this level?" Trenfor asked, voice low, expression unreadable.

"Seven," the priest replied. "All senior clergy under direct Vatican oversight."

They moved deeper, where ancient brick met modern imposition. A brushed steel door with a biometric scanner blinking nearby. The contradiction of ancient and modern security measures wasn't lost on Trenfor.

"Here?" Trenfor asked again, meaning how far down the permissions go at this level.

"Four. Myself included." Benetti's tone thinned, growing taut with the weight of implication.

The third barrier responded to a Latin passphrase and a retinal scan. When the system unlocked with a mechanical sigh, the scent shifted with incense giving way to limestone and latent decay. They were well beneath the curated past, in territory where time had forgotten its rhythm. At last, they reached a simple wooden door reinforced with dark iron bands.

Benetti paused, the final key, a silver one glinting unnaturally in the low light. "This violates multiple protocols," he said quietly. "Without Cardinal Monteverdi's personal authority and your particular résumé, you wouldn't be standing here."

"I understand the risk," Trenfor replied.

The lock turned with a sigh, and the reliquary chamber opened like a confession.

It was smaller than expected, modest even. But the walls whispered with weight. Glass-fronted cabinets held relics that had outlasted empires: bone fragments, threads of fabric, ink-blackened parchment, each one a nail in time's coffin. A sanctum of belief.

Benetti led him to a cabinet in the far corner. The glass pane hung open, and inside, only a ghost of dust remained.

"The ceremonial maps," Benetti said. "They were here. Three days ago."

Trenfor examined the latch. It was pristine. "No forced entry."

"None," Benetti confirmed. "The cameras show nothing. This space is sealed. No public access."

"Inside job," Trenfor said, and the phrase landed like a verdict.

Benetti's composure thinned. "We have partial digital scans of the maps. Incomplete, but perhaps useful."

He moved to a workstation embedded discreetly in a wall alcove. The contrast between stone and circuitry was striking: the modern world stitched into antiquity like a skin graft.

A few keystrokes brought up pale digital reproductions, parchment overlaid with geometry so intricate it looked almost organic.

"These were drawn in the fourth century," Benetti said. "But they're based on older knowledge, possibly Second Temple or even pre-Exilic. They chart the sacred geometry of Rome's martyrdom sites."

Trenfor leaned in. At first, the patterns felt chaotic. But as he toggled layers, a structure emerged, one that connected martyrdom sites in a shape both familiar and disturbing. Not a cross, but a reverse cruciform. An inversion.

"May I?" he asked.

Benetti stepped aside.

Trenfor adjusted scale, contrast, and map overlays. The alignment was unmistakable: Peter's traditional execution site linked to the ancient Roman circus route with lines converging not in reverence, but in reversal.

"This isn't sacred geometry," Trenfor said. "It's anti-sacred. A cruciform inversion."

He pulled out his encrypted device and transmitted the imagery. Three rings. Then a voice.

"Receiving. Standby... Confirmed match." The voice said over the device linked to CIG. "The Ashen Veil uses similar geometries in spiritual disruption sites. This Rome pattern is evolved. They're definitely turning martyr sites into frequency inverters."

Trenfor ended the call and turned to Benetti, who stood motionless, his face pale in the monitor's glow.

"Tesla once theorized that vibration and resonance affect more than energy," the priest said softly. "That they could cross boundaries and into consciousness, into spirit. His papers were suppressed. But the Church archived them."

"Show me the original storage chamber."

Benetti led him deeper, to a smaller vault sealed by a final key. Inside: bare stone shelves. Most were empty now, but Trenfor saw it immediately, disturbed dust. Clean gaps where time should have rested undisturbed.

From his coat, Trenfor produced a penlight. A quick twist, and ultraviolet washed the room in violet hue.

"What are you—"

Benetti's voice trailed off. Symbols appeared, slowly, then all at once carved invisibly into stone. Drawings written in invisible ink. Some spiraled outward like diseased flowers. Others mimicked sacred runes... but twisted, wrong.

"These weren't meant for human eyes," Trenfor said. "They're visible only in specific wavelengths. Like the ones found at Kursi. At Jerusalem."

He circled the chamber, pausing at one glyph whose angles bent light in ways that made the edges shimmer. "They didn't hide them from us. They coded them for something else. Something that sees in frequencies we don't."

Benetti crossed himself. "What do they mean?"

"They're building a mirror altar," Trenfor replied. "This one is only half."

He turned, eyes sharp. "The other is in Ethiopia. They're syncing them. Tuning them like instruments. What happens here reflects there. What's worse is they wanted these symbols here purposely. It demonstrates they have penetrated even the Vatican. It represents that the seat of Christian authority is calling for the old gods return from this inner sanctum and at the highest levels."

"And the worldwide protests? The widespread ceremonies?"

"Distractions," Trenfor said flatly. "Stagecraft to keep us looking at the wrong symbols. The wrong places. So we can't pinpoint their intended altars. But we know. They need to command authority over these two altars that represent the primary seats of Christianity."

Benetti's voice dropped to a whisper. "God help us."

Trenfor's eyes returned to the sigils. "He will. But He expects resistance first."

Lake Tana, Ethiopia

The mist clung to Lake Tana like a spirit reluctant to depart, wrapping the water in a gauze of silence. Sarah adjusted the strap of her gear bag, wincing slightly as it dug into her shoulder. The Ethiopian soil, rich and red, had already left its imprint on her boots. Boots purchased at a climate-controlled REI, now baptized by the weight of this strange, sacred land.

"We should not delay," Kebede murmured beside her, his voice low but urgent. "The monks prefer arrivals before the sun makes its climb."

He moved with quiet assurance through the undergrowth, his pace steady, his posture alert. In the fading light of their first meeting, she'd mistaken him for a typical fixer, competent, respectful, hired guide. But that impression had frayed. Kebede prayed with a grip that clenched a wooden cross like a ward against something more than metaphor. And two nights ago, she had overheard a conversation in which his name was spoken with reverence by monks who called themselves the Remnant. Not guides. Guardians.

They reached the lake's edge. A narrow wooden boat rocked gently in the shallows, its frame darkened by decades of mineral-rich water. The boatman, as weathered as the vessel itself, said nothing. His eyes never quite meeting Sarah's, his hands speaking a dialect of silence learned from wind, rope, and water.

"Tana Cherkos," Kebede said as they pushed off from the shore, setting course for the next island sanctuary, "sheltered the Ark for nearly eight centuries. From Solomon's Temple to this island. From this island to Axum."

Sarah nodded, her mind already sorting the detail into her mental catalog. She glanced down at her equipment, checking that her camera and 3D scanner were safely secured. She was here to document, officially. But the pull in her chest said she was here for something else entirely.

As the mist began to lift, the island emerged in the distance as their boat approached. First as a silhouette, then as terrain. Basalt rock, black and veined with ancient scars, rose from the water like a fortress shaped by prayer. Gnarled fig trees clung to the cliffs with roots that resembled grasping hands. And at the shoreline, three monks stood in absolute stillness, as though they had been waiting since the beginning.

"The brothers of St. Stephanos," Kebede said. "There are those who claim they descend from the Levites who first carried the Ark."

The boat scraped against stone. Sarah stepped out and was met by the eldest priest. His face reflected a topography of age and sunlight, but his grip firm, alive. *"Enqwa wädä Bēta Kidāna Qädāmawi mäṭṭāḥ,"* the priest said softly.

"He welcomes you to the House of the First Covenant," Kebede translated. But Sarah felt the weight of far more than words in the man's soft Ge'ez greeting.

They ascended slowly along a stone path worn smooth by generations. Sarah noticed the details instinctively such as the orientation of trees framing the lake's horizon, carved stones laid not for aesthetics but for ritual geometry. The past hadn't been buried here. It had been curated.

The monastery itself was built not upon the rock, but of it. Its wooden beams and basalt stones had darkened to the same hue, giving the impression that it had grown from the earth like a relic rather than a structure.

The entrance was low, forcing even Sarah to duck. Its arch bore markings that predated Christianity, eclipsed by crosses etched later, asserting dominance or continuity, depending on one's theology. Inside, the scent changed. Gone was the raw wind of the lake. Here lingered old incense, beeswax, stone, and silence.

They passed through chambers, each one darker, narrower, more intimate, until they reached a central room where a single slab of volcanic stone commanded the space.

"Here," Kebede said, "the Ark rested when it was brought inside."

Sarah knelt, photographing the slab from multiple angles. Then Kebede led her outside, to an open-air altar farther up the ridge.

"There," he said, pointing to a flat stone exposed to sun and wind. Four indentations were visible, each one rectangular, precise, carved deep into the basalt. Indicating the Ark's resting place when outside.

Sarah crouched beside them, slowly running her fingertips along the grooves. The measurements matched those she had memorized: the Ark's dimensions as described in Scripture and supported by countless commentaries and theories. But this was not theory. This was stone. This was physical.

Her hand tingled with a subtle warmth she couldn't explain and a sense of reverence seemed to wash over her.

A monk arrived with a silver key and opened a nearby structure which was unremarkable from the outside, but heavily locked. Inside, Sarah saw them: sacred artifacts. Ancient, preserved.

"The priestly implements," the monk said in thickly accented English, surprising her. "Breastplate holders. Pans for purification. Bowls for sacrifice."

"How—?" she asked.

"When the Ark moved to Axum," Kebede said quietly, "these remained. Animal sacrifice ended after the Second Temple was destroyed. These items were no longer needed. But they were not discarded."

With permission granted, Sarah set up her 3D scanner. The hum of the modern machine filled the ancient silence of antiquity. She worked quietly, cataloging every curvature, each hollow basin, the age-worn edges of divine instruments, the outer grounds, the inner temple.

When finished, she asked to see the grounds beyond.

One monk nodded and led them behind the monastery. Terraced stone steps descended to a carved channel that once carried spring water for ritual use.

"Water flowed during ceremonies," Kebede explained. "But the spring dried a generation ago."

Sarah documented it all, but Kebede stepped closer, voice low and urgent.

"The watchers sense instability," he said. "Livestock won't drink. Mirrors fracture without touch. GPS devices reset. And a diver went missing three days ago near the submerged ruins to the east."

Sarah blinked. "Submerged ruins?"

He nodded once.

That night, they offered her a simple meal of injera, lentils, and water. Then she was shown to her quarters: a small room with only a cot, a stool, and a basin. No electricity. No sound but the hush of wind through fig trees.

She sat on the cot, pulling her tablet from its case along with batteries for her devices. The cross Trenfor had given her rested against her collarbone like a weight.

The tablet connected through an embedded Elemental Gear uplink.

A notification pulsed.

INTERNAL MEMO – ALL STAFF

Sender: *Corporate Communications / Outreach Director*

Sarah tapped.

A familiar face filled the screen. A man from her childhood appeared. A trusted presence once known simply as "Uncle Lucas."

"Valued team members and spiritual progressives," he began. His voice hadn't aged. "As we reach the culmination of our awareness campaign, you are invited to stand witness at the dawn of a new global consciousness."

His words were polished, strategic. References to planetary healing. Liberation from oppressive spiritual systems. Rebirth through elemental harmony. Events worldwide.

And then:

"Those near our ceremonial sites, particularly our family in Europe and Africa, will witness the convergence. Document it well. The rest will follow."

The video ended with the Elemental Gear logo. But beneath the animation, Sarah saw it. A symbol. Ancient. One she had seen etched in ashes in Israel. A mark that predated Christianity. A glyph of power. A symbol being used to summon unseen dimensions according to Trenfor.

The tablet slipped slightly in her grip.

This wasn't marketing. This wasn't sustainability.

This was theology being weaponized.

This was ancient ritual in designer packaging.

And she was standing on its altar and somehow directly in its path.

CIG HQ, North Carolina

The cold blue glow from the wall of digital displays turned Doug McCraken's face into a map of furrowed lines and flickering shadows. He stood motionless in the center of the Christian Intelligence Group's subterranean operations center, hands clasped behind his back, as data fed ceaselessly across multiple screens; satellite sweeps, intercepted messages, tremor overlays, and spectral resonance readings. The hum of machinery filled the room like a held breath. Analysts moved with crisp economy, each one aware that something was building. A spiritual convergence masquerading as a humanitarian movement.

"Sir, Miriam's team is ready," said a young analyst, voice tuned to the room's hush.

Doug nodded once. "Put them through."

The central screen shifted. Miriam appeared, seated at a modular command hub in the Israeli field station. Around her, equipment cases were stacked that lent the appearance of a geological expedition. It was cover, of course, for cryptographic surveillance in North Africa and beyond.

"We're tracking elevated encrypted traffic," she began without preamble, fingers already blurring across her interface. "Several activist cells have been penetrated. Ashen Veil's network is using a quantum-phase cipher that resets every seventeen minutes. But we've isolated recurring structure."

Doug leaned forward. "Show me."

The left-hand display populated with cascading blocks of decrypted code. Amber highlights pulsed where key phrases had been unlocked.

" '*Twin altars set to breathe as one*' shows up in over 75% of our intercepts from the last 48 hours," Miriam said. "No direct coordinates, but symbol clusters are being reported worldwide. Hidden marks emerging at known spiritual sites. This is a timed activation set for 72 hours, possibly less."

Doug exhaled through his nose. "The eclipse."

Miriam nodded. "Rome's eclipse window intersects precisely with Lake Tana's zenith alignment. Unique to this decade. We've never modeled this configuration."

Another face joined the feed, Noam, Miriam's lead cryptographer.

"They're embedding cipher keys in ritual language. Blended Ge'ez and decayed Latin. Not just linguistics, but metaphysical semantics. Each phrase acts as a dual-code, its meaning fracturing and reassembling depending on spiritual context. It's pretty sophisticated. They've done their research."

Doug's jaw clenched subtly. "Tremor overlays?"

A new visual bloomed: a global map laced with ethereal lines, delicate, magnetic threads pulsing with spiritual energy. Two nodes pulsed brighter than the rest: Rome. Lake Tana. Not earthquakes. Not ley lines. Heads nodded.

"Rotational mirror vortices," Miriam said. "Each site generates a spiritual current. But paired like this, they act as a binary harmonic. Like quantum entanglement, but across dimensional boundaries."

"Like twin loudspeakers in phase," Noam added. "Creating a resonance field that amplifies both. It may be designed to resonant across dimensions worldwide. It's pretty much the scientific explanation of how the rituals work or at least impact reality."

Doug said nothing for a long beat. Trenfor's findings beneath the Lateran Basilica weren't isolated. They were one side of a mirrored ritual. Frequency. Pattern. Inversion. This was architecture, not of stone, but of spirit.

A movement at the periphery caught his attention. A junior analyst, barely out of seminary, approached like an altar boy bearing a sacrament, tablet in hand.

"Sir," he said, voice trembling slightly. "Father Benetti granted full access to the martyrs' archive. We found something buried in the fifth-century records."

Doug raised a brow. "Show me."

"A hidden journal, sir. Written by a convert named Agapitus. He infiltrated Diocletian's court as a secret believer.

He describes a failed… 'awakening' pre-fifth century. A pagan rite designed to open dimensional gates via twin temple sites. One in Rome. One in Alexandria."

Doug scanned the transcript. Statues bleeding. Spontaneous fires. Mass delusions. Agapitus called it a *false resurrection.* A rift torn open, held at bay only by fasting, prayer, and martyrdom.

"Historians wrote it off as political instability," the analyst continued. "But Agapitus was adamant. The veil thinned. Something tried to cross through the dimensions. It was momentarily horrific."

Doug lowered the tablet slowly. The command center had stilled around him. On-screen, Miriam waited. Her team watched. Silence had become its own liturgy.

"Activate emergency watchposts," Doug said finally. "Full-spectrum sensors. Seismic. Electromagnetic and spiritual. I want sensitivity pegged to maximum."

The room ignited in quiet movement.

"Miriam, we will dispatch mobile units to the periphery around Lake Tana. If this is a resonance field, they'll be using distributed amplifiers. Protestors will be unknowingly placed at nodal points."

"We've already prepped three teams with spectrum-analysis gear," she said. "They're in motion."

Doug turned to the comms station. "Notify our assets inside the Vatican and the Ethiopian Orthodox synod. Use epsilon-level encryption. They need to know: this isn't ceremony or a dry run. They understand the science. They won't make the same mistake they made in the fifth century.

It's why they've been so meticulous leaving signs and holding mass protests across continents to magnify the vibrations."

He paused, letting the weight of it settle.

"They're trying to undo the exorcism of Legion. Not summon new entities, but *re-align ancient ones already here.* It requires human will. That's the loophole. And they're harvesting it through misdirected free will under the banners of justice, ecology, and peace."

The comms officer froze for half a second, then nodded and began transmitting.

Doug's mind raced; resources, countermeasures, prayer grids, sacramental defenses. Somewhere inside the Vatican, someone had leaked the ossuary maps. They now faced an ancient intelligence with modern logistics. A ritual long in rehearsal.

"Open a Vatican joint probe. I want every suspect with access to relic archives reviewed. Cross-reference with Ashen Veil activity. I want a name within twenty-four hours."

Around him, analysts accelerated. This wasn't espionage. It wasn't terrorism. This was sacred geometry deployed as weaponry. It was spiritual terrorism.

"This attempt is going to happen," Doug said aloud, to no one and everyone. "It's synchronization. The Ashen Veil isn't just opening a door. They're *tuning the atmosphere* to what's already here. Like tuning forks priming the veil. They've replaced much of God with pagan worship under the world's nose to prepare the way."

He turned to the spiritual advisor, a gray-haired woman who had remained silent, a prayer shawl folded in her lap like a shield waiting to be drawn.

"Deploy prayer teams to all convergence points," Doug said. "Continuous cover until this is neutralized. They're amplifying. So must we."

She rose wordlessly and moved to the secure line.

Doug turned back to the pulsing map. The line between Rome and Ethiopia flickered like a heartbeat. Rome was an obvious center of attention. The populated center of Christianity. But Ethiopia was more remote. It's Christian origins forgotten. Trenfor was in position. Sarah, whether she knew it or not, stood at the other end.

Only the Remnant remained with her.

"God help them both," Doug whispered, beneath his breath. "And God help us all… if we're not too late."

Lake Tana, Ethiopia

The stone walls of the monastery guest quarters exhaled the day's heat in slow, resentful breaths, like ancient lungs unwilling to forget. Night had fallen over Lake Tana, but the air remained heavy, thick with incense residue, sacred memory, and traditions that echoed a certain truth that Sarah struggled to understand.

She sat cross-legged on the edge of her narrow cot, the rough linen of her pants catching on the grain of the wood. Around her neck, Trenfor's wooden cross hung low, cool against her skin. She absently turned it between her fingers, the small object grounding her even as the world she knew continued to fracture beneath her feet. Its weight felt disproportionate, less jewelry, more artifact. A symbol pressed into her palm not as a gesture of faith, but of warning.

The tablet in her lap cast a soft blue glow, throwing angular shadows across her face and into the creases of the stone wall behind her. On-screen, footage cycled from six continents. Protests. Processions. Ashen Veil demonstrators moving in symmetrical rings, clothed in unbleached linen, chanting phrases that sounded like liturgies stripped of God. From Oslo to Tokyo, Buenos Aires to Cape Town, it looked choreographed, ritual disguised as grassroots. The language was universal: eco-justice, ancestral healing, divine liberation. The branding, she realized with professional clarity, was brilliant. Social justice. Equality for all. Complete with pre-printed signs that looked the same from one end of a continent to the other.

It sounded good. It was *too* good.

She recognized the signatures, visual harmony across cultures, regional tweaks to appeal to the aesthetic palette of each city, unified fonts, curated chants. A single mind had shaped this campaign, someone fluent in iconography, in the bypassing of the rational mind. Someone who understood how beauty and justice could become weaponized under the right light. Pagan themes wrapped in Christian words. Disguised morality and superiority.

She flipped screens. Christian leaders now spoke across livestreams and pulpits, urgent but restrained. A Southern pastor in Atlanta quoted Paul: *even Satan masquerades as an angel of light.* A Greek priest read from Revelation. A Vatican spokesman offered a carefully worded repudiation of "the misuse of Christian imagery for post-religious ideological aims."

Elsewhere, the debate had already been hijacked. Protesters called religious leaders extremists if they disagreed with the call for justice.

On a global news panel, a pair of pundits clashed with the performative polish of actors trained in ideological theater. Some religious leaders supported the protests. The first, a religion professor in flowing sleeves, declared the Ashen Veil a movement of "spiritual reclamation", a rising of the divine feminine suppressed by patriarchal dogma.

"This is a return," she said, slicing the air with her hands, "to a global sacred consciousness unbound by institutional constraints."

Her opponent, a bowtied firebrand, pushed back with exasperated fury. "Their methods *are* the fascism they accuse others of. Look how they silence dissent, demand uniformity, redefine truth. They're not fighting oppression, they're manufacturing it to justify ritualized outrage."

Sarah muted them both. The performance continued in pantomime, hands flying, eyes narrowing, but the silence was a relief. Her thoughts had already shifted.

She thought of her father, Elemental Gear, summer camps and fundraisers, off-the-record meetings she hadn't thought twice about until now. Of the video, *his* voice, speaking in smooth, reassuring tones about "Dawn

Reclamation" and the coming convergence. He had called it a celebration.

She closed the news feed and opened her secure app. No new messages. Nothing from Trenfor since his cryptic note three days ago:

"Discovered something beneath the basilica. Going dark. Trust no one at EG. I know it's complicated with your family."

She sat motionless for a long moment, staring at the empty inbox. Then she closed the app and opened her 3D imaging software.

It was a professional impulse at first, checking the day's scans. The stone slab where the Ark was said to have rested. The channels in the rock. The arrangement of support pillars. She rotated the rendering, zooming, recalibrating. Something was wrong, or right. Something she hadn't seen in person was now undeniable from this angle.

It had *pattern*.

The layout wasn't random. The geometry, subtle from the ground, was unmistakable in 3D. The slab. The carved terraces. The water flow lines. It all obeyed a logic. Not architectural. Not even religious. *Resonant.* Like circuitry. Or sigils. It resembled an electronic circuit with organization. The key sites she had been asked to record were not random points.

She opened a second window. Loaded Trenfor's reference point: Rome. Specifically, satellite imaging of the Lateran Basilica. Trenfor had told her, once, that it was built over an earlier holy site. He hadn't said more. But he hadn't needed to.

She aligned the models. Adjusted rotation. Calibrated scale.

The screen dimmed. Then brightened. And the geometries snapped into alignment.

Two mirrored blueprints. One carved into volcanic stone in northern Ethiopia. The other layered into Roman catacombs and cathedral foundations. Their core structures, separated by continent and millennia, fit together like halves of a forgotten machine. Glyphs and sigils that didn't just match, they responded. Complementary, not identical. *Engineered to face each other.*

"That's not possible," she whispered.

But it was.

She zoomed in on the twin circles at each site's center. Surrounded by sacred inscriptions. From different cultures. Different eras. And yet, they spoke the same design language. The same frequency. Similar configuration of key points.

Her tablet buzzed slightly in her hands. The processor lagged under the strain. Then the image clarified.

It wasn't just symbolic. It was *functional.* Architecture as alignment. Spiritual topography encoded in stone. It looked like a large electronic layout connecting the continents. Mirrored.

Her throat tightened.

"They built them to face each other," she said aloud, her voice trembling into the warm, incense-soaked air.

The realization landed in her chest like a falling star. These weren't isolated worship sites. They were terminals or just activation points. And if the Ashen Veil was right, if their data was complete, these sites were connected over the millennia.

The cross around her neck slipped forward and bumped the edge of the tablet.

The screen flickered.

For one breathless moment, the symbols on the display seemed to dim as though reacting. Not to touch, but to presence. To authority.

Then the moment passed.

Coincidence. Or something deeper.

She looked back at the screen. The circles still glowed. Still aligned. Still waiting.

This wasn't about relics anymore. It wasn't about simply securing 3D imaging of an ancient site.

It was something more, understanding the power of patterns and symbolic language reaching toward something beyond the physical. She had followed data and dirt, glyphs and geography, but now the evidence was whispering in a different tongue to her. Two civilizations could not have coordinated the same patterns she was seeing across continents, cultures, languages and time without superior knowledge or intervention.

The Ark. The archaeology. The geometry of sacred design. The worldwide chaos.

It wasn't just her seeing the patterns. It was the patterns seeing *her*. Then she realized something in the heat of the Ethiopian night.

She wasn't merely an observer. And she was seeing the hand of a superior designer greater than man.

Chapter Twelve

Lake Tana - Ethiopia

The chapel crouched against the cliffside like a weathered sentinel, its basalt walls scarred by time and crowned in moss. Though carved by ancient hands, it bore the weight of centuries without protest, the kind of structure that didn't beg for reverence, but commanded it.

Sarah Whitfield sat at the edge of the last stone bench, her shoulder brushing intermittently against Kebede's as the sound of sonorous chants deepened. The monks had formed a crescent before the altar, their ochre robes absorbing the candlelight that danced across the room like breath made visible. Etched into the walls behind them were ancient symbols, some faded to mere ghosts, others glinting faintly under the play of light. She recognized one or two of the images. The realization startled her.

The scent of incense, dense, bitter, unplaceable, clung to the air. It wasn't just ceremonial. It masked something older. Something alive. The chants in Ge'ez throbbed low through the nave, rising and falling like a deep river current. The rhythm bypassed her intellect and pressed into her skin. Against every scientific instinct she'd clung to, Sarah felt it, the tremble in her gut, the vibration in her spine. Like standing too close to a power line, the vibrations moved within her.

She leaned toward Kebede, her whisper barely audible. "What are they saying?"

Without taking his eyes off the altar, he replied, "Psalm 68. A war psalm. God rising. Enemies scattered before Him." His voice was quiet, but each word felt iron-forged.

Sarah nodded, but her skepticism strained. And yet, the monks' cadence, their devotion, it wasn't pageantry. It was conviction. Ancient and unshaken. She imagined their movements and chants had not changed in hundreds of years.

When the chant dissolved into silence, the stillness that followed wasn't empty. It was alert. A white-bearded monk stepped forward, eyes luminous in the flickering glow. He began to speak in Amharic, not performatively, but as one entrusted with sacred things.

"He speaks of the Ark's journey," Kebede whispered. "From Solomon's Temple to here at Lake Tana and then to Aksum. Hidden in time of war. Preserved in time of silence."

The monk's hands moved slowly, painting invisible maps through the air. His voice followed the old contours of oral tradition, rising with memory, falling with warning.

"Each church in Ethiopia houses a replica of the Ark," Kebede said softly. "Protection through saturation," Kebede said sofly. "What better place to hide a tree than in a forest?"

Sarah turned to him. "Replicas?"

Kebede nodded. "The Kebra Nagast speaks of it. The true Ark was brought here, hidden from conquest, shielded from misuse. The tabot in each sanctuary is a sacred copy. But one true ark remains. The seat of the Most High."

The monk raised a small wooden replica of the Ark above his head. His voice surged with quiet fire, and the entire room leaned toward it like iron filings to a magnet.

"He speaks of guardianship," Kebede translated. "Of covenant. That each generation must not only protect the vessel, but the holiness it bears. It is not the object, it is what it was made to hold. It is the covenant it was meant to represent. Like a legal document between man and God," Kebede said. "Binding. Conditional. Enforced."

Sarah looked around. The few villagers scattered among the monks weren't passive observers. They were torchbearers. Watchers. There was no superstition in their eyes, only a sobering awareness. This wasn't folklore to them. This was real. Living. Defended.

For the first time since stepping into this ancient land, Sarah felt her doubt retreat, not shattered, but displaced. As if a new framework had silently taken its place. For the first time, she was conscious of her soul.

The service ended with a final chant, shorter and more urgent, as if a message had been delivered and now needed guarding. One by one, the worshipers rose and left. Kebede stayed. So did she.

"I found something," she murmured when only one monk remained, extinguishing candles along the far wall. "In the imaging scans. Twin circles and astronomic configurations. Geometric overlays in how the structures here are aligned. The patterns of how they chose to house the Ark and accompanying structures are not random."

She hesitated, then added, "I sent it to Trenfor."

Kebede's face barely moved, but something sharpened in his eyes. "You chose well," Kebed said quietly. "Trenfor will share it with CIG."

"CIG?" she echoed, the letters foreign and faintly unsettling. "What is CIG? And who *is* Trenfor, really? He's not just some archaeologist, is he?"

Kebede stood and offered his hand. "No. But this isn't the place to discuss such things." He cast a glance around the dimming chapel, where darkness was beginning to overtake the last remnants of flame. "Come. We'll talk somewhere more secure."

She took his hand. It was rough, calloused by time, earth, and more than a few battles not found in textbooks. As they passed through the threshold, the final candle winked out behind them, the chapel now cloaked in silence.

Outside, dusk had bled into the hills, and Lake Tana gleamed like molten bronze under a sky veiled in prayer.

"You're part of it too," she said, not asking. "You and Trenfor."

Kebede stopped, the wind catching the edge of his robe. "We all serve in different ways," he said. "Some with swords. Some with words. Some with fire no one else sees."

He turned to her, face solemn. "And now, it seems, you are among us."

The words didn't frighten her. They settled on her shoulders with gravity and a strange relief. Not burden, but a sudden clarity that whatever answers awaited her, they would change everything she thought she understood about the world and her place in it.

Whatever lay ahead, she was no longer outside it.

Kebede's quarters embodied the paradox Sarah had encountered throughout Ethiopia, ancient wisdom coexisting with startling modernity. The stone walls were bare, save for a simple wooden cross and a shelf of leather-bound texts whose spines bore titles in Ge'ez and Amharic. A narrow bed occupied one corner, the blanket pulled tight with military precision. But the object that disrupted the monastic calm sat atop an old wooden desk, a sleek silver laptop, gleaming like a visitor from another world.

Moonlight spilled through a high window, casting long, clean shadows across the floor. Kebede gestured for Sarah to take the room's only chair.

"We have a secure connection," he said, voice low despite the room's silence. "These walls were built for prayer... and secrets."

He moved with deliberate economy, hands gliding across the keyboard. Authentication prompts flashed and disappeared. Sarah noted multiple encryption protocols. A compact satellite relay blinked steadily green from the windowsill, its hum barely audible.

Kebede noticed her glance. "The modern Church does not reject technology. Wisdom discerns the tool from the idol."

The screen resolved into the image of a man in his late fifties, silver-haired, with the bearing of a career soldier. His face was lined but alert, eyes sharp, scanning. But what held Sarah's attention was the symbol on his lapel: a red crusader's cross intersected by a vertical sword. Behind it, a world map gleamed faintly, edged with coded detail. Ephesians 6:12 was etched to the left of the blade. On the right: 2 Timothy 1:7. At the crossguard, an all-seeing eye. And flanking it in crimson: the letters "C" and "G." Below, the Latin phrase she'd once looked up after spotting it in Trenfor's notebook - *Lux in Tenebris.* Light in darkness.

"Kebede," the man said with a nod. "Is the connection secure?"

"Yes, Director," Kebede replied. "This is Sarah Whitfield."

His gaze turned. The screen's distance did little to mute the intensity. He looked at Sarah, not as an introduction, but an evaluation.

"Miss Whitfield," he said. "Trenfor mentioned you. You saw the mirrored geometries and astronomical alignments at the Ethiopian monastery." A pause. "Your contribution is valuable to out assessment. Thank you for stepping into this."

Sarah leaned forward. "Stepping into what, exactly? Who are you?"

"My name is Doug McCraken. I lead the Christian Intelligence Group - CIG." The statement carried no bravado, only fact. "We monitor global spiritual movements, protect sacred sites, and when necessary... we intervene."

"Intelligence group? You're spies?" she asked, her tone half-joke, half-accusation.

Doug allowed the corner of his mouth to smile. "Well, I guess you could say we are like the CIA of the spiritual world, part intelligence, part surveillance, part exploration. Except our arena isn't national security. It's eternity. Our scope extends beyond the physical world as we're more of an interdimensional watchdog."

He tapped a key. The screen split, revealing infrared imagery. Thermal overlays of her measurements onto the twin sites CIG was following appeared. But these were sharper, layered with pulse waves, algorithmic symbols, and geometric lattices she hadn't seen before. Data flowed across the screen like blood through a beating heart.

"Those are my measurements," Sarah whispered. "But your scans go deeper and you've mirrored them with what looks like the Vatican area."

Doug nodded. "We've been watching both sites. Ethiopia's activated first, but Rome is the crescendo. The coordinates form a resonance pattern we've seen before. In Jerusalem. In Alexandria. In Babylon."

Behind Doug, she noticed now what she hadn't at first, banks of monitors, tech teams analyzing real-time feeds, satellite trajectories, even lines of ancient script transcribed and studied by specialists. It wasn't a church. It wasn't a base. It was both. A war room.

"That looks like a command center," she murmured.

"Spiritual warfare command," Doug confirmed. "The Ashen Veil isn't staging a protest. They're manufacturing a false flag. Christian violence, pre-fabricated and pre-blamed. Chaos will erupt, and the cross will take the fall."

He changed the feed again. Images appeared, protest signs already printed in multiple languages: *Christians Out. End the Tyranny of the Cross.* Edited clips of riots, staged violence. A false narrative waiting to go live.

"They've scripted everything. They only need a spark to light it."

Sarah's blood turned cold. "My father's foundation funded part of this, archaeological digs, cultural exchanges."

Doug's expression softened, just slightly. "He's been compartmentalized. He believes he's funding interfaith scholarship. Eli's kept him blind to the spiritual intent."

"Eli?" she said. "He left Israel. Where is he now?"

"Rome. He'll lead the ritual." Doug's voice dropped an octave. "But he won't act alone. They'll need a vessel. A host."

Sarah's pulse slowed as the meaning sank in. "You mean actual possession."

Doug didn't answer. He didn't need to.

She turned to Kebede, searching his face for irony, metaphor, even hyperbole. None came. His eyes were clear. Grave.

"The spirits they seek," Kebede said quietly, "cannot act in this dimension without an anchor. They need embodiment. Consent. Man must invite them to return and that's what they are planning."

Sarah's breath caught. The strange geometries she'd studied, the eerie synchronicity across continents, it hadn't been architecture. It had been a design for something... alive.

"They want to reopen what God sealed," Doug said. "To thin the veil between dimensions. It's not science fiction, Miss Whitfield. It's ancient technology. The kind Enoch warned about."

Her stomach twisted. The Book of Enoch, Kebede had mentioned it in the chapel. Fallen angels. Forbidden knowledge. Giants. The Watchers. Warnings that had sounded mythological until now.

"And Trenfor?" she asked, voice hollow.

"He's in Rome," Doug said. "Collecting evidence. Watching the rehearsals. But they're almost ready. The window is narrow."

The screen flickered again, an atmospheric disruption or a spiritual tremor, she wasn't sure which. She was no longer in the world she thought she understood.

She was in theirs.

The Vatican - Rome

The maintenance jumpsuit hung loose on Trenfor's frame, its drab gray fabric blending perfectly with the work crews bustling around the scaffolding of Santa Maria della Pietà, a centuries-old church tucked into a quiet Roman quarter undergoing extensive restoration. He moved with the ease of familiarity, a coiled length of cable slung over one shoulder, giving him the appearance of a technician assigned to the renovations. No one questioned his presence. He had already intercepted the job sheet and forged his clearance badge. His disguise was convincing because it didn't try to be anything more than unremarkable.

But it wasn't the church itself he had come to investigate.

Behind the building, separated by a tall masonry wall and accessible only through a narrow archway, lay a secluded courtyard no longer in public use. It had once served as a cloister garden but was now overgrown and forgotten except by the group that had quietly leased it for "performance rehearsals." They called themselves cultural preservationists. Trenfor knew better.

He moved through the side entrance, bypassing the inner corridor where actual workers repaired stained glass and vaulted ceilings. A locked utility gate led to a passageway that overlooked the hidden courtyard. He took his place at a darkened maintenance panel behind a slatted vent, peering through the narrow openings.

Below, the scene was already unfolding.

Ceremonial fire bowls cast flickering shadows along the old stone walls, their glow falling on seven participants arranged in a precise formation around a central figure. Eli Weiss moved among them with choreographed authority, his voice carrying clearly in the echoing space.

"The alignment must be perfect. This is a rehearsal, but the geometry must hold even in practice."

Trenfor's gaze followed Eli's hand as he gestured toward white chalk symbols drawn onto the cobbled courtyard, two overlapping circles intersected by lines and notations. It mirrored the geometry Sarah had uncovered in Ethiopia. His fingers brushed the concealed camera inside his jumpsuit, switching it on with a quiet touch. A faint vibration confirmed it had begun recording.

Eli continued, "The real ritual aligns with the eclipse. This is merely preparation. Precision will determine whether the veil opens or remains closed. Let's get this right."

At the center of the formation, a man lay motionless on a canvas mat, his limbs splayed like an offering. The chanting began, a dissonant blend of Aramaic and another language Trenfor couldn't place, throaty, ancient, and intentionally unsettling.

To the side, a pile of banners lay against the wall, their slogans already printed: *Christians Out—No More Tyranny of the Cross.* Trenfor spotted video equipment and digital media labeled with dates in the coming week, evidence of premeditated propaganda. It was a false-flag operation in the making. Plans had already been made to act on responses to the rituals that had not occurred yet.

"Begin again," Eli ordered sharply. "This must be flawless when the eclipse reaches its apex."

As the chanting resumed, one of the participants, a young woman in less-worn ceremonial garb, lowered her arms and hesitated. "But… do we really blame the Christians for this? Isn't this… manipulation?"

Eli's voice shifted. A darker tone crept in, resonant and unsettling, as though two voices now spoke as one. "They burned our libraries. Desecrated our altars. You mistake cunning for deception, child. We are merely restoring balance."

The girl didn't move, but her face paled. "Still… lying to incite hatred."

"Silence," Eli said, stepping closer. "You don't understand what's at stake. The convergence must occur, and the world must be ready to receive what comes through our work."

From Trenfor's vantage, the air around Eli seemed denser, as though the firelight recoiled from his presence. A presence was speaking through him, one that didn't belong to this world. Trenfor had felt it before, in remote villages, during spiritual tremors. It wasn't just symbolism or fervor. Something was already pressing against the veil.

Suddenly, the man on the mat arched violently, then sat upright with unnatural ease.

"The vessel responds," he said. His voice rang hollow and doubled, like an echo behind an echo. "The twin sites must ignite as one, releasing their energy. The shadow will fall, and the gate will open."

Trenfor captured the final exchange, heart steady but senses on high alert. This was no dry ritualistic reenactment, it was a calibrated test. They were measuring resonance and effect.

He slipped away as carefully as he had arrived, retracing his steps through the maintenance access and back out into the Roman streets. A few blocks away, he ducked into a café, ordered an espresso, and encrypted the footage into a data package for CIG.

The confirmation code arrived moments later.

Trenfor downed the espresso, the bitterness suiting the weight of what they expected. The Ashen Veil was definitely preparing more than a protest.

They were preparing a gateway. And the eclipse was coming fast.

Lake Tana - Ethiopia

Mist curled low over Lake Tana like a veil reluctant to lift, its silvery tendrils gliding across still waters untouched by wind. Sarah sat beside Kebede on a weather-worn outcropping that jutted into the lake, their silhouettes framed against a horizon slowly catching fire with the first blush of dawn. The silence between them was not empty, it was reverent, heavy with the weight of things that defied simple answers.

Sarah broke the stillness at last, her voice soft, like a confession whispered in a confessional.

"I went to Sunday School," she said softly. "But this isn't that."

Kebede didn't answer immediately. He let the words hang there, suspended between the visible and the unseen. Her tone didn't need correction. It needed witness.

"The Bible I learned had angels with wings and harps," she continued. "Not… what Doug described. Not Watchers or portals or dimensional geometry."

A heron cried in the distance, its lonely call echoing across the water.

"I heard one of the monks quote something, 'those who fell from high places.' What was that about?"

Kebede finally turned, his face sculpted in profile by the rising light. "The Ethiopian Church preserved writings that others discarded. Some, like the Book of Enoch, weren't lost, they were dismissed. But the early Church knew them. Even quoted them as this was the accepted view of the early Church."

He opened a leather-bound book from his satchel, its script ancient, inked in Ge'ez. Sarah leaned closer as he traced lines with reverent precision.

"This speaks of the Watchers," Kebede said, his finger resting on the ancient text. "Angels who abandoned their assigned places in heaven and descended to earth in rebellion. They took human wives and sired offspring that were neither fully human nor angel."

"The Nephilim," Sarah murmured, surprised the word came unbidden. "Giants."

Kebede nodded. "Genesis gives a whisper of them. Enoch tells the rest. These giants corrupted mankind. The knowledge their fathers taught them, warfare, sorcery, alchemy, spread violence like a contagion. Forbidden knowledge with only one purpose: to twist creation. But it was more than just sexual sin. Their goal was to genetically and spiritually hijack the Messianic bloodline."

He turned to another passage and read aloud:
"Bind them for seventy generations in the valleys of the earth, until the day of their judgment."

"Their fathers were bound," Kebede said quietly. "Cast into a prison, another realm that 2 Peter 2:4 calls Tartarus. These Watchers were sealed away, unable to walk the world again, including their general Semjaza. The New Testament authors that you remember assumed their readers already knew the Enoch version. So, they didn't re-explain it. They did reference the Enoch version. It was a well-known early text."

Sarah frowned. "What happened to the giants?"

"Their bodies died in the Flood," he said, "but their spirits had nowhere to go. They were not fully human, so they could not pass on. They were not fully angel, so they could not return. They were left in between. They roam, oppress, and possess because they crave physicality. This is one of the reasons why they beg in Luke 8:31 for Jesus to not send them into the Abyss. They wished to enter pigs instead. They know their fathers are in the Abyss and once sent there, they will never return."

"The Shedim," Sarah said slowly.

"Yes," Kebede replied. "Demons. Homeless spirits, ever seeking flesh. Their fathers are bound in darkness, but the children of that rebellion still roam the earth, restless, hungry, and dangerous. That is why opening that veil is so terrifying. When it opens, it isn't just demons. It is much worse. Something ancient and more powerful is released. Alive, intelligent, and aware but legally restrained from acting. Fallen angels much more dangerous than demons such as Semjaza mentioned in Enoch. He was Satan's field commander who led the attempt to corrupt mankind and the bloodline in this manner. When Peter and Jude speak of angels in chains, they are talking about him and his cohort. The rest of the world kept the shadow, Ethiopia kept the map and the case against them."

He flipped again, showing her a passage where *mountains split and stars fall*, eerily echoing CIG's seismic tremor maps.

Sarah stared at the water. "So that's what the Ashen Veil is trying to do. Bring them back. The fallen angels and the Shedim."

Kebede's voice was low. "Yes. The door simply must be opened."

A fish broke the surface, the ripples spreading out like an echo from another world.

"Why would God allow that?" she asked. "Why create a system where they could return?"

Kebede smiled, not dismissively, but with the sorrowful clarity of one who had wrestled the same question. "Free will is heaven's greatest gift and hell's favorite loophole. God doesn't force our choices. That includes the choice to invoke darkness. If mankind insists on their return, God is just."

Sarah thought of Doug's war room, the resonance maps, the twin rituals converging on sacred geometries. "So these texts, Enoch, the Kebra Negast. They're warnings?"

"And tools," Kebede said. "Instruction for those who will stand in the gap. Every culture has stories of doors between worlds. Some opened them willingly. Others, like our ancestors, chose to guard them. Isaiah warned of a time when people would call evil good and good evil. We live in that inversion now. Truth is inverted, evil celebrated, and what is holy mocked."

The first golden rays broke over the distant hills, transforming the mist into molten gold. Sarah reached instinctively for the wooden cross at her neck, Trenfor's gift. At the time, she had received it as an emblem of sentiment. Now it felt like armor.

"He knew," she whispered. "When he gave this to me. Trenfor knew what we were really facing."

Kebede nodded. "Faith isn't just comfort. It's a weapon. It's light. And sometimes, it's the only map you get in the dark."

Sarah studied the cross again. Its simplicity made it easy to overlook. But it had endured for millennia while empires crumbled. Symbols mattered. So did belief.

"I've spent my career crafting narratives," she said. "Stories that move markets. Shape public opinion. But this… this isn't branding. It's reality."

"And reality," Kebede said gently, "has always been stranger than fiction, especially the part we're trained not to see."

She stood slowly, holding the cross like a tether. The lake before her seemed older than time. She thought of her father. She thought of Trenfor and Eli. The cities poised on spiritual fault lines. The veil thinning.

"Then teach me," she said. "Tell me everything. What these rituals do. How to stop them."

Kebede's expression became solemn, but not without hope. "We begin with sealing," he said. "With learning how to close what has been opened. How to bind what seeks to roam." He gestured toward the monastery now emerging in the early light. "And we pray. Not passively, but as soldiers without being timid. We dismantle their points of invocation, like the nails Trenfor is tracking. And we invoke an authority they cannot counterfeit."

He paused. "And we have faith."

"Like a grain of mustard seed," Sarah said.

Kebede turned to her, surprised. "You know the verse?"

"I remember it from Sunday School," she said. "I've heard preachers explain it a hundred times. A mustard seed is small. So, you only need a little faith to move mountains."

A faint smile crossed his face.

"What?" she asked. "Why do you look amused?"

"Because that is what is often taught," he said gently. "But it is not what Jesus meant."

Sarah frowned. "What do you mean?"

"When the disciples asked why they could not drive out a demon," Kebede said, "Jesus answered plainly: *Because of your little faith.* Not because they had too little power, but because they lacked the right kind of faith."

"But the mustard seed is tiny," she said. "That's the whole point, isn't it?"

"Only in translation," Kebede replied. "The Greek text in Matthew 17:20 uses the word *hōs*, meaning *as*, not *the size of.* Jesus did not say faith the size of a mustard seed. He said faith *like* a mustard seed in the original language."

Sarah's brow furrowed. "So what kind of faith was he talking about?"

"The kind his listeners understood instinctively," Kebede said. "First-century farmers knew mustard well. Not as a garden plant, but as chaos."

She leaned closer as he continued.

"Black mustard could grow twelve feet in a single season. It spread fast. It overwhelmed fields. Once it took root, it was almost impossible to remove. To a Jewish farmer, mustard wasn't quaint. It was trouble. It wasn't the analogy they expected and that's what made the analogy so powerful. Like they understood the book of Enoch, they understood mustard seed."

Sarah smiled faintly.

"Mustard roots go deep," Kebede went on. "Cut it back and it returns. Leave a few seeds behind and the ground is reclaimed. It refuses to stay small. It refuses to be contained."

"And that," Sarah said slowly, "is the faith Jesus meant."

Kebede nodded. "Faith like a mustard seed is alive. Aggressive. Expanding. It changes the landscape. It is big and powerful." He glanced at her. "Jesus could have said wheat. Or olives. Or figs. But he chose mustard. The plant no farmer wanted invading his land."

"Interesting," she murmured. "I never heard that in Sunday School either."

"Serving in the Kingdom of God is not tidy, Sarah," Kebede said. "True faith doesn't stay in its place. It invades. It displaces what was there before. Birds nest in its branches even the unclean, the unexpected." He met her gaze. "Faith isn't revealed by how small it begins. It's revealed by how much it grows."

The lake stirred beside them. The monastery stood behind them. And somewhere between the two, Sarah felt the shift, not into belief, but into resolve. Her intellect no longer denied the spiritual dimension. Her heart no longer dismissed the ancient warnings as myth.

The cross warmed against her skin, a flicker of presence or maybe the sun. It didn't matter. What mattered was that she was ready.

Chapter Thirteen

The Vatican - Rome

The shadow slid across the sun, slowly swallowing it, warping the sense of time. St. Peter's Square sank under a half-light that seemed to mute the world, turning the ancient stones a spectral gray. The obelisk at its center, an Egyptian relic far older than the basilica it now adorned, stood like a sentinel waiting to be awakened for its original purpose.

Trenfor moved through the crowd like smoke through a seam in the throng of onlookers, clothed in a janitor's uniform that concealed more than his name. His manner was unassuming, his pace measured, but his mind was aflame. The Ashen Veil had taken the square under the guise of a protest, their slogans blaring against centuries of tradition:

"Faith was Built on Blood."

"Science over Faith."

"No One Path Owns Truth."

"Equity for all."

The media adored the theater. Cameras orbited the crowd like vultures, oblivious to the deeper currents beneath the spectacle. Eli Weiss had orchestrated more than a protest: this was like ritual. One masked in progressive defiance but ancient in its core: the invocation of forgotten gods under the shroud of an eclipse.

Trenfor's earpiece clicked on.

Doug's voice in his ear. "Thermal imaging confirmed. Object's inside the box. Metallurgy matches Roman-era iron. The tomb-designated nail."

Trenfor's eyes scanned the central ring. A woman stood beside Eli, young, solemn, draped in dark linen. Her gaze was shuttered, as if some internal blind had closed to light long ago. The small box she held at chest height was black, unadorned, yet heavy with purpose. Participants reached toward it as if it radiated energy, pressing talismans to it, and whispered invocations.

They don't even know what they were holding, Trenfor thought. Or maybe they do.

The oil-and-ash sigils at the obelisk's base were drawn more visibly now in deliberate geometry. He recognized Akkadian spirals. Phoenician serpent glyphs. Inverted Hebrew. Language twisted.

And then, the chanting began.

"*Before the Light,*
Before the Word,
We summon those who were.

From ash and stone,
From blood and breath,
Rise now and claim your world."

Eli's voice then carried like wind through hollow stone, speaking no tongue he knew, yet the sound turned his stomach. It wasn't human speech. It was mimicry. Like a cracked phonograph spinning ancient syllables in corrupted rhythm. Eli's attention was on the crowd.

Trenfor stepped forward.

He carried a scarf in his hand, frayed and faded, borrowed from a Coptic priest in Jerusalem years before. The cloth was holy, but it also made the perfect distraction. One he had practiced as a child in cheap hotels, dreaming of stage magic. Now the stakes were souls, and history dependent on his skills in sleight of hand.

He approached the woman holding the box with calculated humility.

"Forgive me," he said in accented Italian, tinged with Slavic consonants. "This scarf was blessed by my grandfather. I want to touch the relic, just once."

The woman tilted her head. Her eyes bore into him like frost through stained glass. She looked briefly to Eli, but his eyes were now closed, consumed by his invocation. She nodded once.

"Touch it," she said. "Let it take what's yours and absorb your desire."

Trenfor bowed slightly and stepped close. He let the scarf hover above her hands, briefly blocking her view of the box she held. He draped the scarf gently over the lid, holding it with his right hand. His left hand simultaneously disappeared beneath the folds. With his left hand now hidden by the scarf, he lifted the lid. Then he felt it. The metal edge of the nail met his fingertips. Smooth, cold, heavy. With a sleight of hand masked by cloth and faith, he swapped the relic with a copper-colored pen wrapped in oxidized foil he had palmed. Lid closed. Cloth withdrawn as he now palmed the nail relic. A magic trick he had practiced just for the occasion.

Doug's voice chirped in his earpiece. "We saw the motion via drone. Looks clean. Do you have it?"

Trenfor simply nodded, knowing the drone was watching. He slipped the nail into an inner pocket of his uniform, briefly feeling a spiritual tremor as it rested. Crucifixion memory in iron.

He stepped back, turned to disappear into the crowd. Then a single word, flat, certain.

"You."

Eli's voice sliced through the chant like a blade through silk.

Trenfor paused.

The square held its breath.

Eli stood still, his eyes open now, locked on Trenfor. Behind him, the assistant checked the box, opened it, glanced at the decoy and said nothing. The optics held intact. The illusion seemed to work.

But Eli felt it. Not with sight, but with something darker.

"The current shifted when you stepped here," Eli said. "The air stopped obeying."

Trenfor said nothing.

Eli stepped closer, the crowd tightening in instinctive awareness. His hands twitched with unspoken power.

Trenfor breathed once, then spoke. Declaration, not defiance.

"No weapon formed against me shall prosper," he said, voice calm as stone. He paused before continuing. "And every tongue that rises against me in judgment… I shall condemn.

For the weapons we fight with are not the weapons of the world."

The words struck. Thunder aimed at the spirit.

Eli flinched. His body trembled. Several nearby protestors collapsed or recoiled, their bodies reacting to a power they couldn't name or see. The crowd's chant faltered. Then silence.

The assistant staggered, one hand clutching her pendant.

Trenfor's earpiece echoed again with Doug's voice. "Massive resonance drop. Spiritual disruption confirmed. The signal field around the obelisk is breaking. You *rattled* something."

Then suddenly, a spark. Fire erupted along the oil-glyph lines at the base of the obelisk. Someone had thrown fuel early. Panic ignited alongside flame.

"This wasn't the moment!" someone screamed. "It's not time yet!"

Chaos bloomed as a flame climbed the ancient monolith.

Tourists scattered. Protestors shouted. The Vatican guards rushed the edge. Sirens wailed. Firelight licked the symbols as if mocking them.

Eli stumbled backward, caught between rage and confusion. His mouth moved without words. His eyes, once confident, now wide, confused, *afraid.*

A figure in clerical robes rushed through the chaos. Whether bishop or Vatican observer, Trenfor couldn't say. But the man pulled Eli away from the flames just as the obelisk's base cracked from the thermal stress.

Smoke rose. Screams echoed. And through it all, Trenfor stepped away, head low, uniform smudged, relic secure.

Doug's voice came over the earpiece. "Did you hurt him?"

Trenfor spoke as he weaved through the crowd. "No. God's word did. And whatever was inside him."

Trenfor continued to slip through the crowd like wind retreating behind a storm, the nail pressed to his side pocket, heavy with the weight of salvation and war.

"The word dropped the resonance field. That's confirmed," Doug said over the earpiece.

Trenfor broke free from the crowd and headed toward a Vatican entrance. "Well, scripture when spoken does reverberate across boundaries. That scripture from Isaiah and 2 Corinthians didn't just disrupt the square. It shook the unseen." Trenfor then looked up before ducking into the Vatican side entrance.

Above, the eclipse reached its zenith, light smothered by darkness.

But in the square below, the veil had already torn a bit, until something ancient lost its grip.

Lake Tana - Ethiopia

The same shadow that had swept across Rome dimmed the sky above Lake Tana. While Rome had vanished beneath the total shadow, Lake Tana dimmed only partially, the sun veiled, not erased. The partial eclipse mirrored in the still waters surrounding the monastery island. Sarah Whitfield stood among the Remnant Watchmen monks, her practical khakis and breathable button-down standing in quiet contrast to their earth-toned robes. The eclipse had turned their world to ink and hush. No wind stirred. Even the birds had vanished. The air itself seemed to be waiting.

Unlike the chaos unfolding in Vatican City, here there was order, intentional, ancient, and unshaken. The monastery rose from the island like a memory made of stone, its weathered walls the color of sunbaked clay. Around its perimeter, the lake water trembled as if aware of the celestial event, ripples spreading in concentric waves from no visible cause.

On the distant shore, dark figures shifted. Ashen Veil protestors denied access to the island. Their hands moved with ritualistic precision, banners raised, chants lifted into the half-light. But their words fell flat, scattered by a presence they could not see.

"They waste their energy," Kebede said, his gaze fixed on them with calm detachment. "They begged to set foot on this island. But we remember. We still honor the ancient seals. Some doors," he added, "must never be opened."

Sarah watched the protestors with narrowed eyes. "Different than what I saw on TV. More frantic. Less choreographed."

"They strike against a wall they cannot perceive," Kebede replied. "But the wall stands."

He turned, and Sarah followed him through a colonnade of stone pillars each carved with geometric designs she had mapped for weeks. Here, sacred geometry and ancient theology met like breath and lungs. The monks were already taking their places across the courtyard, aligning their bodies to points on an invisible grid traced into the architecture by long-dead hands and mapped by Sarah.

Blue and crimson sashes marked their roles, their postures fluid, synchronized. Then came the sound: low, resonant chanting in Ge'ez, shaped by a language older than most alphabets. The monks began Psalm 91.

"He who dwells in the shelter of the Most High shall abide under the shadow of the Almighty…"

The Psalm's cadence thudded through Sarah's boots. Not imagined. Real. Like the earth itself was stirring.

Then came the barking.

Dogs on the far shore broke into guttural howls. Hackles raised, they circled, snapped at air, stared across the lake as if watching something approach.

Sarah stiffened. "What are they barking at?"

Kebede's face was still, but his voice carried a note of gravity. "Animals see what we do not. There are frequency spectrums beyond human vision. Some creatures are born with eyes that can see what the veil hides. Humans only see a portion of the visible light spectrum."

Sarah followed his gaze.

She saw nothing but lake and sky. She perceived nothing that the barking dogs seemed to sense.

But just above the water, the veil thinned. Images visible only at the edges of the light spectrum and invisible to the human eye swirled. Only the animals could see the spectacle unfolding over the Lake.

A second world emerged, one of radiant power and dreadful shadow. The eclipse marked more than a cosmic coincidence. It was a hinge in the heavens outlining the darkening sky.

From the upper atmosphere descended a host of celestial beings. Even in the fading light, their wings shimmered with glory, their robes embroidered in verses that pulsed like flame. They bore no swords, only radiance and law. They were not armed as soldiers, but anointed as executors of divine authority, strengthened by the prayers of man.

Then, from the east, the sky split again.

Where light had gathered, darkness poured. Demonic spirits slithered and snapped into being. Amorphous forms of smoke and malice. Ragged limbs clawed at nothing. Horned faces twisted with hatred. They rose in numbers and speed, summoned not by accident, but invitation.

"They called us," one shrieked in a language that reeked of rot. "They gave consent. The humans opened the gate!"

A towering angel, radiating with the weight of heaven's judgment, stepped forward. His voice was thunder layered on thunder, but the monks heard nothing. Only the demons heard.

"Not here," the angel declared. "This ground is sealed. By covenant and by blood."

The demon laughed, pointing its jagged hand toward the distant protestors. "They cry out! They invoke! They mock your name and claim ours! We have been invited."

The angel did not flinch. "They cry into a void. The gate was sealed before they were born."

But the demons came anyway.

They surged forward like a storm, noisy, lawless, convinced of their claim. And in the skies above Lake Tana, the first blows were exchanged.

Flashes of invisible power erupted as angel met demon, light colliding with darkness in blasts of raw, legal force. Each monk's spoken verse became a strike. Every repetition of the psalm forged a blade in the hand of a guardian.

Back in the courtyard, Sarah could feel the tension rising. The monks raised their hands, the cadence of Psalm 91 increased.

"You shall not be afraid of the terror by night…"

Kebede moved to the center and traced a symbol in the air, one of the glyphs Sarah had reconstructed. She now realized they weren't merely decorative. They were locks. Keys. Wards.

"Faith is not only a shield," he said softly, "it is permission. It is authority. The word has power. Prayer focuses the will."

The chanting grew.

Above them, angels pressed back the swarm, but not without resistance. One demon broke free of the fray, screaming across the invisible boundary over the island after being struck by a gleaming angel. Dogs on the shore scattered, yelping. The moment the spirit hit the perimeter, it disintegrated in a soundless flash, shredded by unseen geometry forged in prayer and sanctified stone.

But the battle raged on.

Demons shrieked, accusing, justifying, insisting their right to trespass. They spat twisted scripture. They mimicked the monks' chants in mockery. But the voices of the faithful burned hotter.

Sarah's phone notification buzzed.

ROME: RITUAL FAILED. NAIL SECURED.

She stared. Then turned her face upward, toward nothing she could see, but everything she could now feel.

She stepped forward and joined the monks, her voice steady:

"With long life will I satisfy him and show him my salvation."

The words rang like iron in the unseen realm. With the final recitation, the heavens split with holy fire.

The demons screamed, retreating, falling back into shadows, into the earth, into the depths from which they came. Some fell like ash into the waters, dissolving into the lake. Others vanished in curls of smoke. The skies shimmered once more, then stilled.

And the dogs… fell silent.

The partial eclipse broke. A sliver of sun returned. Light spilled across the monastery.

Kebede turned to Sarah, his expression unreadable but his eyes full. "You stood in both realms today. And both were moved."

On the far shore, the Ashen Veil began dispersing. Their protests withered. Some dropped their signs. Others got into vehicles and drove away, dust trailing like a funeral procession.

The monks resumed their duties lighting lamps, preparing food, tending wounds not physical but spiritual. Sarah walked to the edge of the island and looked out across Lake Tana. To the eye, it was an uneventful evening. A routine service. Anticlimactic. But she felt it. She felt something.

To the eye, nothing had changed.

And yet… everything had.

Hours later, the small wooden boat slipped silently through the whispering reeds, leaving the monastery island behind. Sarah sat near the bow, the shadows of evening stretching long across the lake. Her fingers skimmed the water's surface, disturbed only by the gentle oar strokes of the elder monk at the stern. The sun, freed now from the eclipse, bathed Lake Tana in a soft, amber glow, the kind that made everything seem calm even when it wasn't.

She was supposed to feel peace. And for a time, she had. But the tension in her chest had returned, slow and crawling.

Was it the missing nail? The silence that followed victory? Or that strange sensation that the air itself was listening again?

"You are troubled," Kebede observed from across the boat. His voice, as always, was quiet, but the wind carried it easily.

Sarah hesitated. "The Ashen Veil ritual failed. But it feels too… neat. Too easy."

Kebede's weathered hands folded atop his staff. "Victory in the spiritual realm often brings retaliation in the physical. Darkness may be pushed back, but it never concedes without looking for another door." He tilted his head toward the approaching shoreline. "They have many doors. And they watch for cracks. That's the pattern. Pushback in the spirit, retaliation in the flesh. We are simply partners with our brethren who watch the other side. Your unease may come from that dimension, not ours."

Sarah nodded, gripping the worn edge of the boat. The reeds rustled like whispers as they drew near the dock. Birds called to one another in the dusky air. The entire lake felt like it had exhaled after the eclipse, but the breath hadn't gone far.

"What will you do now?" Kebede asked.

She touched the wooden cross at her neck, Trenfor's gift, a carving as rough as it was dear. "I need to reconnect with Trenfor. We've both seen parts of something much larger. The Ashen Veil failed today… but it doesn't seem like we've won. The other nail is still missing."

The boat bumped gently against the dock. A younger monk leapt to tie them off. Sarah slung her pack over her shoulder, her notes, her sketches, her recordings and reached to help Kebede disembark.

Then, the treeline moved.

Three men emerged from the tree line without warning. They appeared like wolves. Steel caught the lamplight, rifles, slung casually in hands that knew how to use them.

The tallest man barked something sharp in Amharic.

Kebede froze, then stepped protectively in front of Sarah. "Pirates," he said calmly. "He says you are foreign… valuable."

"What?" Sarah whispered.

"They say there are those who will pay for you."

Sarah stepped back, heart pounding. "Tell them I'm just a researcher. I have nothing of value."

Kebede relayed it, but the men laughed. A short, muscular one responded, and Kebede's expression darkened.

"They've been watching us. They know about your work."

Sarah's muscles tensed as the third man stepped forward, hand outstretched. She jerked away. The men fanned out, cutting off escape. Their movement was coordinated, practiced.

Kebede raised his staff, eyes burning. "You will not take her."

The leader responded with a rifle butt to the Kebede's temple. The crack echoed across the dock. Kebede dropped to the dock, blood pooling beneath his head.

"Kebede!" Sarah cried, lunging forward, but rough hands grabbed her, twisting her arms. One tried to yank her necklace. She tucked it beneath her shirt, feeling the cross press against her chest, wooden, but embedded with more than prayer.

One of the younger monks in another boat raised a small radio, shouting in Amharic. But they were still in the water, still too far. The gunmen didn't care. They dragged Sarah toward the treeline, their boots pounding the dock.

She didn't scream.

Instead, she catalogued in her mind: The path. The limp in the second man's gait. The serpent tattoo behind the leader's ear. The stumps on the third man's left hand.

"You've made a mistake," she said coldly, even as branches closed behind her. "They'll come for me."

The leader's grin was all teeth. "No mistake," he replied in accented English.

They vanished into the forest.

Behind them, her backpack lay abandoned, papers fluttering in the evening breeze, maps and sacred geometry scattering across the dock like leaves from a broken tree. One monk knelt by Kebede, applying pressure to the wound, while another called into the radio in strained tones.

The Vatican - Rome

Far away, beneath the Vatican, Trenfor stood before a holographic display in a dimly lit chamber. Around him, the walls pulsed with data: satellite feeds, spiritual resonance graphs, seismic overlay.

Doug's voice broke through the low hum of celebration over secure communications. His face suddenly appears on a video feed.

"We have a situation," he said, urgent but contained.

Trenfor turned. The elation from Rome was still fresh in his eyes, but it vanished as Doug continued.

"Sarah's team just sent a distress signal. Attack on the dock. She has been abducted by armed men."

A still image flickered onto the screen where Sarah was last seen, Lake Tana bathed in post-eclipse calm. But peace was an illusion. Somewhere beyond that shimmering surface, Sarah had vanished.

Trenfor's gaze dropped to the cross carving he held in his palm, the twin to the one Sarah wore.

He closed his hand.

The war was not over. It had just changed rooms.

Chapter Fourteen

African Continent Airspace

The wooden cross in Trenfor's hand radiated warmth, subtle, unmistakable, and not entirely physical. Identical to the one he had given Sarah, the grain matched perfectly, even the tiny imperfection at its base. He held it with the quiet reverence of a man handling both a memory and a mission.

Outside the aircraft window, the African night unspooled ahead of him, black velvet streaked with starlight, vast and silent. Somewhere far below lay Lake Tana, its waters no longer still, and beyond that, a village cloaked in shadow.

The plane hummed steadily through the sky. Cabin lights had dimmed, casting passengers in a muted cobalt glow. Most were asleep, tilted awkwardly in their seats, heads resting on pillows or windows, unaware of the struggle unfolding a continent below. Trenfor sat upright, unmoving. Sleep was a luxury he could not afford, not tonight.

He tucked the cross into his breast pocket, directly over his heart, then subtly adjusted the nearly invisible comms piece in his ear. A single press on his watch activated the encrypted channel.

"Doug, I'm secure," he whispered.

A soft crackle, then Doug's voice responded: "We read you. Tactical team is in position. Coordinates locked."

Trenfor shifted slightly, eyes scanning the cabin. "ETA less than five hours to Addis. After that, immediate transfer to Bahir Dar. The cross I gave Sarah is still broadcasting her location. Embedded tracker, low signature. Signal's holding steady. She's in a rural settlement east of Lake Tana according to the GPS signal its transmitting. Pirate territory. An uncontested and unforgiving area."

Doug's voice was sharper now. "We're tracking it. Satellite images confirm movement in the area. Heat signatures indicate around twenty-eight individuals. Civilians and armed males. Possibly captives."

Trenfor's jaw clenched. "What about the others? Any sign of the Ashen Veil students?"

"Unconfirmed," Doug replied. "Thermal reads bodies, not affiliations. But here's what we do know. The international media's running with a story that several eco-protesters disappeared three days ago. They'd planned a demonstration near the Ethiopian Highlands. Their last post tagged them in transit with a local escort."

Trenfor exhaled slowly. "They were sympathetic and unfortunate protestors. They actually thought the pirates were anti-colonial freedom fighters and would not harm them."

"And they got used," Doug said.

"They got scammed, and believed their own misinformation," Trenfor corrected. "Then they got betrayed. The Ashen Veil turned environmentalism into religious zeal. They trained these kids to believe they were holy warriors for the Earth. But the pirates don't worship Earth. They worship power. And power doesn't make allies. It makes trades."

Doug hesitated. "There's more. Your old friend's stirring."

"Kebede?" Trenfor asked.

"Concussed, banged up, but functional. Docs ordered seventy-two hours bedrest. He's not listening. He's already asked for a field briefing."

Trenfor allowed himself a brief smile. "Give him the briefing, but keep him in the rear. I need his mind, not his blood. His understanding of local hierarchies will be essential. Pirates will negotiate, but only with force."

"Speaking of force," Doug added, "we've secured air clearance. The Ethiopians are happy to let this play out quietly. They're dealing with enough on their northern borders. They don't want international scrutiny. U.S. Special Forces from Djibouti are on standby. Four-hour response window. And we've got one asset in play now, an armed Predator drone, Reaper-class, loitering at altitude with two Hellfire missiles and infrared optics."

"Rules of engagement?"

"Your discretion. They were combing the region looking for the missing protestors when we told the U.S. military that we had people on the ground in the region."

Trenfor's fingers tapped the edge of the armrest. "Keep the drone high. I want the pirates uncertain, not panicked. Unless I say otherwise."

A flight attendant approached, her movements practiced and silent. "Something to drink, sir?"

Trenfor shook his head politely. "No, thank you."

She nodded and moved on, the ice in her tray clinking gently as she passed.

"Any change in signal?" he asked once she was gone.

"Still solid," Doug replied. "She's not moving. Looks like they're holding all captives in a single location. Some kind of fortified cluster. Satellite images show walled compounds. Dirt roads. No vehicles in or out since yesterday. There is a river nearby with boats on it."

Trenfor nodded, though no one could see him. "Good. Keep eyes on the comms net in the area. Any encrypted chatter or sudden outages, flag it."

"Already watching. Anything else?"

He paused, reviewing the logistics in his mind. No gaps. No delays. "Have transport waiting at Addis. Unmarked, low-profile. I'll fly the next leg alone to Bahir Dar that will put me on Lake Tana. Alert the Remnant."

"Done," Doug said. Then, softer: "Be careful, Alex. Glad you gave her that tracker. But this one feels different."

"It is different," Trenfor replied. "But the mission's the same. She's still alive. That's all I need."

The line went dead with a quiet click. Trenfor leaned back into his seat, the hum of the engines a soft lull in the pressurized silence. He reached once more for the wooden cross. The grain of it felt like memory and conviction fused together. If a fight waited in the valley below, it would not be his first.

But it might be the one that mattered most.

Addis Ababa, Ethiopia

Heat wrapped around Trenfor like a cloak as he stepped onto the tarmac of Bole International Airport in Addis Ababa. The scent of jet fuel mingled with roasted spices and humans in motion, a thick swirl of activity that pulsed beneath the African sky. He kept his stride measured and economical, his bag light, only essentials. Always only essentials.

He moved through the terminal with unspoken authority. Travelers instinctively shifted aside, responding to something silent, yet unmistakable in his presence.

Three men in plain clothing waited near the domestic gate, unremarkable but vigilant. Their gazes swept the crowd with trained precision, their subtle posture shifts signaling recognition. Former military, now Remnant operatives embedded across East Africa as CIG's eyes and ears in regions where official visibility meant risk.

"Dr. Trenfor," the eldest greeted, his Sudanese accent clipped and direct. "Your connecting flight is ready. You'll board within the hour."

Trenfor gave a brief nod and followed them toward the internal terminal for the short flight to Bahir Dar. As they moved, the lead operative, Solomon, kept his voice low.

"The target village sits on the lake's eastern arm. Isolated. Tribal governance. The locals follow beliefs older than any church or mosque. Their shaman claims descent from Makeda, Queen of Sheba."

"Spiritual concerns, or political?" Trenfor asked.

"Both. They've harbored pirates for years. In exchange for sanctuary, the village receives protection and a cut of the loot. The arrangement makes them suspicious of outsiders."

"They'll be more than suspicious once I arrive," Trenfor noted.

Solomon hesitated. "No man should walk into that village alone."

Trenfor's eyes remained forward. "I won't be alone."

Near Lake Tana

The small domestic flight from Addis Ababa to Bahir Dar near Lake Tana was uneventful, and within an hour of the short hop, Trenfor stepped off the twin-prop plane into the warm air of Bahir Dar. At the edge of the airstrip, a battered SUV waited with its engine idling.

Two hours later, just outside town, they reached a safe house cloaked behind a market stall facade. Inside, Kebede sat at a wide table layered with maps, thermal printouts, and satellite photos. His head had a small bandage, but his posture was erect and alert.

He stood as Trenfor entered.

"Don't stand on my account," Trenfor said. "You should be resting."

Kebede managed a faint smile. "You didn't think I'd let you face them alone, did you?"

He gestured toward the spread of images. "The village is here," he pointed, "wedged between high ridges and the lake.

Only one road in by land, and they'll be watching it. The pirates use papyrus boats, tankwas. Hard to trace, easy to hide on the river banks of the village."

Trenfor studied the overheads. "And Sarah?"

"Here." Kebede tapped a structure on the eastern edge of the compound. "Storehouse, reinforced clay and wood, one visible entrance. It's where the tracker pings Sarah's last location."

"And the shaman?"

Kebede's expression darkened. "He's called 'Makeda's Son.' No real name. A mystic with wide influence. Pilgrims come from the highlands to receive his blessing. He claims royal blood. But more concerning, he collects relics. Religious items. I think he believes they increase his spiritual authority."

Trenfor's mind connected dots. "If one of the Ashen Veil protestors had the second nail... it would've drawn his interest."

"Exactly."

In an adjoining room, Trenfor changed into local garb, simple cotton, weathered sandals, a trader's tunic dyed with the muted colors of travel. He looked like a man used to long walks and longer silences.

Solomon handed him a staff with a steel-reinforced core. "Communicator is hidden in the collar of your clothes. Signal will relay through the drone once you're in range. After that…"

"I know," Trenfor said, adjusting his small earpiece. "I'm on my own."

By late afternoon, Trenfor approached the village on foot, the sun sinking toward Lake Tana's glittering horizon. Dust clung to his sleeves. Thorn trees lined the path like sentries.

Children were the first to see him, their games silenced as they watched him pass. Elders leaned on walking sticks, eyes narrowed, following his every move. Whispers passed like wind in dry grass.

"Spirit-walker..." someone muttered in the dialect of Gojjam.

Men with AKs appeared near the houses who were clearly pirates. They loitered with deliberate threat, their movements relaxed but alert, weapons slung low. A few exchanged mocking comments, but none stepped forward. They were waiting.

At the center of the village stood a large round hut painted in ochre spirals and dark blue glyphs. The door opened.

A man stepped out, tall, gaunt, draped in robes adorned with shells, feathers, and thin bone talismans. His face was painted with ash and red clay, etched with angular runes. Bracelets of carved wood and animal teeth hung from his wrists, chiming with each movement.

Makeda's Son.

He locked eyes with Trenfor.

Then he froze.

His eyes widened, not in aggression, but in alarm. He took a slow step backward, one hand rising instinctively to his chest.

Whispers stirred among the villagers.

"The spirits speak against him..."

"He walks with the shining ones…"

Makeda's Son turned to the pirate standing beside him and muttered something low and urgent. The pirate glanced between Trenfor and the shaman, puzzled.

But Trenfor said nothing. He walked with steady steps toward the center of the gathering, each stride carrying the silent pressure of conviction. Perception was a weapon here and belief ammunition. If they believed he walked with powers they couldn't name, that belief could shield him longer than any armor.

And belief, Trenfor knew, was already in motion.

The forming crowd parted as Trenfor stepped into the village's heart, where a man lounged on a makeshift throne, a raised wooden platform covered with rugs and shaded by a canopy of faded tarpaulin. Gold glinted from the man's smile, but the amusement never touched his eyes. A web of scars traced across his cheek and forearms, some earned, some carved intentionally, like the tattoos of a man who wanted the world to remember his pain.

He leaned forward, arms draped lazily over the armrests, his fingers idly tapping the worn grip of a pistol nestled at his side.

"You walk into our village alone," he said, his English lilting with a coastal East African accent. "Either you are very brave… or very foolish."

His gaze flicked briefly to Trenfor's walking stick. Assessing. Measuring.

The pirate's look told its own story: a long scar split one brow and dragged his mouth into a permanent sneer. His gold teeth, real ones, not cheap caps, spoke of successful raids and rich ransoms. His clothing was scavenged Western wear: cargo pants, combat boots, and an open tactical vest decorated with handmade fetishes of cowrie shells, bits of carved wood, fragments of bone. A paradox of modernity and the occult.

Trenfor stood still as stone. Not aggressive, not submissive, just centered. When he spoke, his voice was calm, but carried like steel through the sudden hush.

"I'm here for the girl you took."

The pirate's eyebrow lifted. "Girl? We have many girls. Local. Travelers. Do you collect them?"

Trenfor didn't flinch. "Sarah Whitfield. American. Taken three days ago. And the other college students you may have hidden. You need to release them. All of them."

A murmur ran through the onlookers. Some villagers leaned closer. Others backed away.

The pirate's gold-toothed grin widened. "Ah… our honored guests. They arrived full of fire. Passionate young fools with eco-manifestos and zero survival instinct. But they're alive."

He waved a hand casually. "The woman, Sarah, she carries knowledge. Real knowledge. The others have companies that support them, which have money. We haven't harmed them. That would lower their value."

Trenfor said nothing, his silence pressing against the pirate like a presence.

"But everything has a price," the pirate added. "So… how much is she worth to you?"

Before Trenfor could respond, the painted shaman stepped forward from the shadow of the main hut. His bones clattered with each movement, and his ochre-painted eyes locked onto something unseen beyond Trenfor.

He bent low to whisper into the pirate's ear.

Trenfor caught only pieces:

"…not alone…"

"…an army walks beside…"

"…shining ones… watchers… death..."

The pirate's cocky grin faltered. His gaze swept the village perimeter, suddenly unsure as he was trying to see what the shaman described. But then he forced a laugh, sharp and brittle, his men echoing it, too loud, too fast.

"My spiritual advisor sees ghosts," the pirate said with mock cheer, waving at the retreating shaman. "He believes you're surrounded by spirits. Armies of light and shadow. But I see only one man, dusty and tired, armed only with a stick."

Trenfor's face remained unreadable. "Your advisor is wiser than you."

With deliberate calm, Trenfor lifted his right hand skyward, palm open. His thumb brushed the near-invisible button at the base of the walking stick's handle, activating the uplink.

Into his collar mic, he murmured, "Confirm strike on Alpha. No personnel aboard their craft."

Confused glances darted between the pirates. Some raised weapons. Others looked skyward.

A whistle soon pierced the air, high, sharp, and rising.

The Predator's missile struck a skiff moored at the lakeshore, two hundred meters away.

The explosion shattered the illusion of control.

A geyser of fire and lake water roared skyward. Wood splinters rained down like needles. Shockwaves rolled through the village, shaking the huts, knocking over buckets, rattling bones strung over doorways. Women shrieked. A dog howled. Men fell to their knees, shielding their heads.

Trenfor didn't move. He hadn't blinked. Hadn't lowered his hand.

Silence fell like a curtain.

Every eye turned to him.

He let his hand fall.

"You've got one chance," he said softly, like someone announcing weather. "Release the hostages. Now."

The pirate leader's bravado cracked. Sweat broke across his temple. He glanced at his men, then at the shaman, who now stood off to the side, arms folded, chin lifted in grim vindication.

"Perhaps…" the pirate said, his voice dry, "perhaps we misunderstood your intentions."

He coughed. "They were not prisoners, you understand. Guests. For their own protection."

"Of course," Trenfor replied. "And now their stay is over."

A negotiation followed, not with words, but with silences, narrowed eyes, and the cold logic of leverage. The pirate wanted face-saving concessions: a staged release, no more explosions. Trenfor gave him just enough to allow retreat without humiliation.

Doug's voice buzzed faintly in Trenfor's earpiece.

"Thermal confirms all hostages alive. Minimal movement. Still in the east structure. U.S. Special Forces still on standby. Predator's holding pattern resumed. Ethiopian military has perimeter sealed. No incoming threats."

Trenfor offered a nod so small it could have been a breath.

The pirate leader barked at a subordinate in a coastal dialect.

"Bring the guests. Tell them their escort has arrived."

As the man disappeared down an alley of reed huts, the pirate's eyes settled on Trenfor again.

"You're not what you seem."

"Truth needs no disguise. Angels walk unseen while demons wear justice like a mask."

Trenfor said. "You should learn the difference."

Smoke curled in the distance from the shattered skiff. Its burning skeleton cast long shadows across the river, a silent reminder that hung in the air more effectively than any verbal threat.

The door to the eastern hut creaked open, sunlight piercing the shadows inside and illuminating a cloud of dust. Four figures emerged, shielding their eyes. They moved slowly, hesitant, half-expecting violence. Sarah came last, supporting a limping young woman.

Trenfor assessed them instantly. Bruises, dehydration, fear. Sarah's cheek was mottled with purple, her clothes ragged. But her eyes, sharp, unwavering, met his.

"You hurt?" he asked, voice low.

"Nothing serious. The students tried to resist. This is Maya, sprained ankle." She nodded toward the girl beside her.

He leaned in, slipping a transmitter into her hand. "Get them clear. Press the signal once you're a hundred meters out. It alerts a team outside to pick you up."

But she didn't move.

"There's something else," she murmured. "I saw the shaman take a carved wooden box like in the photos Doug sent from Rome. Yesterday. The shaman brought it from outside the village."

Trenfor's jaw tensed.

"He kept it covered, but I saw the carvings. The students said a box came with them from Italy. But the ones who carried it... never arrived."

Trenfor gave the faintest nod to the students. "Take them. Now."

Sarah understood. With quiet authority, she turned and began leading the students toward the valley trail.

Then Trenfor faced the shaman.

"You have something else that doesn't belong to you," he said calmly.

The painted man stared back, unreadable. But after a beat, he turned and disappeared into his hut, returning with a small, carved wooden box.

Trenfor didn't take it. Instead, he removed a slender black device from his pocket and held it near the box. A red light blinked to life. Trenfor then stepped away from the shaman.

"Doug," he murmured low enough that the shaman could not hear. "You getting this?"

"Affirmative. No metal signature, but explosive trace confirmed. Likely booby-trapped. That's not the Vatican relic."

Trenfor then locked eyes with the shaman. "Open it."

The holy man froze. He turned to the pirate leader, voice low and urgent in Amharic. Trenfor caught fragments:

"…meant only to delay…"

"…spirits will not protect…"

But the pirate had grown agitated. Suspicion flared in his eyes, then anger. He barked something sharp, shoved the shaman aside, and thrust the box toward Trenfor.

"Open it," he said, smiling coldly. "You came all this way for a gift. It would be rude not to open it."

Trenfor tilted his head slightly. Then, with a sudden flick, he hurled the box away from them.

The explosion was sharp and surgical. The box detonated near a cluster of rocks, blasting a crater into the dry earth. Shouts and screams erupted. Dust spiraled into the sky.

Trenfor hadn't moved.

The pirate leader stumbled back, reaching instinctively for his pistol, but Trenfor was already there. Trenfor caught the pirate's wrist, pressing it downward with steel precision, trapping the weapon in its holster.

Trenfor's voice was low but clear. "The theatrics are over. Now, where's the real box?"

The pirate hesitated, sweat blooming at his temples. Around them, his men held their weapons in uncertain hands, exchanging glances. The shaman had retreated, his face pale beneath the paint.

Trenfor gestured toward the charred remains of the boat on the lakeshore. "Or do I call down another gift? Because you know I have friends nearby. Don't you?"

He didn't wait for an answer.

"Do not try to deceive me, my friend," Trenfor continued. "Did your spirits not warn your shaman of who walks with me?"

The pirate's eyes flicked past him, to the hills, to the sky, to things unseen. Trenfor let the silence settle, heavy and purposeful.

Trenfor followed the pirate's gaze, but not to the hills or they sky.

To the edge of the village.

A shadow peeled itself from the wall of the shaman's hut. It caught Trenfor's eye as the motion was too deliberate to be chance and too smooth to be fear. The pirate didn't notice.

Trenfor recognized Kebede emerging from the shadow with the economy of a man who had learned long ago how not to be seen. His robe hung loose, his posture unhurried blending in with other villagers. Barely visible in his left hand, Trenfor saw him carrying a small wooden box.

Their eyes met for a fraction of a second. It was all Trenfor needed. He let his shoulder relax just slightly. Enough for the pirate to notice the shift, but not so much for it to be misread as uncertainty.

"Enough," Trenfor said calmly, lowering his hand. "Your performance is meant to frighten men who still believe fear has authority. You may keep your illusions. Your payment for keeping your guests safe. They'll turn on you soon enough. I will leave. I will also call down fire on any who follow." As he spoke, confusion rippled quietly through the men around them.

Trenfor watched as Kebede melted into the crowd, the nail already gone from the village that had never truly possessed it. Trenfor then turned and walked away giving a final glance toward the pirate leader, not as a threat. A verdict.

Sarah stood at the edge of the clearing, her arms wrapped around herself despite the afternoon heat. From this vantage point, the village resembled a theater set abandoned mid-rehearsal. Huts were arranged in a loose circle, the central square still echoing with the tremor of confrontation. Beyond it, the path sloped toward the river, where broken Ethiopian reed boats, *tankwas*, drifted lazily in the shallows, rudderless and splintered.

The students had been escorted to safety. She'd watched them vanish over the ridge, flanked by Ethiopian personnel. But she hadn't followed.

Not until she knew Trenfor was safe. And not until she knew what had happened to him.

The last of the pirates were slipping into the hills, machetes and sacks of ill-gotten goods clutched to their chests, eyes flicking skyward as though the heavens might again speak with fire. Their bravado had vanished, leaving behind a silence that clung to the village like smoke.

She turned at the sound of soft footsteps ascending the path. Trenfor emerged from between the huts, his walking stick tapping rhythmically against the earth. His shirt clung damply to his frame, collar rumpled, but his stride was steady, measured. His face gave away nothing.

"You have it," Sarah said quietly, more statement than question.

Trenfor stopped beside her, his gaze sweeping over the village as though calculating the distance to some unseen edge of the world.

Then, casually, he glanced toward Kebede, who stood a few meters away with a grin tugging at the corners of his mouth. Kebede opened a small box just enough to reveal the relic nestled inside, iron dark and sacred, then shut it again without a word.

Sarah's brow furrowed. "Do they know?"

Trenfor's smile was faint, enigmatic. "The wise fisherman doesn't reach into the crocodile's mouth when the net's already full. They have no idea."

"You think they'll come looking when they discover it's gone?"

"I told them I didn't believe they had the real relic," Trenfor said. "I agreed we'd quit while we were ahead. It was to let them save face. When the shaman discovers it's gone, he'll blame the pirates. The pirates will blame him. Confusion buys us time."

She studied him. "So, the pirates just let you walk away?"

"I gave him something better than a threat," Trenfor said. "I left them with uncertainty."

She arched a skeptical brow.

Sarah looked back down toward the lake, where curls of smoke still twisted lazily from the shattered decoy. The village below seemed smaller now, diminished beneath the weight of what had just passed.

"You speak in riddles more often now," she said. "Since Kursi."

"Riddles are how ancient truths survive in dangerous places," Trenfor said. "Besides, clarity gets people killed. The Ethiopian military will move in soon. The students are safe. That's all that matters for now."

She gave a faint laugh, though it carried no mirth. Only fatigue, and the strange relief of surviving something they had barely understood.

"What about the shaman?" she asked softly.

Trenfor's gaze narrowed, his voice quieter. "He's too busy wondering whether the gods he pretended to serve just abandoned him."

As Trenfor and Sarah turned to leave, the air felt strangely quiet, too still, as if the land itself held its breath.

A scruffy village dog stood near the edge of the huts, ignoring Sarah and Trenfor passing just feet away. Its ears then flicked toward a sound no human could hear. The animal's head tilted, eyes sharpening, nostrils flaring as something unseen shimmered into focus.

Above the village, invisible to the human eye, the light fractured, colors bent, rearranged until within the dog's field of vision, which was beyond the spectrum visible to the human eye, a figure stood tall and radiant where Trenfor had just walked. Robed in a brilliance no cloth could weave, the angel faced the village, its expression solemn.

A gleaming sword, too real to be metaphor, was in the being's hand. With reverent slowness, the angel slid the blade back into its scabbard, the metal whispering as it disappeared.

Then, as if to the heavens or perhaps to no one in particular, the angel spoke, the words resonating on frequencies no human ear would register:

"The weapons we fight with are not the weapons of the world. They have divine power to demolish strongholds."

The angel turned once more toward the path, where two servants of the kingdom, one weary, one awakening, walked away into the failing light.

And the dog, satisfied, sat back on its haunches and resumed licking its paw.

Chapter Fifteen

Ethiopian Orthodox Church, Ethiopia

Dappled light filtered through the narrow-arched windows of the Ethiopian Orthodox church, casting honeyed patterns across the worn stone floor and setting centuries-old icons aglow. The air was thick with incense, sweet, ancient, sacred, as Sarah and Trenfor sat side by side on a carved stone bench, their shoulders almost touching. Around them, the church stood as a witness to time: walls that had absorbed a thousand years of prayer, frescoes that had listened to the whispered devotions of pilgrims long gone. Their voices, when they spoke, seemed to join that quiet chorus, soft against the gravity of history.

Sarah traced her finger along the bench's edge, following the curve of a symbol etched into the stone. Her auburn hair caught the light as she tilted her head, creating a halo effect that felt strangely fitting within these consecrated walls.

"I'm heading back to Israel tomorrow," she said, breaking the silence. "My professors want to see the 3D imaging I captured at Lake Tana." Her voice carried the enthusiasm of someone who'd finally found her footing. "The tech we're using now, it can detect subtle material variations invisible just five years ago. There's so much we might uncover."

Trenfor nodded, his profile sharp beneath the soft blur of painted saints. "The nails will be transferred to the university under strict protocols," he said. "I've arranged for a specialized team. Artifacts like these require security beyond what museums are accustomed." He paused, scanning the ancient sanctuary. "After that, I'm heading to CIG headquarters in North Carolina. Debriefings on all of this before going back to New York."

The phrase "all of this" hovered between them, too vast to define in a sentence, weighted with everything they'd seen, uncovered, survived. Sarah's fingers stilled.

They sat in companionable silence, the kind forged only through shared trials. A shaft of sunlight drifted across the stone floor, illuminating dust motes.

"What does it all mean?" Sarah finally asked. Her voice was softer now, uncertain in a way her professional persona rarely allowed. "I feel like I've been standing on a fault line I didn't know existed, and now it's shifting beneath me. Everything's coming loose. The relics, the manuscripts, the rituals. It doesn't fit in the neat box academia taught me. And it definitely doesn't fit in the Sunday School I remember."

Trenfor folded his hands, calmly, almost prayerfully. "Ethiopia's Christian heritage is unlike any other," he said. "While Europe stumbled through the Dark Ages, monasteries here preserved ancient knowledge, copying texts, safeguarding traditions, holding onto truths the West forgot. They maintained a faith that remembers what most churches eventually edited out."

"Which is?" she asked quietly.

"That the unseen world isn't metaphor, it's real." He looked up toward a golden icon of St. Michael, its contours glowing in the sunlight. "Modern Christianity tends to psychologize the supernatural. Angels become metaphors, demons become dysfunction, and miracles are coincidences dressed in piety. But the early Church, especially here, never stopped believing in the spiritual reality that surrounds us. The Ethiopian church kept the canonical works recognized by the rest of the world but held on to the writings that informed the early church as well. The wealth of ancient knowledge here is deep."

Sarah shifted. "But what about science? Doesn't it contradict all of this? I mean, carbon dating, stratigraphy, data modeling. These are the tools I trust."

Trenfor smiled, but it wasn't dismissive. "Einstein once said, *'Science without religion is lame, religion without science is blind.'* And he wasn't wrong. Theology that's afraid of science isn't theology, it's dogma. If it's true, it should welcome scrutiny. Science asks how. Faith asks why. Neither can afford to pretend the other is irrelevant."

He gestured around them. "The people who built this place didn't divide knowledge like we do now. They believed wonder and wisdom could live together."

Light shifted again. Outside, the hum of cars, the murmur of voices, signs that the modern world kept turning. But inside, time felt layered, past and present folding into one moment.

"Who are you really?" she asked, voice laced with curiosity and something deeper, a recognition of the mystery he carried as she looked deeply into his eyes as if for the first time.

He didn't answer right away. When he did, the words came slowly, intentionally.

"I was once a seeker of forbidden knowledge. Ancient rites and philosophies that promised truth but delivered shadows." His jaw tightened. "Then I went to war. Real war. And I saw things, felt things, that no textbook could explain. It wasn't power I found. It was presence. A presence deeper than death."

He turned to her fully now. "John, the beloved disciple, wanted to know God's heart. That's why he writes about love. I'm a soldier turned scholar. I wanted to know God's mind." He paused. "And it is vast. Beautiful. And not easily known. But that's the call. That's why I wake up each day."

The silence that followed was reverent, not awkward.

"You'll find your path too," he said gently. "You're asking the right questions. That tension you feel, that's the beginning of wisdom. A great physicist once said it's better to have questions that can't be answered than answers that can't be questioned."

A bell then tolled deep in the stone walls, slow, resonant. Sarah closed her eyes for a moment and let it pass through her like breath. When she opened them, she wasn't looking at Trenfor.

She was looking at the icons, at faces worn by centuries of light, of smoke, of searching. And she felt, just faintly, the veil between her understanding of things had thinned.

Jerusalem, Israel

Sarah's Jerusalem apartment sat four stories above a narrow street where vendors sold fresh bread each morning and children played soccer in the late afternoons. Now, as evening settled in, the small space felt intimate rather than cramped. The windows were open to catch the breeze that was warm, but welcome. A desk fan whirred in the corner, rustling the edges of maps and notes scattered across her work table. Above it, a framed reproduction of an ancient Hebrew text hung on the wall, a quiet reminder of why she'd come here, to uncover what lay buried beneath the layers of accepted history.

She sat cross-legged on the small sofa, tablet balanced against her knees, scrolling through international headlines. The blue light cast her features in a spectral glow as the unraveling of the Ashen Veil played out in real time.

"Global backlash intensifies against Ashen Veil as documents reveal coordinated disinformation campaign," read one headline from a British outlet.

"*Environmental groups distance themselves from radical faction as evidence of falsified climate data emerges*," read another.

She tapped into a video report. A stern Italian journalist stood outside a police station in Naples, flanked by flashing lights that strobed rhythmically behind her.

"Eli Weiss, prominent leader of the Ashen Veil movement, was taken into custody today by Italian authorities on charges of financial fraud and incitement of violence," the reporter announced.

"Investigators claim the organization funneled millions through shell companies, with large sums still unaccounted for. Encrypted messages recovered from Weiss's devices reportedly discuss coordinated disruptions at religious sites across Europe and the Middle East."

The camera shifted, revealing a man being ushered through a side entrance. His face was obscured, but the hunched posture was unmistakable, the same Eli who once delivered impassioned sermons about impending ecological collapse. Now, his silhouette looked smaller. Diminished.

Sarah swiped to another feed. This time, the Vatican's spokesperson stood before a bank of microphones, framed by the stately columns of St. Peter's. "Father Marco Benetti has been placed on administrative leave pending an internal investigation," the man intoned gravely.

"We have credible evidence that ancient manuscripts were stolen from Vatican archives then shared with Ashen Veil leaders. Father Benetti has been identified as having access to these manuscripts and facilitating their secret removal from the Vatican. It is unclear why the progressive Ashen Veil organization sought access to these ancient texts as workers continue to repair damage from recent protests by the group."

Behind him, Vatican staff were shown scrubbing graffiti from the basilica's exterior, quietly erasing the visible marks of a deeper spiritual vandalism.

Sarah closed the tablet and exhaled. The movement that had once roared with certainty now folded in on itself like a structure built on hollow ground. There was something inevitable, almost judicial, in the way lies collapsed and how they required an ever-larger scaffolding until the weight of them became unsustainable.

She reached for her phone, hesitated, then tapped the contact. The line connected quickly, but her father's answering "Hello" came slowly, hesitant and heavy.

"Sarah?"

"I've been watching the news," she said quietly.

A long sigh followed, more weary than defensive. "It's… not good."

"No," she agreed. "It's not."

"I pulled all our funding," he said after a pause. "The foundation. My personal accounts. Everything. It got away from us. I thought we were fighting for justice and for the planet, but…" He trailed off.

When he didn't finish the sentence, Sarah did.

"Good intentions don't equal truth, Dad. I'm learning how to tell the difference."

The fan in the corner continued its steady whir, marking time. Outside, the city softened into dusk: a distant car horn, laughter from a nearby café, the melodic call to prayer rising from a mosque several blocks away. Multiple voices. Multiple truths. All layered atop one another in the same fading light.

"You sound..." Her father's voice paused, searching. "Different. I haven't heard from you in over a week. I was worried. When I heard some of those Ashen Veil kids were kidnapped near your dig site, I…" he stopped. "You weren't involved in all that, were you?"

Sarah glanced at the framed text on her wall. Then at the notes, the maps, the quiet breadcrumbs of a journey that had shifted something deeper than she could articulate.

She thought of the Ethiopian church. Of Trenfor's voice echoing in that sacred space. Of fault lines and the wisdom that begins where certainty ends.

"I'm okay," she said simply. "I'll tell you. Just not yet."

Her words hung there, neither evasive nor premature, but precisely enough. An acknowledgment that something had changed, and not all change fits neatly into explanation.

CIG HQ, North Carolina

The CIG headquarters rose from the North Carolina mountainside like an apparition of symmetry, human ingenuity woven into the contours of ancient stone. Panels of glass and steel mirrored the forest canopy, each surface catching light like a lake catches sky. To the casual observer, it might resemble an elite research facility or tech campus. But to those who knew, the architecture was a parable. Its seamless design spoke not just of excellence, but of alignment between heaven and earth, between truth and mystery, between the seen and the unseen. An embassy at the boundary of realms.

A row of international flags fluttered in the highland wind above the entrance, not merely decorative but declarative, a visual shorthand for the global reach of a quiet war few understood. The fabric shimmered in the morning sun, like a mosaic being rewritten by the breeze.

Etched above the doors, solemn and unadorned, were words from 2 Corinthians:

"The weapons we fight with are not the weapons of the world." II Corinthians 10:4.

It was not a boast, but a boundary marker. Words for initiates, not tourists.

Trenfor stood at the foot of the stone steps, eyes fixed on the inscription. Though he'd returned from Ethiopia the day before, he lingered here as if crossing the threshold required more than a passport. It demanded reckoning.

Footsteps approached from the gravel walk. Doug McCraken emerged, flanked by a rising column of steam from the two coffees in his hands. He offered one wordlessly. Trenfor accepted with a nod. No greeting necessary.

For a long moment, they stood in silence, the mountain air crisp around them.

"Do you ever wonder," Trenfor said at last, eyes still on the carved words above, "if the world has the faintest idea what's really behind what they see on their screens? The politics, the protests, the market shocks...?"

Doug took a sip before answering. "Not until something cracks. Not until the surface breaks open and the deep things bleed through."

Doug adjusted the shoulder holster beneath his coat, the leather creaking faintly, a subtle reminder that the battle wasn't metaphorical. "People are like children standing at the edge of a vast ocean. They think they've grasped its mysteries because the tide kissed their toes."

He smiled, but it didn't reach his eyes. "They feel the spray and call it the sea. But a trench lies beneath."

Overhead, a hawk wheeled silently in the rising thermals, its wings outstretched in a lazy spiral. Both men glanced upward, tracking it instinctively.

Doug continued, his voice quieter now. "The spiritual and the physical aren't two worlds. They're one, layered like light through stained glass. What happens in one echoes in the other. The ancients knew this. We've forgotten."

He gestured toward the building. "That's why we're here. To keep watch at the convergence points. To be translators. Bridges. Even guardians."

Trenfor nodded, his jaw tightening slightly.

"The relics," he said. "The stolen texts. The nails. They weren't just targets, they were keys. The Ashen Veil thought they were opening doors to knowledge. But they were prying open seals they didn't understand."

"Half-truths," Doug said, his voice suddenly hard. "Always more dangerous than lies. Lies you can spot. Half-truths come dressed like light."

The flags above stirred again. Cloth and color. Borders and nations. But both men knew the real battle lines weren't drawn on maps. They were drawn in hearts and in heavens.

For a time, they stood in stillness. Not hesitation, but preparation, the pause before movement. The silence before the shofar.

Then Trenfor stepped forward, ascending the steps with quiet resolve. The Scripture above the door seemed to pass through him, not just carved into stone, but engraved on bone and soul.

Inside, the hum of activity greeted him, analysts parsing intercepted transmissions, scholars restoring fragments of lost scrolls with spectral imaging, operatives coordinating with field teams across continents. Ancient knowledge paired with modern tools. Timeless truths requiring real-time vigilance.

As the doors closed behind him, the world outside receded. Trenfor's awareness narrowed into focus, into calling. The scent of incense still lingered from the Ethiopian church.

Sarah's questions still echoed. The nail still pulsed with implications.

A mission complete. A page turned.

But the war, the ancient, cosmic war, wasn't over.

The inscription above the door remained behind him for the next to see. A reminder. A charge. It said all that needed to be said.

"The weapons we fight with are not the weapons of the world." II Corinthians 10:4.

Ethiopia

Heat shimmered along the road like a living thing.

The dirt track cut through the Ethiopian highlands in a pale ribbon, flanked by tall grasses that swayed in the afternoon wind. The tall grass golden, dry, whispering against one another as though trading secrets older than language. Somewhere beyond the hills, Lake Tana reflected the sun in fragments of silver, patient and watchful.

A lone dog trotted along the road's edge.

Its coat was the color of dust and ash, ribs faint beneath its skin, ears alert to sounds no human noticed anymore. It paused, nose lifted, as a gust passed through the grass, carrying with it the scent of earth, old stone, and something sharper. Not danger. Presence.

The dog's ears flattened.

The air changed.

To human eyes, nothing happened. The road remained empty. The grasses continued their slow, rhythmic sway. Heat pressed down with familiar weight.

But the dog saw the light bend.

Colors fractured where no colors should have been with edges bleeding into one another, the light spectrum stretched thin like fabric pulled too far. Where the road dipped between two rises, a shape stood that did not cast a shadow. Tall. Still. Wrapped in a radiance that did not burn, yet made the air tremble around it.

The dog did not bark.

It simply lowered itself to the ground instead, tail still, breath shallow, not in fear, but in recognition. Animals knew what humans had forgotten: that the world was layered, that sight was not the same as seeing.

The figure did not move. It did not need to.

Then, as quietly as it had appeared, the distortion eased. Light returned to its proper place. The road was only a road again. The grasses sighed. The heat resumed its familiar weight.

The dog rose, shook the dust from its coat, and continued on.

Far away, in places of glass and steel, analysts watched screens and scholars debated texts. In lecture halls and monasteries, questions were asked that had been asked before, though few recognized them. Science refined its instruments. Theology refined its language. Both strained toward the same horizon.

And here, where the modern world rarely looked, something ancient remained awake. Ever alert. Ever alive. Often beyond the perception of man.

The samurai had understood this once: that rain was not an enemy simply because it soaked you; that death was not terrifying when accepted as part of life; that clarity came not from resisting reality, but from standing fully within it.

You did not fear the rain if you accepted you would get wet.

You did not fear the unseen if you accepted it was already there.

The wind passed again through the grass, bending it toward the road, toward paths yet walked and wars yet unnamed. Somewhere, far beyond the hills, the bells of an old church rang, steady, unhurried, unconcerned with whether the world still understood why.

The dog did not look back.

And the land remembered.

For we wrestle not against flesh and blood, but against principalities, against powers, against the rulers of the darkness of this world.

—Ephesians 6:12

Author's Note on Theology & Fiction

Nails of God occupies the space between faith, history, and imagination.

The Christian tradition has always wrestled with unseen realities such as spiritual authority, ancient powers, and the cosmic consequences of human activity and rebellion. Scripture offers glimpses of these truths, while history and archaeology provide context but not always certainty.

This novel does not claim to resolve theological mysteries or establish new doctrine. Instead, it explores what it might look like if ancient spiritual realities intersected with the modern world and how faith, doubt, and courage respond under pressure.

Readers are encouraged to engage the biblical texts directly, to question boldly, and to remember that truth does not fear examination.

Historical & Scriptural Notes

Several historical locations, ancient texts, and theological ideas referenced in this novel are rooted in real scholarship and tradition, including:

- Second Temple Judaism and early Christian history
- Archaeological debates surrounding crucifixion practices
- Ancient Near Eastern understandings of spiritual powers
- Biblical references to Watchers, principalities, and spiritual authority

Primary biblical passages referenced include Genesis 6, the Gospels, Daniel, Ephesians, Colossians, and Revelation. Extra-biblical literature (such as intertestamental writings) is referenced for historical context, not doctrinal authority.

Any liberties taken were done in service of the narrative.

Acknowledgments

This novel would not exist without the patience of family, the sharpening influence of scholars and mentors whose work came before it, and the quiet encouragement of readers who believe stories still matter.

Soli Deo Gloria.

About the Author

Phillip M. Stephens is a clinician, researcher, and author whose work bridges medicine, history, science, faith, and the human condition. With academic training in health science and years of experience in clinical and emergency medicine, his writing reflects a lifelong interest in how belief, evidence, and unseen realities shape human behavior. He writes non-fiction for the mind and fiction for the soul.

Nails of God continues his exploration of faith under pressure, spiritual conflict, and the enduring questions at the intersection of science and faith.

Also see: ***The Fifth Dimension:*** A Christian thriller of spiritual warfare and unseen realms.

Call to Action

If you enjoyed *Nails of God*, please consider leaving a review on Amazon. Reviews help readers discover new books and allow stories like this to continue.

To know what we believe is only the beginning. To understand why is to see more clearly. Scripture has endured every honest examination. And for those drawn beyond what is seen, the work goes on.

Also see other works by this author at:

www.PhillipMStephens.com

Thank you for reading and remember to pray daily. Your prayers join a global fellowship of believers, strengthening the world-wide work of the Christian Intelligence Group.

www.ingramcontent.com/pod-product-compliance
Lightning Source LLC
LaVergne TN
LVHW041110080826
845145LV00007B/1755

* 9 7 8 0 9 7 4 7 1 0 8 3 9 *